The Last Bullet

MORGAN HILL

Multnomah Books

THE LAST BULLET
published by Sage River Books
© 2003 by ALJO PRODUCTIONS, INC.

International Standard Book Number: 978-1-59052-278-3

Cover illustration © 2003 by Rene Milot. All rights reserved.

Printed in the United States of America

For information:
Multnomah Books
12265 ORacle Boulevard, Suite 200
Colorado Springs, CO 80921

Library of Congress Cataloging-in-Publication Data

Hill, Morgan, 1933-
    The last bullet / by Morgan Hill.
        p. cm.
    ISBN 1-59052-278-8
  1. Nebraska--fiction. 2. Wagon trains--Fiction. 3. Cheyenne
Indians--Wars--Fiction.
I. Title.
    PS3562.A256L65 2003
    813' .6--dc21

                                    2003011817

Chapter One

Clay Bostin lay motionless, staring bleakly toward the darkening sky. His lean, six-foot-four-inch frame was spread-eagled on the grass, wrists and ankles lashed tightly to heavy wooden stakes.

The drumming sound of galloping painted ponies was quickly diminishing. The savage Black Hawk and his merciless warriors would return only when the rain had passed. They would come to gloat over his dead body. It would be most interesting to them to see if he had withstood the torture of the deadly rawhide until death released him, or if he had taken the easy way out.

Bostin focused his eyes on the slender, taut rope that was stretched just an inch above his forehead. The evil genius of Black Hawk had fashioned a diabolical apparatus of instant death. Breaking limbs from a nearby cottonwood tree, the vengeful Cheyenne chief had mounted a single-shot .44-70 Spencer rifle at Bostin's feet. Tying it securely to the limbs, which were sunk deep in the Nebraska sod, the rifle lay in the two Y-shaped crotches, aimed directly at the tall man's head.

Threading the rope through additional crotched limbs, the Indian cocked the hammer and touched the tightly drawn rope to the trigger. All Bostin need do was lift his head one inch. Pressure on the rope would trip the trigger. Lowering his gaze toward his feet, he looked at the muzzle. It seemed to stare at him as a single menacing eye.

The prostrate man cast another glance overhead. There was rain in those dark thunderheads. Black Hawk knew it.

Holding his head still, Clay strained his muscular arms against the stakes. They would not budge. The painted Cheyennes had driven them deep into the sod.

A wave of panic washed over him, followed by a settled, cold dread. The rawhide strips which thronged his wrists and ankles would shrink when soaked by the oncoming rain and slice unmercifully into the flesh. This was plenty to dread, but the real horror lay in the two narrow rawhide cords which circled his head just above the eyebrows.

When these began to shrink, they would slowly but surely crack his skull, like bands of contracting steel. Death would hover near him in savage mockery, inviting him to lift his head and end the paroxysm of torture with a bullet.

The wagon was burning freely now, about thirty feet to his left. He dared not look. There was no need. The sickening smell of burning hair and flesh was sufficient. The rampaging Cheyennes had shot Gil and Clara Rodman and their two boys after binding Bostin to the stakes. Helplessly, he had heard the bark of the rifles, the thudding of the bodies as they slumped to the earth.

The savages had not taken time to lift their scalps. They dumped the four bodies inside, then quickly set the prairie schooner on fire.

Clay Bostin's thoughts drifted back to two days earlier, when he had come across the Rodmans' camp on the trail to Fort Laramie. Gil Rodman had purchased the general store in the fort and was brining his family from Omaha to live there.

Rodman invited him to dismount and join them for supper. When he learned that Bostin was also headed for the fort, he suggested they travel together.

Everything had been fine until two hours ago. Black Hawk and ten of his bucks rode in on them suddenly. Clay knew something was terribly wrong as the Indians' faces loomed larger. He had not seen warpaint on an Indian for nearly four years.

At first it appeared that the savages were going to allow Bostin and his friends to proceed. Bostin had relaxed his guard.

Black Hawk was visibly disturbed about something. The warpaint emphasized the fact. When Bostin inquired about it, the young hostile chief only grunted that the Cheyenne were tired of White Eyes' forked tongue and mistreatment of their people. All White Eyes must die. Seizing him suddenly, the Indians held guns on the frightened family. When Bostin was clearly no threat, they shot down the Rodmans and their young sons.

The prostrate man pondered his predicament. Why had Black Hawk not shot him down as he did the others? Was a quick death too easy for the son of an Indian agent? Black Hawk's father, Running Horse, had known Derek Bostin for many years. Their relationship had been good.

Clay had seen the young son of Running Horse on several occasions during his growing-up years. Black Hawk had always shown hostility toward white men. As he grew into manhood, he displayed a stronger will and a more fiery spirit than his aged father. When the old chief died, there was general fear throughout the territory that Black Hawk would stir up trouble.

Over three years had passed now since Black Hawk had become chief of the Northern Cheyenne Tribe. Not one white man had been killed by Cheyennes since the bloody uprising which took place during the last year of Running Horse's life.

Whites in the territory had agreed that they had been hasty in their assessment of the young chief. So pleased were they with the tribe's behavior, the whites had recently named a growing and thriving town in southern Wyoming Territory after them.

Apparently the hatred for white men had smoldered deep in Black Hawk's heart, like a dormant volcano. The fire was there all the time. Something, somewhere, was done by white men very recently which triggered the eruption of that fire.

Clay Bostin cast a disconsolate glance at the black sky overhead. Any minute now the rain would come in torrents. The wind was picking up, popping in his ears with a heavy, hollow sound. It caused the flames of the burning wagon to roar.

A heavy gust swept over the prairie. Clay focused nervously on the taut rope just above his forehead. The gust of wind caused the rope to vibrate. His line of sight flicked to the hideous muzzle of the Spencer. The rope quivered along its length, the vibrations extending to the knot on the trigger.

Clay Bostin had faced death before, but never had the grim reaper held him in such a helpless position. He had faced Comanche, Blackfoot, and Cheyenne bullets and arrows from the time he was eighteen until he turned twenty-nine four years ago, when peace settled over the territory.

Bostin wore a deep scar on the left cheekbone of his handsome, angular face, a reminder of a Comanche tomahawk that had brought death to within a hair's breadth during fierce hand-to-hand combat.

As the son of Derek Bostin he fell into guiding settlers across the prairies of Kansas and Nebraska. His lifetime among Indians had made him the perfect man to lead wagons westward through Indian country.

There was within Clay Bostin a deep reverence for the wide open spaces and a spirit of adventure that this kind of life satisfied.

As he lay in the grass with the circulation ebbing in his hands and feet, he reminded himself that yesterday he had complained to Gil Rodman that things had been pretty dull. There had been no raids on the wagon trains he had led in four years. He recounted some of the bloody battles to Rodman, including the one that gave him the scar. Overhearing the conversation from inside the covered wagon, Clara Rodman had interrupted to say that she was thankful the Indians were peaceable.

While Clay's bay gelding followed the wagon on a lead rope, he explained to Gil that he had returned to Omaha, ready to lead a small wagon train to Cheyenne. A telegram was awaiting him there from General Lucius Henniger at Fort Laramie. The general wanted him to return to the fort by July first. He wanted Bostin to ride as scout for a cavalry brigade through Ute country in Colorado.

There was no way he could guide the train and make Fort Laramie by July first. Quickly, he found a replacement to lead the train. He had left Omaha riding hard for Wyoming. The day before he had come upon the Rodman camp, Bostin's horse had thrown a shoe. There was no choice now. He would have to travel slowly. Hence his quick acceptance of Rodman's invitation. Clay had wired an instant reply to General Henniger. Knowing he was coming, the general would wait.

Another gust of wind sallied the rope up and down the posed trigger of the Spencer. Clay wondered if he would hear the shot if it fired. Or would the bullet end his life too quickly?

A jagged bolt of white fire lashed angrily across the black-clouded sky. A sharp clap of thunder followed. The rain would soon come, virtually spitting death at him from above.

Suddenly, Bostin was aware of movement somewhere near.

Shifting his eyes back and forth, he listened. As far as he knew, the Cheyennes had taken his and the Rodmans' horses.

Again, there was movement. A rustling sound. Straining his ears, Clay listened intently. It sounded like a small animal as the noise came closer. A jackrabbit approached inquisitively, examining this strange, unfamiliar sight in its territory. Since the man had not moved, the animal experienced no fear.

Sniffing heavily, the rabbit touched Bostin's right knee with his nose, working upward. A cold claw of fear squeezed Bostin's heart. If the rabbit touched that rope...

Again he glanced at the threatening muzzle. The rabbit was now sniffing near his rib cage. He could shout and frighten the little furry beast away, but if the rabbit ran into the rope which hovered menacingly above his forehead, Clay Bostin was a dead man.

His heart pounded in his breast.

The rabbit paused, studying Bostin's pulsating lungs. Clay remembered that the rope remained at the level just above his head until it rounded the two sticks which protruded from the sod near the stakes that held his hands. From that point the rope angled upward through two other crotched sticks. Then it ran through two more, at sharp angles, where it brushed dangerously against the trigger. One slight bump on the rope by that rabbit...

He was moving closer to the rope!

Bostin's eyes shot again to the rifle. The hammer, locked back in firing position, seemed to mock him.

The little beast of the prairie suddenly disappeared from view. Clay Bostin waited breathlessly. He could not hear the rabbit.

Another bolt of lightning cut the sky. The rabbit lunged in fear, bumping Clay's side. He waited as if finding solace from the threatening storm in Clay's body. Thunder boomed.

Lightning popped again, the bolt coming near the ground. The frightened animal suddenly turned in the direction of the rope and skitted away. Bostin bit hard, cording his jaw, closing his eyes. The Spencer did not fire. Looking at the rope, Clay saw that it was firm and motionless. The jack rabbit had leaped the rope and was gone.

The prostrate man heaved a sigh of relief. His body trembled. For the moment, he was still alive. As long as he was alive, there was hope. Small, maybe. Remote, maybe. But *hope*.

A drop of rain hit Bostin's face. His eyes shot upward. Another drop struck him in the right eye. He blinked it away. *Strange*, he thought. *I've always loved the feel of rain in my face.* Now it was signing his death warrant.

The rawhide cords that pressed his brow seemed to tighten. *Just your imagination*, he told himself. *Two drops of rain won't shrink them.*

The cold dread within him was unleashed like a flood, swarming through him like ice water. Savagely, he rebuked himself for succumbing to the rushing dread and icy fear. Self-control was absolutely necessary. Every muscle in his body screamed for release, but Clay held on until the wave of panic passed, then relaxed. He felt hot beads of sweat form on his face.

Lifting his eyes upward, he studied the sky overhead. He had felt only two raindrops. The clouds were swirling angrily. Heavy winds were driving them hard. A faint ray of hope rekindled itself in Clay Bostin's breast. Maybe...maybe the winds would be kind to him and blow the storm away! If the rain did not come and he had a little time...

There had to be a way out of this. Maybe tomorrow someone would come by. That was highly possible. This was the main trail between Omaha and Cheyenne. Many travelers from St. Joseph also angled northward and picked up the trail before getting this far west. There could easily be somebody coming tomorrow.

The cold dread touched him again. *Black Hawk would be back.*

Clay Bostin fought the intruding pessimistic thought. He must maintain the proper attitude. His survival depended on it.

If he gave up, he was doomed for sure.

The sky was growing darker now. Soon it would be night.

Lightning and thunder played intermittently across the broad expanse overhead. Still, only light drops of rain touched Bostin's face.

Time seemed to crawl.

Eventually, darkness fell. *That storm has to have an edge somewhere*, Clay told himself. He reasoned that every moment without a downpour was another moment closer to the end of the storm.

Suddenly, a bolt of jagged white flame split the dark sky, lighting the whole world. A sharp clap of thunder retaliated angrily. And then it came.

Rain.

Torrents of it. Heavy, devilish rain. Within moments, Clay Bostin was soaked. The cords on his wrists and ankles were soaked, as were the death dealing bands on his head. Clay eyed the shiny barrel of the Spencer as it reflected a flash of lightning.

As the rawhide on his head began to tighten, he wondered how long he would be able to stand the horrid pressure.

There was a double flash of lightning, which hung in the sky for a long moment, turning the world a pallid blue-white. Bostin looked at the rifle again.

Chapter Two

Rachel Flanagan pulled the slicker from under the wagon seat and unrolled it. Studying the dark, swirling masses overhead, she spoke to the old man holding the reins. "Bucky, I think we're in for a good one."

Bucky Wiseman turned his leathered features toward the young woman. In his sixty-seven years on earth, he had never beheld eyes that were a deeper blue, nor hair so rich an auburn. Even in the gathering darkness the golden highlights of deep red flitted alluringly in her hair. Her skin was soft, and smooth as ivory. He found himself wishing he were twenty-five again. "Guess so," he said with a faint smile. "Seems we oughtta be pullin' over and battenin' down the hatches."

Rachel leaned out, looking at the ten wagons behind them. The wind was gusting, flapping the canvas covers vehemently. Coming around the rear wagon, Dale Roy appeared, trotting the big buckskin. As he pulled alongside the lead wagon, he smiled at Rachel and said, "Bucky, let's pull over when we get to that draw up ahead!"

"Right, Mister Roy," said Bucky.

The guide wheeled the buckskin and rode toward the wagons, pausing momentarily at each one.

A bolt of lightning pierced the black sky. Bucky's team shied slightly at the unexpected flash. Thunder rolled.

As the designated spot drew closer, the sky darkened. Rachel slipped into the slicker as rain began pelting her face. Lightning bolts played tag across the heavy sky, followed by intermittent claps of thunder.

During one of the bright flashes, Bucky Wiseman blinked his eyes, fixing them on an obscure object dead ahead.

"What is it?" asked the lovely Rachel.

"Not sure, honey," Bucky said, squinting. "I'll study it during the next flash."

Suddenly, lightning split the dark sky, followed by the low rumble. And then the rain came. Great sheets of it.

Rachel pulled the hood of the slicker tight around her perfectly fashioned face. Blinking toward the old man, she said, "Did you get a good look at it?"

Bucky nodded. Lifting his voice against the wind, he said, "Yep. Not sure, but it looks like the shell of a burned-out wagon."

"Probably old," observed the girl. "Probably been there a long time."

"Prob'ly," agreed the old man.

Several moments passed.

As the lead wagon drew abreast of the charred remains of the prairie schooner, a double flash of lightning turned the Nebraska plain a pallid blue white. The light seemed to hang in the sky for a long moment.

Abruptly, Bucky jerked on the reins, pulling the wagon to a halt. Rachel thumbed the rain from her eyes. "What's the matter, Bucky?" she called as the elderly man began to climb from the wagon.

"There's a man staked to the ground over here! Gonna see if he's alive!"

The sky was radiant with light again as Bucky approached Clay Bostin. The flinty eye of the weathered Wiseman saw the threatening Spencer. He waited until the next flash to examine the area. He was quick to line his sight on the threaded rope drawn tight over the man's forehead.

When the lightning bolted again, he stooped carefully, looking at Bostin's twisted face. Wiseman's jaw slacked. Lifting his voice above the booming thunder, he shouted, "You just hang on, mister! We'll get you out of there!"

Bostin's eyes flew open. He had not heard Bucky's approach. "Watch...watch the rope!" He gasped. "Rifle!"

"I see it, son!" said Wiseman. "Hold on. I'll be right back!"

Dale Roy was dismounting beside the lead wagon as the old man returned. "What is it?" he called loudly.

"Indians have a young feller staked out over there. He's still alive. Looks like they burned his wagon."

Bucky reached inside the wagon for his lantern, when he saw Roy moving toward Bostin. "Hey, Mister Roy!" he bellowed. "Don't get too close! There's a rifle fixed on him. Touch the rope, you'll kill him!"

Roy froze.

Leaning out of the weather, Wiseman fished under his slicker for a match. Finding one, he thumbed it into flame and touched it to the blackened wick.

Raindrops sizzled on the chimney of the lantern as the gray-haired man sloshed through the wet grass. As he passed the wagon train guide, he said, "Come hold the lantern for me."

Rachel blinked against the rain, watching the two men moving within the yellow circle of light. Three men approached from behind. Rachel could hear others coming.

"What's happening?" one asked, eyeing the circle of light.

Wiseman looked at Bostin's twisted face. He wouldn't last much longer. Directing Daly Roy to lift the lantern higher, the old man eyed the rawhide witch was biting into the man's wrists and ankles. It would take time to cut them loose without cutting skin.

There was only one answer. He would have to jerk the muzzle of the rifle out of line with the man's head. The Spencer would fire on contact, but Wiseman would just have to move the muzzle fast enough to make the bullet strike sod instead of flesh.

Stepping over the threaded rope, he spoke softly to the pain-wracked man. "Son, I've got to snap that muzzle off to the side. It's the only way. Okay?"

Bostin blinked his agreement.

Dale Roy held the lantern close as Bucky knelt in the wet grass. First flexing his crooked fingers, he lowered his hand slowly and ever so carefully closed them over the lower end of the barrel, just behind the muzzle.

Holding his breath, he swallowed hard. Abruptly, Bucky jerked the barrel toward him. The hammer snapped hollowly. Cursing violently, he jerked the limbs free of the ground and tossed the rifle in the general direction of the huddled group, limbs flailing. "See if the chamber's empty!" he shouted.

Within thirty seconds, Wiseman worked the razor sharp tip of his hunting knife under the rawhide cords on Bostin's head and cut them loose. By the time two more minutes had passed, Clay Bostin was free of the stakes. Bucky had not once punctured skin.

The tall, rawboned man was carried to Wiseman's wagon. One of the men hollered that he had found Bostin's boots, hat, and gun stuffed in a heavy clump of grass.

Clay was conscious, but his head throbbed violently. The pain in his wrists and ankles was already subsiding. He felt dizzy and nauseated as strong hands hoisted him into the covered wagon.

Outside, he heard the voice of the guide shouting above the din of the storm. "Circle 'em right here, boys! We'll park here for the night!"

Inside the wagon, Bucky Wiseman piled boxes on boxes, making room so Clay could be comfortable. Rain continued pelting the canvas cover.

Rachel Flanagan turned in the seat and crawled through the opening in the canvas. Bostin's eyes were closed. He was still in tremendous pain. Once his head was down, the nausea passed.

Looking closely at the two slender blue rims indented in his forehead, Rachel said, "Bucky, do you suppose his skull is cracked?"

Bostin opened his eyes at the sound of the soft, feminine voice. His vision was impaired. He could see a blurred face, set in a background of deep red, but the features would not come clear.

Bucky adjusted the lantern, shedding more light on Bostin's face. Answering the young woman's question, Wiseman said, "Can't tell, honey. If it is, he won't make it. A cracked skull needs professional attention. We're three hundred miles from the kind of help he'll need."

Rachel's brow furrowed. "We've got to get the circulation going where the cords have turned the skin blue."

Bostin felt a soft hand lift his own. "We must work on the wrists. Ankles, too." He heard the soft voice say. It seemed to fade in and out.

"Have someone heat some water," Rachel told the old man.

"Right away," said Bucky, opening the flap. Descending from the wagon, he closed the flap.

It sounded to Rachel like the rain was easing up. Clay Bostin tried once again to bring Rachel's face into focus. Suddenly, it seemed to go into a spin. She was saying something to him, but the words were lost in the filmy black shroud that seemed to envelop him.

In the yellow light of the flickering lantern, Rachel Flanagan studied his features. It was a commanding face...strong and angular. The square set of his jaw told Rachel that he was a man of strong will and purpose. A jagged scar stood out on his left cheekbone, white against the suntanned and windburned face. This was a rugged man. A man who lived his life in the elements of nature.

Her thoughts turned to Alvin. Alvin Penell was just the opposite of this man. His banking career was his life. Alvin was soft and pale. He detested the heat of the sun, the bite of the wind. Alvin was a good man, though. Certainly he would make Rachel a fine husband. He was intelligent, steady, and reliable. These were the characteristics which had landed him the position in San Francisco's largest bank.

Certainly his record was impressive. Twenty-seven years old...and already *assistant vice-president!* With the influx of people to San Francisco, new banks would be established. Rachel had convinced herself that Alvin would be a bank president before he was forty. *Just think of it,* she told herself. *You'll wear the latest fashions and the finest jewelry. You'll be somebody, moving in the social circles as Mrs. Alvin Penell!*

It was all cut and dried for Rachel Flanagan. Alvin had shown real promise all through grammar school. The Flanagans were close friends with the Penells. Both lived in the same fashionable neighborhood in Chicago.

When other boys showed interest in courting Rachel (and there were many), Walter and Elsie Flanagan were quick to discourage them. Their minds were made up from the time the auburn-haired beauty was sixteen. She would marry Alvin Penell. It was expected, of course, that the marriage would not take place until Alvin had graduated from the University of Chicago and was well established in his chosen field.

The young banker had done well at Chicago's First City Bank. He caught the eye of a west coast tycoon whose main interest was banking. Penell was offered the position in San Francisco. He accepted and moved to the west coast. He would send for Rachel once he was settled in.

Now the time had come. Twenty-four-year-old Rachel Flanagan was on her way to be united in holy matrimony with Alvin Penell. She had ridden the train as far as Omaha. The railroad was pushing west. She could have gone as far as Plains City, some fifty miles further, but Dale Roy's train was leaving from Omaha. Walter Flanagan had booked her with Roy because of his long and perfect record in guiding wagon trains west. He was assured that there had been no Indian trouble on the route for some time. He and Rachel's mother had kissed her good-bye at Chicago's Union Station, feeling perfectly at ease concerning her safety.

Something deep stirred inside Rachel Flanagan as she bathed Clay Bostin's rawhide wounds with hot water. The only men she had ever been really close to were her father and Alvin Penell. There was something about this man's rugged manliness...the square of his jaw...his hard muscular frame...

The man stirred two or three times in the night, opened his eyes briefly, then lapsed again into unconsciousness. It was nearly dawn when he awakened again, spoke a few mumbled words, and relaxed. This time, Rachel noticed a change in his breathing. He was now resting in normal slumber.

Chapter Three

Clay Bostin opened his eyes and blinked against the bright light. The morning sun was filtering through the canvas covering on the wagon. He looked at his surroundings. *Where am I? What am I doing in a covered wag—?*

It all came back to him like an onrushing flood. Gil Rodman's wagon burning. The stakes. The Spencer. The storm. The pain. Voices. Pain. Nausea. A lantern...a soft voice...blurred recollections.

Slowly, Bostin raised his head, pausing on his elbows. He expected dizziness, but it did not come. Cautiously, he lifted himself to a sitting position. Suddenly, he realized that under the blankets which covered him he didn't have a stitch on!

Easing toward the slight opening, he peered out. Several men were hunkered around a large fire, scraping forks on tin plates and sipping steaming coffee. Bostin's stomach growled. The aroma of bacon and coffee brought saliva to his mouth.

Looking back in the wagon, he searched for his clothes. Nothing. He remembered that the Cheyennes had heaped his hat, boots, and gun in a clump of tall grass.

Bostin was planning his next move when the rear flap opened abruptly, exposing a hardy old face. The man's skin was like wind-blown mahogany. Around the cheekbones it had a ruddy look. The corners of the eyes were heavily wrinkled. Heavy locks of silver hair protruded form a dirty, sweat-stained hat. The lower part of his craggy face was clouded with white prickly stubble.

"So you're awake, young feller!" The husky voice crackled, as one whose vocal cords had been strained by years of shouting against the wind at a wagon team.

Pulling the blankets tight around his slender waist, Clay Bostin said, "Yessir."

The old man smiled, revealing a large gap where his upper two front teeth had been. His gray eyes glinted with a warmth to which Clay was drawn instantly.

"You hurtin' much?"

"My head's sore, but it only hurts when I touch it."

"Good!" ejaculated the old gent, twisting his head and squirting a stream of brown juice.

"Uh...do you know where my clothes might be?" Bostin asked.

"Shore do, son. They's about dry. I hung 'em over one of the fires. May have a slight smoky smell, but they'll be dry ennyhow."

"I've smelled like something worse than smoke before," Clay smiled.

"Like some coffee, son?"

"Love it."

The old man disappeared and returned quickly with a steaming cup. "This'll heat yer innards," the weathered man said. "I'll go git yore clothes. We found yore boots and hat, along with yore Colt. Boots won't be dry."

He turned away, then came back. "Whut's your name, son?"

"Clay Bostin."

Reaching toward Bostin, the old man said, "I'm Bucky Wiseman."

Clay smiled and gripped the bony hand, feeling a stab of pain in his wrist.

"Drink that coffee, Clay. I'll be right back."

By nine o'clock Clay Bostin was seated near one of the fires, wolfing down food heartily. Questions were being fired at him rapidly from the crowd which encircled him.

"Hush up and let him stock his gizzard," commanded Bucky Wiseman good-naturedly. "He can talk his lungs out once't he gits some fuel in the burner."

The womenfolk busied themselves with cleaning up the camp as a band of men gathered circular-fashion around Clay Bostin. The inquisitive children had been sent to play.

"This here is Clay Bostin, men," advised Wiseman loudly. Looking at Bostin, who was still seated, he said, "Clay, I won't bother yuh with all their names, but I would like to have yuh meet Mister Dale Roy, the boss of this here train."

Clay stood to his full six feet, four inches. His two-inch riding heels lifted him that much higher.

Dale Roy was a meaty man, thick through and through. He had a heavy set of shoulders, topped by a bull-like neck and formidable head. He stood just under six feet.

"No need to stand up, Bostin," said Roy, extending a husky hand.

"Time I was forcing my knees to hold me," said Bostin calmly.

"I take it some renegade Indians burned your wagon and staked you out," said Dale Roy.

"Not renegades, sir," replied Bostin. "Black Hawk himself. Painted up like he's going to war with the world."

Roy's face blanched. A murmur broke out among the dozen men. Bucky Wiseman used a couple of cursewords Clay could not distinguish, turned away from the circle, and spit.

"Wasn't my wagon," continued the tall rawboned man. "Belonged to a family named Rodman." Fixing his gaze on Roy, he said, "You haven't looked in the ruins?"

"Huh-uh," said the husky man. "We assumed you must have been traveling alone."

"You'll find what's left of four bodies," said Bostin grimly.

Three men separated themselves from the group and walked toward the charred remains of the Rodman wagon.

Clay waited, looking toward them.

"He's right," one of them called.

"Like to give them a decent burial," said the tall Bostin to the wagon train leader.

"Sure enough," replied Roy.

Bucky Wiseman cut in. "Black Hawk say whut riled him?"

"Not really," answered Bostin. "Just that he was tired of the white man's lies and mistreatment of his people."

"Things have been so peaceful," interjected Horace Nething, one of the wagon owners. "I talked to several scouts and agents before starting out. Every one of them said there was no danger." His voice was shaking.

"Something has sparked this," said Dale Roy.

"You have guns and ammunition?" Clay Bostin asked Roy.

"Yes. We're pretty well situated. Most of the men have Winchesters. A few have sidearms. Chester Manley, here, has a double-barreled shotgun."

"I've got a Sharps .50 buffalo," chimed in Bucky Wiseman with a cackle. "Make a hole in an Injun you could drive a wagon through."

"Shucks, Bucky," said one of the men on the fringe of the circle, "you could spit one of them streams between your teeth and knock one of 'em's head clean off!"

Hearty laughter made the rounds.

"You really think we're in for it?" Dale Roy asked Bostin.

Nodding, the tall, dark man said, "I was born and raised at Fort Laramie. Been around Cheyennes all my life. I've fought them, along with the Comanche and Blackfoot. When they put on warpaint, white people are going to die."

Roy shook his head. "I've only made this run twice before. Been guiding trains the southern route for years. Always got them through, but I came up here 'cause I was tired of fighting Apaches."

"That explains why I hadn't heard of you," Clay said casually. "I thought I knew the names of the guides that run this route."

Roy turned to the men. "Guess we better call a meeting, fellas. Gonna have to decide whether to turn back or keep going."

"Whatever you decide," remarked Clay Bostin, "it better be fast. Black Hawk will be coming back to check my body."

"Meeting in five minutes!" bellowed Dale Roy, as the nervous group disbanded.

Bostin looked down at the wrinkled Wiseman.

"How did you get that rifle loose without it going off?"

"You don't recollect?"

"Don't seem to. Pain in my head was keeping me occupied."

"Well, I jist took a good holt on the end of that there barrel and give it a yank," said Bucky, reenacting his deed.

"I don't recall hearing it fire."

"It didn't." Bucky twisted his face. "Thet dirty Injun didn't even have it loaded!"

Clay Bostin's face went hot. The cunning Black Hawk had made him think there was a way to release himself from the slow, torturous death. If he had succumbed to the pain and lifted his head to quickly end it all, the effect of the hammer striking on an empty chamber would have intensified the horror of the ordeal.

"Where's the rifle?" Bostin asked, boiling with anger.

"Got it in my wagon," said Bucky.

"Good. Keep it there. One of these days I'll see the Hawk again. I'm gonna personally jam it down his throat!"

"I'll be cheerin' yuh on, too!" shouted Wiseman.

The sudden rush of anger reminded Bostin of his injured head. Gingerly, he ran the tops of his fingers over the deep ridges in his forehead.

"Buy the way, Bucky," said the tall man, cooling down, "I want to thank you for saving my life."

"Yer jist welcome, pardner," said the old man, his voice crackling, "But I was jist the feller who cut you loose. It was Rachel who sat up with yuh all night, nursin' yer wounds."

A blurry picture leaped into Clay Bostin's mind. A soft face. Red hair. A soothing voice. "Rachel?"

"Yeah. Rachel Flanagan. Purtiest little Irish lassie yuh ever set yer peepers on! Taken care o' you like yuh was a sick calf!"

The travelers were gathering for the meeting. Clay's eyes ran a quick scan of the female faces. "Where is she Bucky? I sure want to thank her."

"She was sleepin' in Mrs. Peabody's wagon," said the old man pointing. "Didn't go to bed till sunrise. I reckon she'll be a-getting' up now, though. Everybody's got a vote in this decision."

The tall intruder remained on the fringe of the crowd, keeping one eye on the Peabody wagon. Dale Roy stepped up on a wooden box, elevating himself above the crowd. Gaining their attention, he put a serious tone in his voice.

"Folks, we got bad news. Is everybody here?"

"All except Rachel Flanagan," said a middle-aged woman.

"Better wake her up, Mrs. Peabody," Roy said kindly. "She needs to be in on this." Lining his sight on Clay Bostin, he motioned to him. "Mister Bostin, will you come over here?"

Clay watched Mrs. Peabody stick her head through the opening at the rear of the wagon. Steadily, he approached the spot where Dale Roy stood on the box.

Roy lifted his voice. "Folks, you all know about the man we picked up in the storm last night. His name is Clay Bostin. There's Indian trouble in the area. I'm gonna ask him to tell you about it."

Stepping off the box, Roy said to Bostin, "Guess you don't need the box, do you?"

Clay smiled down at the shorter man. Turning serious, he said, "Folks, the Cheyennes are on the warpath. We don't know what triggered it, but they shot down a family I was traveling with yesterday and staked me out to die."

A heavy moan swept through the crowd. Conversation began immediately. The thick-bodied guide stepped up on his box and quieted them.

"Maybe it was just an isolated incident," came the voice of a woman.

Looking at Bostin, Roy said, "Tell 'em."

"They were painted up for bloodshed," said Clay. "I was born and raised among the Cheyenne. My father is the Indian agent at Fort Laramie."

"He knows them," cut in Dale Roy. "He says they're on a killing spree."

Roy was proceeding to warn of the dangers of continuing westward when Clay Bostin's eyes beheld the sunlight dancing on the auburn hair of Rachel Flanagan. As she walked toward the crowd, the movement of her head highlighted the golden texture of its rich color. He thought the Lord must have worked overtime on this stunning creature. Her deep blue eyes were unusually large, set in a perfectly formed face with skin as delicate as a rose petal. She was not dressed to attract attention, but neither did her modest clothing disguise her well-formed figure.

Suddenly, Bostin motioned to Bucky Wiseman. As Dale Roy continued his speech, Clay met Bucky a few steps away from the crowd, behind a wagon.

"Gotta ask you a question," Clay said nervously.

"Yeah?"

"Who took off my clothes and wrapped me in the blankets?"

The crafty Wiseman looked the tall man square in the eye, face sober. "Rachel did."

Bostin's face flushed. Wiseman kept a stolid countenance.

"Yeah, she said that scar on your right knee was shaped like a half-moon." The wiry old man was about to burst. Bostin broke into a sweat.

"How can I ever look her in the eye?" stammered the red-faced man. "How can I—"

Bucky screwed up his face, buried it in his hands, and muffled a burst of laughter. Clay's eyes sagged.

"You old codger!"

Wiseman bent over, holding his sides. Tears touched his leathered cheeks.

"I oughtta stake your bony frame to the ground and leave you here for Black Hawk!" Clay said, relief apparent in his voice.

"It'd be worth it just to remember that look on your face," chuckled the old man, gaining his composure.

Clay cuffed him lightly on the chin and returned to the crowd.

"...the decision is yours," Roy was saying.

"What are our chances, Mr. Bostin?" asked Avery Wilson, another wagon owner.

Dale Roy shot a glance toward Bostin. The latter said, "Not the best, sir."

"Even if we turn around, what's to keep them bloody savages from following us and launching an attack?" asked another.

"Nothing," replied Clay. "You're already deep in their territory now. Either way, it's going to be might dangerous. But at this point, you're closer to Omaha than you are to Fort Laramie."

"Are you saying that Fort Laramie is our closet military protection west?" another asked.

"There are patrols that come as far as North Platte," said Bostin advisedly. "They'll probably be beefed up, once word of the new hostilities reaches the fort." His gaze fell on Rachel Flanagan. Her blue eyes met his. Someone was asking another question.

"...very big numbers?"

Clay found it an effort to pull his gaze from Rachel to the voice in the crowd, but he did it reluctantly.

"I beg your pardon, sir," said Bostin. "I didn't hear your question."

"I said, do the Cheyennes attack in very big numbers? I mean, can a train this size hold them off?"

"Hard to say," answered the tall man. "There's thousands of them. No one can predict how many Black Hawk might bring against this train."

"You said *bring*, Mister Bostin. Don't you mean *send?*" came another voice.

"No. Black Hawk is young and vicious. He leads the pack like a hungry wolf. It was Black Hawk himself who staked me out yesterday.

A heavy murmur moved through the crowd.

Another man spoke up. Clay saw Rachel turn to look at him. "We have guns, Mister Bostin, but we're not Indian fighters. Don't you think it would be best to turn around and head for Omaha?"

Before Clay Bostin could reply, a big, square-shouldered man, who looked to be in his mid-fifties, broke in. "If you think there's a good chance there'll be some cavalry at North Platte, Mister Bostin, don't you think the wise thing is to push on? We're certainly closer to North Platte than we are to Omaha."

A slender youth, whom Clay judged to be about nineteen, was standing right next to the big man who had just spoken. He turned to the big man and said, "But, Pa, we'd just be getting deeper into hostile territory. Besides, if the Indians attack us before we get to North Platte, how are we going to hold them off? I think Lon Berry is right. We're not Indian fighters. What are we—?"

"Shut up, Jeremy!" loomed the big man, disgust written on his face. "You can hide in the wagon when the Cheyennes attack. I'm sure there's a *girl* in the train who can handle your gun!" The boy ducked his head.

"All right!" shouted Dale Roy. "Enough arguing. I know that all of you have wrapped your whole lives up in this journey. You are headed west to begin anew and build great futures for yourselves. It will be hard to turn back. Majority rules. Everybody over twenty gets a vote."

Clay Bostin scanned the crowd. He could predict the outcome. His eyes fell again on the face of Rachel Flanagan. She was looking at him. Where their eyes met, a warm smile formed on her lips, exposing a set of white, even teeth. Bostin's blood seemed to warm.

"Everybody for turning back, raise your hand," said Dale Roy loudly.

The main pointed out as Lon Berry lifted his hand. The frail young woman who stood at his side, holding an infant, followed suit. The young man named Jeremy shot his hand upward. As it reached ear level, his eyes fell on the stern face of his father. Jeremy's hand hovered where it had stopped, trembled slightly, then eased down slowly.

"Guess I don't have to ask the other question," said Roy. "Let's get rolling."

"Could I say one thing?" asked Clay Bostin.

"Of course," said Roy.

"Shouldn't you tell them what to do in case of an attack?"

The stout man's face flushed. Lifting his voice he said, "If I shout for you to form a circle, do it quickly. Bucky will lead. Women and children in the wagons, flat on the floor. Men bell down under the wagons. Better have your guns ready. Martin Manor's wagon—the one with the red wheels—has the bulk of the ammunition. Get yourselves a good supply right now. We'll pull out in ten minutes."

Roy turned to Bostin. "We put the bones of your friends in a box. We'll have the burial later. Right now, I think we'd better light a shuck out of here before Black Hawk shows up."

"Agreed," said Clay nodding.

Bucky Wiseman, standing next to his new tall friend, said, "You can ride in my wagon with Rachel and me."

"Rachel rides with you?"

"Yep," said the oldster with a twinkle in his eye.

"She knows a real he-man when she sees one. Can't hardly keep her eyes offa me!"

Rachel was standing beside the wagon as the two men approached.

Ignoring Wiseman, she tilted her face upward. "Mister—Bostin is it?—I'm Rachel Flanagan."

It took the tall man about three seconds to find his voice. "I...I understand I owe you a big thank-you," he said.

"It isn't necessary," she said, smiling. "Just to see you up and walking is thanks enough."

The auburn beauty turned to mount the wagon. Quickly, the tall man offered his hand. "May I?"

"Certainly," she replied, placing her soft hand in his.

Chapter Four

Wagon wheels grated on rocks as the train moved westward. Before them lay the vast prairie. The land lay flat, broken by an occasional low butte and sometimes a shallow stream, usually lined with trees. The green spring grass swayed under the soft breezes which played haphazardly across the open fields.

Dale Roy rode morosely alongside Bucky Wiseman's lead wagon. Occasionally, he dropped back along the line of eleven prairie schooners, answering questions and carrying on brief conversations.

Rachel Flanagan sat between Wiseman and Clay Bostin.

Bostin's eyes carefully scanned the vast purple and green expanse, searching for any sign of movement.

Worry was etched on Rachel's face. "You've been through many battles with Indians, Mister Bostin?" she asked nervously.

The wagon swayed heavily as he answered without taking his eyes off the prairie. "More than I care to remember, ma'am."

"The scar on your face, was it—?"

"Yes, ma'am. Comanche tomahawk."

Rachel shuddered. Clay released his gaze from the sunlit prairie for a brief glance at her leaden face. "You afraid, ma'am?"

The young woman nodded, swallowing hard.

Bucky Wiseman spat a dark brown stream off to the side of the wagon.

A look of disgust touched Rachel's countenance. "Must you do that, Bucky?" she asked with furrowed brow.

"Yes'm," offered the old gent.

"Why?"

"Cuz it'd make me sick if I swallered it!" he said with a wry smile.

Clay Bostin laughed. Rachel followed suit. The tension of the moment had been eased.

Again, Bostin fixed his dark brown eyes on the prairie. Before them, a shallow valley came into view. It spread wide, with a gentle slope which bottomed out at a swollen stream. The heavy rain had brought life to the moving waters.

Clay Bostin could still feel the strain that gripped the young auburn-haired woman.

"You headed for Fort Laramie, Miss Flanagan?" he asked, in an effort to take her mind from the threat at hand.

"San Francisco," she answered.

"San Francisco? Long way for a young lady to be traveling by herself."

"Mm-hmm," she hummed, looking straight ahead.

"You have relatives in Frisco?"

"No. Fiancé."

A gray gloom swept over Clay Bostin like a savage ocean wave and settled in the pit of his stomach.

"I'm going to be married in San Francisco," she added.

His mouth suddenly dry, the man with the gray gloom in his stomach said, "He's...a mighty lucky man."

Rachel smiled quietly. Bucky spied a prairie dog sitting erectly beside a large rock. Spewing a straight brown stream, he hit the little animal square in the face. It wheeled and darted into a hold.

"You ever miss?" asked the girl.

"Only when the wind makes a sudden change," Wiseman said dryly.

"Where are you from?" Bostin asked the girl, trying to smother his disappointment.

"Chicago."

"That's a long way from San Francisco. How did you meet your fiancé?"

"We grew up together in Chicago." Rachel's eyes were fixed on the horizon. "Childhood sweethearts."

"Oh."

"He's in banking. Has a promising future in San Francisco."

Slowly turning his eyes on her, Clay said, "With a lovely lady like you beside him, he would have a promising future if he sold pencils on street corners."

Rachel managed a weak laugh. "Why, thank you, Mister Bostin."

Dale Roy pulled his big gelding alongside the wagon. "We'll cross the river, Bucky. Then we'll stop for chuck."

"Gotcha," said the weathered old driver. "Stomach *is* startin' to grumble."

The short side of an hour brought them to the riverbank. The water was swift and muddy. The horses required strong urging from Bucky Wiseman to enter the swollen stream. Reluctantly, they stepped in. Once in the belly-high waters, they strained into the harness and were quickly across.

Under the direction of Dale Roy, the eleven prairie schooners formed a tight circle. The aroma of hot food soon filled the air. Clay Bostin loaded his plate and slowly walked the perimeter of the circle, studying the four horizons. The guide soon joined him.

"See anything?" queried Roy, sipping on a steaming cup of coffee.

Bostin rolled food to one side of his mouth and replied, "No, but I feel something."

"They're watching us."

"Yep."

From the corner of his eyes, Clay saw the big man who had spoken out earlier coming toward them. His son followed close on his heels.

"Catch sight of 'em?" asked the big man.

"No," answered Bostin, flicking him a casual look.

"By the way," said the big man, "my name is Jack Sutherlin."

Bostin gripped Sutherlin's hand, cast a glance to the slender youth who stood behind like a nervous puppy, met Sutherlin's eye, and said, "Howdy."

Sutherlin ignored his son's presence. He opened his mouth to speak, when Dale Roy said, "Bostin, this is Jeremy Sutherlin."

Jeremy reached around his hulky father and shook Bostin's hand. "Glad to meet you, Mister Bostin. Your head feeling all right by now?"

The kid had a winsome smile. Bostin felt an immediate liking for him. His clean-cut appearance and sincere personal warmth were appealing. The only flaw Bostin could detect was the browbeaten look in his eyes.

"Much better, Jeremy," replied the tall angular man.

"How many men did Black Hawk have with him yesterday?" Jack Sutherlin asked Clay Bostin.

"Ten."

"How many we got who can handle a gun, Dale?" Sutherlin asked the thick-bodied guide.

"Fourteen, if you count Jeremy and Billy Adams."

Sutherlin shot a look of disgust at his son. "Guess we better say thirteen, then."

The boy flushed and dipped his chin.

Clay Bostin felt a touch of temper. Looking past the big man, he said, "You ever fire a gun, Jeremy?"

"Yes, sir," replied the youth.

"Rabbits and magpies can't shoot back," said Jack Sutherlin. "His guts will turn to butter if he has to face a hostile Indian."

"You ever fight Indians, Jack?" Bostin asked heatedly.

The big man squared his shoulders, stiffened his neck, and said, "No." Clearing his throat, he added, "But I fought Confederates in the war."

"You gonna tell me you didn't have any fear before going into battle?"

The big man glared hard at Bostin. Jeremy scrutinized his father's florid features. Sutherlin did not answer.

"Give the boy a chance," said Bostin.

"You heard him back there," snapped Sutherlin pointing eastward. "He wanted to turn and run like a yellowbelly!"

The youth took a deep breath. "Pa, I just—"

"None of us are eager to face Cheyenne warfare, Jack," Bostin bit in. Swinging his gaze to Jeremy, he said, "Jeremy, when the Indians attack, you come fight next to me."

Jack Sutherlin spat.

Jeremy smiled. "I'll do it, Mister Bostin!"

Clay Bostin surveyed the surrounding prairie, turned toward Dale Roy, and said, "We'd better get them moving again."

As they reentered the circle, Clay Bostin's eyes fell on a girl who leaned against a wagon, her head thrust back provocatively. Long, blond hair hung recklessly on her shoulders. Bostin guessed she might be sixteen. Fixing her large brown eyes on him, she said,

"Hello."

The tall man touched the brim of his hat. "Miss," he said, nodding.

Walking past her, he said to Dale Roy, "Who's the little flirt?"

"Flirt is right," chuckled Roy. "Her name's Sherry Manor. Her folks have the big wagon there with the red wheels. Thinks she's God's gift to the male species." Pointing across the circle to a curly-headed youth loading a box into the wagon, he said, "See the boy there with the box?"

"Uh-huh."

"Name's Billy Adams. He's sweet on her. She's supposed to be his girl, but all she does is torture him. Needs somebody to whomp her upside the head."

"Why doesn't her pa take her in hand?"

"He can't handle her."

Bostin shook his head. "Didn't you say the bulk of the ammunition was in his wagon?"

"Yep. It's bigger than the others, so we loaded it in there."

"Be a good idea to distribute it evenly in all the wagons," said Clay advisedly. "If the Cheyennes put a hot arrow in that one, we'd lose all the ammunition in one big boom."

"Yeah, you're right," agreed Roy. "I'll have it done when we pull in for the night. Right now, we better get our wheels rolling."

Clay started to object. It ought to be done right now. He was only a guest on this train, he reminded himself. *Better not stick my nose in too heavily.*

Bostin noticed Sherry Manor watching him as she sat on the wagon seat between her parents.

As the wagons fell into line, Rachel Flanagan and Clay Bostin resumed their positions on the seat of Bucky Wiseman's wagon. The elderly man bit off a fresh chaw from a plug of Bull Durham. Rachel crinkled her nose, looked at Clay, and shrugged her shoulders. Bucky caught her gesture. Pushing the soggy plug under her nose, he said "Here, honey, I know yer jist dyin' to git a leetle of this between your own jaws!"

Turning her face away, she gasped, "Yuk! Get that awful stuff away from me!"

Wiseman cackled. "Don't you never say I didn't offer yuh

some."

Soon, a silence settled over the train. The only sound above the usual noise of the wagons was the shrill cry of Esther Owen's baby.

Clay Bostin kept a careful examination on the face of the rolling prairie. The sun worked its way across the sky and began to slide downward.

At first it was just a distant speck. Clay squinted, his face turned toward the southwest. The speck was moving toward them.

Rachel saw him squinting. "What is it?" she asked, trying to fol-low his line of sight.

"Not sure. We'll know shortly. It's moving toward us."

Bucky Wiseman squinted, spat a brown stream, and squinted again. "It's a fly crawlin' on a rock, forty miles away," he said whim-sically. "I got eyes like an eagle."

"You also have a tongue like a salamander," iced Rachel.

Wiseman slapped his knee and guffawed.

The speck soon resolved itself into two men. It was apparent one was limping. As they drew near, Bucky said, "Buffalo hunters."

Stiffening the reins, the leathered oldster halted the wagon.

Rachel set her gaze on the two men. Both were young. Early twenties. Both were dirty and unkempt. They were about the same height and weight...lean, slender. The one who limped was dark, with matted hair protruding from under his filthy hat. It was evident he had not visited a barber in months.

The other was sandy-complexioned, with deep-set eyes and buckteeth. Orange-red hair, as long as his partner's, dangled from his hat brim. The stubble on his face was as red as his cohort's was black.

Both men carried .50 caliber Sharps buffalo guns. One had a battered canteen slung by a strap over his shoulder.

Dale Roy crossed his buckskin gelding in front of Wiseman's team and faced them. Clay Bostin climbed from the wagon.

"Howdy!" said the dark one. There was something about him Bostin did not like. A shifty look in his eyes...or was it the natural curl on the left side of his upper lip?

"Hello," replied Roy, dismounting.

"Name's Dub Smith," said the dark one. "Friend here is Lambert Fielder."

Fielder smiled, revealing a mouthful of oversize teeth.

Bucky spoke softly to Rachel. "Looks like that redheaded hombre swallowed a wagon wheel. Bet he can't close his mouth."

As Roy and Bostin closed in, Smith said, "We're buffalo hunters, from down Kansas way."

"Lose your horses?" queried Dale Roy.

"Yep," replied Smith, his eyes finding the face of Rachel Flanagan. Holding his gaze on her splendid features, he said, "Lamb's horse stepped in a hold. Busted her leg. Had to shoot 'er. We were ridin' double, when a hissly ole rattler sunk his fangs into my horse. He got real sick. Couldn't carry us no more."

Fielder spoke up. "We spotted y'all coupla hours ago. S'pose we could beg a little food? We ain't et in three days."

Clay stepped in front of Smith, who continued to cast glances toward the auburn beauty. His broad upper torso blocked the buffalo hunter's view.

"I noticed your limp," said Bostin. "You hurt?"

"Oh...no," said Smith, lifting his right foot. "Heel came off my boot."

"Where you fellas headin'?" asked the thick-bodied guide.

"Nowhere, really," replied Dub Smith. "We were huntin' a herd about twenty miles due south of here."

Clay Bostin's head snapped. "You were might close to the Cheyenne reservation. Good way to get yourselves scalped."

"Herd was movin' that way, mister. We was jist followin' the herd."

"Government has a treaty," said Bostin curtly. "White man is not to shoot buffalo within ten miles of any reservation."

A cynical sneer finished the wicked curl of Smith's lip. "Dumb savages can't measure miles."

Repulsed, Bostin turned to Dale Roy. "We'd best keep moving. Won't be long till sundown." With that, he returned and mounted the wagon.

"We'll give you boys some jerky, hardtack, and water," Roy told them. "Then we'll be on our way."

"Where you headin'?" asked Smith.

"Ultimately, Oregon," said Roy. "Right now, we're trying to make it to North Platte. Cheynnes are on the warpath."

Dub Smith's eyes widened. "Yeah?"

"Since when?" queried Fielder.

"Few days," said Dale Roy.

The two grisly buffalo hunters eyed each other.

Looking back to Roy, Smith said, "Any idea what put 'em on the warpath?"

"Nothing concrete."

"Would you have room for us till you get to North Platte?" asked the dark hunter. "We need to buy horses."

Dale Roy wiped a hand over his moustache. "I'll have to ask among the wagons." The stout man mounted the big buckskin. "Be back in a minute."

As Roy wheeled the gelding and trotted toward the other wagons, Dub Smith cast another look toward Rachel Flanagan. Rachel's eyes met his. Quickly, she turned to Bostin and whispered, "I don't like him."

"That makes two of us," said Bostin.

"Three of us," chimed Bucky Wiseman.

Shortly, the wagon train guide returned. They could ride with a couple who had space in the back of their wagon.

Clay watched Smith limp toward the rear, followed by Fielder.

"We've got trouble," said Wiseman, spitting sideways.

"*More* trouble, Bucky," said Clay Bostin. "We had trouble before those two showed up."

Chapter Five

Clay Bostin was awakened before dawn. Someone was skulking through the camp. Slowly, he rolled out of the bedroll, eased his Colt .45 from its holster, and strained his eyes against the heavy gloom.

One thing for sure. It was no Indian. The man was making too much noise. Abruptly, a dark form loomed over him.

"Hold it right there!" shouted Bostin, thumbing back the hammer.

"Don't shoot!" came a frightened response.

Clay moved toward him as others, coming awake, began to move in their bedrolls and rustle around in the wagons.

"Don't shoot me, mishter," said the man with a thick tongue. "I...I'm just tryin' to fine my wag—wagon."

The man burped and exhaled the sickening odor of whiskey.

A flame flickered behind Clay Bostin, followed by the bright glow of a lantern. Jack Sutherlin carried the lantern and stopped beside Bostin. The face of the drunken man was fully illuminated. The man covered his eyes, staggering.

"Harry Owen," said Sutherlin, with a loathsome tone. "Drunk again."

Dale Roy's burly frame moved into the light.

"Harry," he said loudly, "I told you if this happened again, your wagon would be discharged from the train."

A crowd was gathering now. A small woman with a tired look in her eyes threaded her way through the circle and appeared in the light. Speaking to the guide, she said pleadingly, "Please, Mister Roy. You can't leave us here with them Cheyennes on the prowl."

"We're going to need every man in this train, Mrs. Owen," retorted Roy. "If Harry is drunk when the attack comes, he'll be a liability, not an asset."

"I thought I had found all the whiskey he had stashed, Mister

Roy. I'll search the wagon again."

"All right, Mrs. Owen," Roy sighed, "Take him and sober him up."

Clay Bostin saw Rachel's face peering sleepily from the back of Bucky's wagon. Moving toward her, he said flatly, "Just a drunk man, Miss Flanagan."

"Mister Owen again," she said with disgust.

"You better catch yourself a little more shut-eye, ma'am," he said in a gentle tone.

"All right," she agreed softly, and disappeared.

Clay thought how beautiful she was, even when first awakened.

Returning to Jack Sutherlin, Bostin said, "I thought you were supposed to be on guard."

Sutherlin's face reddened in the light of the lantern. "I...uh...dozed off for a minute," he said, clearing his throat.

"If Owen had been fifty Cheyennes, we'd all be dead by now," Bostin said hotly.

"Indians don't attack at night, Bostin," snapped the hulky Sutherlin.

"As a general rule, that's true," said the tall, angular man. "It's part of their religion. But every now and then a few crop up in a tribe who aren't very religious."

"I wasn't aware—"

"Appears to me there are a lot of things you're not aware of, Sutherlin," sliced Bostin.

The big man's lips pulled tight against his teeth. "Like what?"

"Your son," retorted Clay curtly. "He's a fine boy. He's—"

"A lot you know about it, *stranger*," cut in Sutherlin, heavily emphasizing the last word. "You just butt out between me and Jeremy."

Clay Bostin knew he had no right to interfere between the big man and his son. However, his sense of fairness threw him in Jeremy's corner in the conflict between the two. Wordlessly, he turned away.

Jack Sutherlin doused the light and returned to his post. Clay Bostin glanced eastward. Dawn had painted the edge of the earth a dull gray.

Breakfast was ready when the sun peeked over the earth's rim.

All the Nebraska plain took on a rosy glow. The meadowlarks praised its beauty, singing to the newborn day.

Clay Bostin scanned the horizon, satisfied himself that all was safe for the moment, and sat down on a keg to eat.

Rachel Flanagan was carrying a hot coffeepot among the men, filling and refilling cups. She had brushed her hair and it was alive with color as it reflected the brightness of the sunrise.

"Good Morning," she said with a warm smile, filling Bostin's cup.

"'Morning, Miss Flanagan," he said, returning the smile. "Did you get back to sleep after the ruckus?"

"No," she replied. "I guess it was just too close to getting-up time." With that, she moved on.

On the other side of the circle, Clay noticed the two buffalo hunters, gulping food like starving wolves. The one called Smith was watching Rachel with even more appetite than he showed toward his food.

Bostin felt a hot rush of temper flash through his body.

As the tall man was scraping the final morsels from his tin plate, Sherry Manor appeared, standing over him. She had used too much perfume. "Good morning," she said, flipping her long blond hair with a toss of her head.

"Good Morning," replied Clay, smiling faintly.

"We haven't met formally...been introduced, I mean," said Sherry warmly.

Clay pulled himself erect. Towering over her, he said, "Guess not. I'm Clay Bostin."

"I know," she said, extending her hand. "I'm Sherry Manor."

"Glad to meet you, Miss Manor," said the tall Bostin, meeting her hand.

"We're from Illinois," said Sherry.

Clay released his grip on the girl's hand, but she held on.

"Did I hear you say you were born in this part of the country?" she asked.

"Yes," answered Bostin. "Fort Laramie. About twice as long ago as you were born in Illinois."

The smile that rode the girl's lips quickly vanished. Releasing his hand, she said, "You...uh...think the Cheyennes will bother us today?"

"Chances are mighty good, little lady," replied Bostin, draining his cup.

"I'm sure glad you're along to help us," said Sherry, walking away.

Bostin could not help but notice the young man with the dark, curly hair who rushed to meet Sherry Manor as she approached her parents' wagon. He was unhappy and made no attempt at concealing it.

Bucky Wiseman was attempting to return a heavy wooden box to its place in his wagon. Clay stepped toward him and said, "Here, Bucky, let me get that."

The leather-faced old man shot him a quick glance. "I can handle it, son." With that, he doubled his effort and heaved the box in the wagon.

The bottom rim of the sun departed form the earth's edge as Clay Bostin helped Rachel Flanagan into the wagon seat and stepped up to sit beside her. Before slacking into the seat, he lifted his gaze upward...and froze.

White puff balls of smoke were rising skyward from the crest of a distant ridge, due west.

Wheeling around, he fixed his gaze to the east.

"What is it?" demanded Rachel.

"Smoke signals."

Bucky was just climbing into the wagon. He shot a glance westward, spat, and cursed.

Without taking his gaze from the eastern plains, Clay Bostin said, "There's a lady present, Bucky."

The old gent cleared his throat. "I...er...ah...I'm sorry, Miss Rachel."

"Apology accepted," the lady said flatly.

Clay Bostin watched until he saw identical balls of smoke appear from a ridge about five miles behind them.

Bostin's voice bellowed, "Hey, Roy!"

The big buckskin galloped from near the tail of the assembling wagons. As Dale Roy reined in, Bostin said, "Smoke signals...east and west."

The big man twisted in the saddle, looking both ways.

"We're in for it," said Bucky Wiseman.

"No doubt about it," agreed Roy.

"Best thing to do, is—" Clay Bostin's words were cut short by a noisy disturbance to the rear. Angry voices were filling the morning air with cursewords.

Dale Roy spun his horse around and touched spurs to its sides. Clay Bostin jumped from the wagon and followed.

Billy Adams, his face livid with rage, was standing almost nose-to-nose with Dub Smith. A wicked sneer curled Smith's mouth. His eyes were cold and passionless. The people crowded around.

"You leave her alone, do you hear me?" shouted Billy.

Roy dismounted. "What's the trouble here?" he said briskly.

Sherry Manor stood between her parents, a sly look in her eyes.

"He's messin' with my girl, Mister Roy," said the young Adams heatedly.

"She come flirtin' my way," said Smith defensively. "She shore doesn't act like she's yore girl. I seen her shinin' up to this tall dude this mornin'." Smith was pointing at Clay Bostin."

"You leave her alone, or I'll—"

"You'll what, curly?"

"Both of you shut up!" bellowed Dale Roy. "We've got hostile Indians preparing to attack us. You two save your fighting energy for *them*." Turning toward Clay Bostin, Roy said, "Bostin, here, just sighted smoke signals."

A gasp of horror swept through the crowd.

"Now, we're gonna proceed as usual," advised Dale Roy. "The best thing is to keep moving. This land is flat enough, we can see 'em coming in plenty of time to form a circle. We need to keep moving toward North Platte. I'm hoping they'll have cavalry there that can escort us on to Fort Laramie. So let's move out!"

As the crowd broke up, Billy Adams eyed the grisly buffalo hunter. "You mess with Sherry again, I'll bust your head, Smith!" he said loudly.

Smith grinned defiantly and walked away, limping on the impaired boot.

Martin Manor eyed his daughter with open displeasure. Sherry tossed her head rebelliously. Manor gripped her forearm and said through his teeth, "You're gonna cause bloodshed, young lady, if you don't stop this. Billy is a fine boy. Much too good for the likes of you. I'm sick of you usin' him like a toy...pickin' him up when he suits your fancy...droppin' him when you want to google-eye at somebody else. Why don't you just be honest with him? Tell him you don't care nuthin' about him?"

"It's my life," Sherry retorted defensively. "I'll live it to please me."

Manor's palm struck her face sharply. The girl stumbled, but Manor's grip on her arm kept her from falling. Mrs. Manor burst into tears.

"Get in the wagon, you little hussy!" hissed her father.

The girl's face had a bright red blotch where the open palm had connected, but as she climbed into the wagon, she displayed no emotion.

As Clay Bostin lowered his lean, muscular frame into the seat beside Rachel Flanagan, his eye caught the ashen pallor of her skin. Fear was evident in her blue eyes.

"I knew that hunter was gonna cause trouble," said Bostin, half to himself.

Bucky Wiseman snapped the reins, speaking to the horses. Once again the wagon train was moving.

"Mister Bostin," said Rachel quietly, "I've never fired a gun, but if you'll tell me what to do, I'll be glad to use one."

"We've just about got one gun for each man, ma'am," said the square-jawed man. "I don't even have a rifle myself. Have to use my pistol. Black Hawk's .44-70 Spencer is back here with Bucky's stuff, but I don't have any cartridges for it."

"When they come, honey," said Wiseman, "we want you *inside* the wagon."

"Get down between the boxes and stay there," added Bostin.

Rachel shuddered, crossed her hands over her midsection, cupped elbows in palms. Her body shook as she bent forward.

The two men eyed each other.

"Well, go on, Clay," said the older man. "I gotta hang on to these leathers!"

Clay Bostin reached his arm around her back and squeezed her shoulder. "It'll be all right, Miss Flanagan," he said, forcing a note of optimism into his voice. "We'll get through this, and in no time at all you'll be on the other side of Fort Laramie, heading for San Francisco."

Straightening up, she looked into his dark brown eyes. Lifting her shoulders, she took a deep breath and let it out slowly. There was an unfathomable something in her eyes. Clay could not read its meaning, but it was there.

"Thank you," said Rachel. "You are a very kind man."

She let her line of sight drift to the vast expanse before them. Bostin's arm was still around her. She had made no move to release it. He kept it there until her trembling subsided, then slowly let go. Acknowledging the movement, she looked at him and smiled.

Abruptly, Dale Roy's big voice pierced the air. *"Here they come!"*

Clay Bostin turned in the seat as Roy rode by. Immediately, Bucky Wiseman swung the wagon to the right. The other wagons followed suit until Bucky closed the circle behind the last wagon.

The tall man leaped from the wagon. He could hear a baby crying as Dale Roy barked orders. Rachel Flanagan's horror-stricken blue eyes were fastened on the face of Bostin.

"Get in the back," he said hurriedly. "Stay there. Please."

As Rachel obeyed, Clay turned to face Jeremy Sutherlin, who held a Winchester seven-shot repeater.

"You told me to come fight with you," said the youth, face blanched.

"Okay, kid...under the wagon."

Bucky Wiseman bellied down beside Jeremy, positioning the big buffalo gun.

Bostin ducked under the heads of the horses, which stood with their noses to the rear of Bucky's wagon. He caught the rhythmic beat of swift hooves before he saw them. A quick glance to the left brought them into view. There were about twenty-five, Clay judged. Half-naked bronze devils, striped with white paint, coming at full gallop.

As Bostin dived under the wagon, gun ready, he could hear Jeremy sobbing.

"Come on, now, boy," said Bostin firmly. "We need you."

Suddenly, the air was filled with bloodcurdling yells, the hideous warcry of the Cheyennes.

"Come on, Jeremy, get ready," implored Bucky Wiseman.

Dale Roy could be heard, urging everyone to hold fire until the oncoming horde was close. The earth trembled under the thundering hooves.

When the Cheynnes came within about fifty yards, they suddenly divided, in order to encircle the wagons. They were coming close now...screeching, whooping, barking like wild dogs. Bucky wet his thumb on his tongue, touched it to the muzzle of the .50 caliber gun.

Jeremy was still weeping.

Quickly Clay holstered his Colt and lifted the Winchester form Jeremy's trembling fingers. Checking the load, he said, "Got any more shells, Jeremy?"

Nodding, the youth reached to his side and slid a large box of cartridges toward the hand of Bostin.

The screeching Cheynnes were closing in. Dale Roy's first shot rang out, followed by a clattering volley from the circled wagons. The deep roar of Smith and Fielder's buffalo guns contrasted with the bark of the other rifles.

Clay Bostin drew a bead on a young painted buck and squeezed the trigger. The Indian clawed briefly at the pain in his chest and toppled form his pony.

Bucky's big gun boomed. A pony went down, spilling its rider. The Indian rolled over and came to his knees. Bostin's gun barked again, dropping the savage flat-faced on the sod.

An arrow hissed, thudded, and twanged into the wagon bed just over their heads.

The air was filled with smoke now. The smell of burnt gunpowder stung their nostrils. Bostin emptied Jeremy's rifle and Bucky's Sharps roared as Bostin reloaded. A bullet nicked dust in Wiseman's eyes. The old man swore as he thumbed away the particles. Another bullet struck the metal rim of one of the wagon wheels and caromed away angrily.

For a brief moment the smoke cleared, and Clay caught a glimpse of Black Hawk, wearing full headdress, astride his albino stallion. The colorless animal faded in contrast with the redskinned, brightly painted savage on its back. Two horsemen suddenly blocked Bostin's view. Bucky's rifle discharged, spewing a cloud of smoke...and Black Hawk was gone.

Within two minutes the howling Cheyennes were pulling away.

A few rifles on that side of the circle were still firing. Clay waited for the sound of Dale Roy's voice to command the cease-fire. It did not come. Sliding backward, the tall man jumped to his feet and ran toward those who still were firing.

"Hey! Stop shooting!" Bostin yelled. "They're out of range! You're wasting ammunition!"

The firing abruptly ceased.

Tossing a circular glance around him, Bostin asked a couple of men, "Where's Roy?"

Both shook their heads.

Darting for Bucky's wagon, Clay pulled back the canvas flap at the rear. Rachel was still flat on the floor.

"You all right, little lady?" he asked, brow furrowed.

Sitting up slowly, she said, "I...think so."

"Let me help you out," said Clay, extending his hands.

Rachel leaned forward, bracing her hands on his sinewy shoulders. She fixed her eyes on his. Clay caught a glimpse of that same look he had seen earlier.

"Dale Roy's dead!" It was the big voice of Jack Sutherlin.

Releasing her, Clay said, "You wait here."

Sutherlin and several others were gathered around the inert form of Dale Roy, lying faceup next to the rear wheel of the Peabody wagon. A feathered arrow was sunk deep in Roy's massive chest.

Two other men were dead, Avery Wilson and Jed Healy. Their wives wept amid the sympathy of the other women. Two others had been wounded.

The young Lon Berry stood at the rear of his wagon, frozen in his tracks. He was holding the flap open, staring wide-eyed into the wagon. Suddenly, he turned toward Jack Sutherlin. His face was a twisted mask of horror. A wild, savage scream escaped his lips as he charged the big man insanely, fists flailing.

Sutherlin sidestepped him. Berry, having flung himself full-force, rolled on the ground. Gaining his feet, he screeched, "*You!* You just *had* to make us keep going! It's *your* fault, Sutherlin! Why didn't you listen to Jeremy?"

Berry charged again. Sutherlin met him with a meaty fist to the jaw. The slender man slumped earthward.

Clay Bostin ran to the Berry's wagon. Peering in, he turned

quickly away, his face blanched. Rachel Flanagan scurried toward him. "What is it?" she gasped.

"Don't look in there!" Bostin said, too late. Rachel was already looking inside the wagon.

"Oh, no—" she breathed, her legs giving way.

She did not pass out, but were it not for the tall man she would have fallen to the ground. Rachel Flanagan began to weep.

Several others were gathering around the wagon. Bucky Wiseman fixed his gaze inside and swore. The young mother had been holding her baby snugly to her breast. A Cheyenne arrow had ripped through the canvas cover, pierced the infant's head, and buried its tip in the mother's heart.

Clay Bostin cast a glance toward Lon Berry, who was now being helped to his feet by Jeremy Sutherlin. Berry's eyes were glassy.

Rachel made her way to the cluster of women who sought to comfort the newly made widows. Other women were tending to wounded husbands.

Harry Owen stumbled toward his wagon under the watchful eye of his wife.

The two buffalo hunters stood aloof, carefully observing the scene.

Martin Manor approached Clay Bostin. "You think they'll hit us again, Bostin?"

"I'm not sure," answered the tall man, "But I wouldn't doubt it. Let's take a look at *their* losses."

Retrieving Jeremy Sutherlin's rifle, Bostin moved through the tight circle of wagons. Martin Manor followed, as did Bucky Wiseman.

Tossing a glance in the direction in which Black Hawk and his warriors had fled, Bostin said, "They'll be back for these bodies. Best thing we can do is get moving again. We'll have to bury our own dead first."

The three men counted six Cheyenne bodies. Five of them had used bows. One of them had an old Remington .44 single-shot rifle.

"Just as well take this rifle," said Bucky, picking it up. On the dead Indian's body he found ten cartridges.

As the three men reentered the circle, Jack Sutherlin plodded forward, face reddened. "What are you doin' with Jeremy's gun,

Bostin?" he demanded rudely.

Clay looked down at the rifle in his hand, then met the large man's burning gaze. "He loaned it to me," Clay said curtly.

Jeremy was standing next to his father.

"Why?" boomed Sutherlin. "You got a gun on your hip!"

The youth's face revealed his utter dismay.

"The boy had never been in a battle before, Sutherlin," said Bostin icily. "He'll be all right next time."

Jack Sutherlin swore vehemently, cast a disgusted look at his son, and stomped away.

Jeremy's face was pinched and pale. Mrs. Sutherlin, who had been listening to her husband's tirade, detached herself from the huddled group of women. Slipping a tender hand around Jeremy's waist, she said, "Don't worry about it, son. Your father will get over it."

Looking straight ahead, the degraded youth said with tight lips, "No, he won't, Ma. I'm a yellow coward. He knows it, I know it."

"That's not true, son," she said soothingly. "I know you. You are as good a man as ever there was."

"You're kiddin' yourself, Ma." Jeremy's face was stolid. "I wish they'd killed me instead of Mister Roy."

Chapter Six

The bodies of the six Cheyennes still lay sprawled in the blood-soaked grass as the wagons pulled away.

Clay Bostin swung into the saddle of Dale Roy's big buckskin. A brief discussion among the survivors and a quick vote had placed the tall plainsman in charge of the wagon train. He would lead them as far as Fort Laramie. The only dissenting vote was that of Jack Sutherlin. Even Jeremy had defied his overbearing sire and raised his hand for Clay Bostin.

Rachel Flanagan cast an approving eye at the tall man in the saddle. She thought of how natural he looked on the magnificent animal, back straight, shoulders wide.

The train's new leader waited until the last wagon was in motion, did a careful scan of the southern horizon, then touched spurs to the gelding's sides. For a moment his gaze fell on the fresh mounds protruding ominously from the sod. He wondered how many more would die before they reached the fort.

Along with those who were just killed, the charred remains of the Rodman family had finally been laid to rest.

Setting the buckskin's pace to hold just to the right rear of Bucky Wiseman's wagon, Bostin fixed his eyes on the fascinating profile of Rachel Flanagan. A coldness swept over him as he thought of her fate if the Cheyennes captured her alive. A sick dread settled in his stomach. He must not let that happen.

From time to time Bostin dropped back along the line. Billy Adams drove the wagon for Maude Healy, whose husband lay beneath the sod of the makeshift burial ground. Lambert Fielder drove the wagon for the other widow. Dub Smith rode on the seat with Fielder. One of the wounded men, Horace Nething, drove with his arm in a sling. Jeremy Sutherlin, feeling quite unwelcome in his father's wagon, voluntarily drove for the other wounded man,

Chester Manley. The latter had taken a Cheyenne bullet in the upper chest. There was serious question whether he would live.

Clay Bostin studied the face of the man who drove the wagon just behind Jeremy Sutherlin. He fixed his eyes for a moment on the woman who sat beside him. These had to be the parents of young Billy Adams.

Pulling alongside the wagon, the man on the buckskin said, "I haven't met you folks formally, but I think your name is Adams."

"Yessir," replied the rugged-looking, handsome man. "*Cliff* Adams, Mister Bostin...and this is Mary Lou."

Bostin touched his hat brim and smiled at Mrs. Adams. Abruptly, two girls poked their heads through the opening behind the seat. "I'm Melanie," said one.

"And I'm Suzanne," chimed the other.

Melanie appeared to be about eleven or twelve. Suzanne would be a year or so younger. Both favored their mother as much as their older brother favored his father.

The tall man touched his hat again, nodded, and said, "Hello, ladies."

Looking at Cliff Adams, Bostin said, "That's a fine boy you have there, Mister Adams."

"Thank you," replied Adams.

"I appreciate his driving the wagon for Mrs. Healy."

"He's glad to do it."

Clay Bostin set his jaw in a serious line. "You might warn the boy, Mister Adams. He should go easy with that hide-hunter. His kind have no scruples. He might do Billy harm over that Manor girl."

An apprehensive look clouded Adams's countenance. His eyes hardened. "She's a tramp, Bostin," he said tightly. "I've tried to get Billy to see it, but he thinks he's in love. She sure isn't worth getting bloodied up over."

"Better talk to him some more," warned Bostin. "For his own good."

"Will do," said Cliff Adams.

Working his way toward the lead wagon, Clay passed Lon Berry. The young man sat in the middle of the seat, holding the reins and staring blankly into space. The wagon train's new leader doubted if Berry would be any help when Black Hawk attacked again.

Spurring the buckskin to a gallop, Bostin raced ahead of Bucky's wagon for about a hundred yards. Reining to a halt, he stood in the stirrups and ran his gaze over the plains in all directions.

Bucky Wiseman squinted at the towering, muscular man on the big gelding. Spitting a brown stream at a white rock protruding from the green earth, he elbowed the auburn beauty next to him and said, "That there is some hunk O' man, honey."

Rachel Flanagan, who was already watching Bostin's every move, said, "Mm-hmm. He sure is."

"That feller you're a-fixing to marry...is he like Clay Bostin?"

Rachel did not answer. She kept her eyes straight forward.

Bucky waited another half minute. "Is he?"

Still she did not answer.

The old gent let the question pass and asked another. "Yuh know he likes yuh purty good, don'tcha?"

"Mister Bostin?" she asked.

"Yeah. It's in his eyes, honey."

Wiseman looked at the side of the train. "Yuh see that yellow flower, Rachel?"

Leaning toward the old man for a better view, she said, "Yes."

"Watch." He spit and hit the small flower dead center. "Whattya think of that?" he cackled.

"I guess everybody's got to have a goal in life," she said.

"How do you feel about him?" asked Bucky, resuming the conversation.

"Who?"

"Clay Bostin, girl. Clay Bostin."

"He's a very nice man, Bucky. I like him."

As the wagons drew nearer, Bostin rode further ahead, until he reached the crest of a gradual rise which slanted sharply on the other side. The steep slope reached its low point about a mile away.

Bostin's eyes focused on a cluster of vague, dark objects. Being familiar with the trail, he knew it was something that was not ordinarily there. Raking the gelding's sides, he pressed the animal into a steady lope. Quickly, the nebulous cluster began to take shape. It was clearly a group of wagons. Some were lying on their sides...others were upside down. From two hundred yards away, the tall man could count six wagons.

Upon approach, a chill came into Clay Bostin's face. The smell of blood and death hung like a bitter pall in the air.

He first saw a dead man, sprawled face down, two arrows in his back. His scalp had been lifted. Flies were crawling through the bright red mass where his hair had been.

Bostin's dark, piercing eyes darted back and forth. He shuddered to see a middle-aged woman, her clothing half off, dangling scalpless and bloody over the side of an overturned wagon.

Three children were lying in a lifeless heap, their bodies riddled with bullet holes. Their hair had not been touched.

The body of an elderly man lay face up, eyes staring sightlessly skyward. Another man lay dead, pinned under an overturned wagon. Both of them had been brutally scalped. Inside the wagon were the bodies of two older women.

Next to another wagon lay a dead saddle horse. Draped over the horse's neck was its rider, an arrow through the side of his neck. *Must have been the guide*, Clay told himself.

Two young men and an elderly man lay huddled together in a heap. They had died a common death. Their hands were tied behind their backs, throats slit.

Clay Bostin felt a hot rage wash over him. This was Black Hawk's ultimate brutality.

Suddenly, from the corner of his eye, he saw two forms lying prostrate on the ground about thirty yards off. Urging the buckskin toward them, he quickly eyed two young women staked to the ground, stripped of their clothing. Both were smeared with blood.

At that moment, he heard the sound of the wagon train descending the slope. Whirling the horse about, he quickly rode to the overturned wagons and slid from the saddle. Rummaging hastily through the nearest wagon, he sunk his fingers into two blankets and ran to cover the bodies of the two young women. Dropping one blanket to the ground, he flipped the other to its full length and knelt down to cover the body, head to feet. His heart leaped to his throat. The girl's head moved. Her lips uttered a faint moan.

She's still alive!

Covering her with the blanket up to her neck, Clay picked up the second blanket and ran to the other girl. Her sightless eyes would never see again. She had died a death of utter horror. He closed the girl's eyes and, spreading the blanket, covered her entire body. A wave of nausea swept over him.

Running to the buckskin, he slipped the canteen from the saddle and hurried to the bruised and bleeding girl. Kneeling, he poured small portions of the cool liquid into her swollen mouth.

Clay Bostin did not want the people of his wagon train to see the bloody carnage, but it was too late. The prairie schooners were stopping, one by one. He could hear the excited voices of some of the people decrying what their eyes beheld.

Within moments, Rachel had located him and was running toward him. Bucky was on her heels.

Clay stood up as Rachel reached him. Her face was white and lined with terror. "Oh, it's awful!" she exclaimed, looking into his face. "They're all dead!"

Rachel's eyes fell on the girl. A sorrowful cry escaped her lips as she moved toward the victim and knelt down. Tenderly, Rachel stroked the young woman's face. Looking up at Bostin, she said, "Let me have the canteen."

As Clay handed it to her, Bucky Wiseman moved beside him.

"Can you cut her loose from the stakes?" asked Rachel.

Quickly, the tall plainsman ran to his horse, pulled a hunting knife from a saddlebag, and cut the thongs which held the girl's wrists and ankles to the stakes.

Bucky looked at the prostrate form and breathed something Clay could not distinguish.

Lifting the girl's head, Rachel spoke softly, stroking her battered face. Slowly, she gave her water.

Casting a glance to the blanket-covered body, Rachel looked up at Clay Bostin. "Another one?"

Clay nodded. Rachel closed her eyes, shaking her head.

"She can ride in my wagon, Clay," offered Bucky.

Bostin nodded again.

"We'd better not move her for awhile," said the lady with the auburn hair. "Let's wait till we're ready to pull out. Just leave me here with her."

The bruised young woman opened her eyes and studied

Rachel's face. She was trying to speak as the two men walked away.

"It's a cryin' shame," said Bucky, wagging his head. "Poor little gal will have nightmares the rest of her life...if she lives."

Entering the area where people had gathered, Clay Bostin looked from face to face. The crowd was stunned.

Jeremy Sutherlin was doubled over behind a wagon, giving up his breakfast. Mrs. Adams was commanding her daughters to remain in the wagon. Lon Berry sat on the seat of his wagon, looking blankly at the bloody scene.

Sherry Manor stood beside her mother, face blanched.

Jack Sutherlin, Martin Manor, Cliff Adams, Billy Adams, and Elmer Peabody had begun digging.

Bostin eyed the two scruffy buffalo hunters, who leaned against a wagon nonchalantly.

"There are more shovels around, fellas," Bostin said curtly. "The quicker we get these bodies buried, the quicker we move on."

Immediately, Lambert Fielder departed from the wagon and hunted up a shovel. Dub Smith shot the tall leader an insolent look and said, "I ain't diggin' no graves."

Bostin felt his face turn hot. "All right, Smith. You get off the train right here. Start walkin'."

Smith's eyes hardened. "You ain't got no authority over me, cowboy," he said angrily.

"That's right, hide-hunter," Bostin said with a raw look. "My authority extends only to this wagon train. Since you are no longer a part of it, I have no authority over you. Start walkin'."

Smith spat and called Clay Bostin a string of bad names. Bostin's temper flared. Three quick steps brought him face-to-face with the unkempt hunter. The tall man's rawboned right fist flashed like lightning, striking the bearded Smith flush on the left jaw. He went down like cut timber, out cold.

Turning to the stunned group of travelers, Bostin said, "We've got to hurry, folks. Black Hawk did this. He's probably watching us right now. We must get to North Platte as soon as possible."

"How far are we from there, Mr. Bostin?" asked Frieda Manley. "Chester is going to die if we don't get him to a doctor. That Cheyenne bullet has got to come out of his chest."

"It's a good three days' travel, Mrs. Manley," replied Bostin. "I mean three days without interruptions."

The woman turned away, face pinched, eyes watery. Maude Healy walked her back to the Manley wagon.

Picking up a shovel, Clay headed for the chosen burial area. Bucky had already joined the burial detail.

"Is that girl Rachel's tendin' to going to make it, Mister Bostin?" It was the voice of Mrs. Manor. Clay turned to answer and saw that Sherry Manor had left her mother's side and was kneeling beside the unconscious buffalo hunter.

"I don't know, ma'am," answered Bostin. "Maybe Rachel could use your help in examining her."

Mrs. Manor cast her daughter a hard look and moved in the direction on Rachel Flanagan.

Before going further, the tall man remembered that he had not seen Harry Owen. Carrying the shovel loosely at his side, he headed for the Own wagon. Inside, Mrs. Owen was wrestling with her two boys, trying to keep them in the wagon, while holding her tiny baby.

Looking through the opening, he said, "Where's Harry, Mrs. Owen?"

Her face was colorless and etched with fatigue. "I don't know, Mister Bostin," she answered wearily. "He's got to be around somewhere."

Clay Bostin turned away and began walking among the wagons. Looking right and left, his eye caught the hunched form of Harry Owen sitting about fifty yards from the cluster of wagons, in the grass. The sun reflected from the whiskey bottle in his hand.

Dropping the shovel, Bostin walked briskly to Owen, who was already bleary-eyed. Snatching the bottle from Owen's strengthless fingers, he dashed it against a half-buried rock, shattering it.

"You got any more stashed, Harry?" demanded the wagon leader.

Owen shook his head, rubbing his bloodshot eyes. "Nope. Tha's the las' one."

Sinking his fingers into the wobbly man's denim jacket, Bostin lifted him to his feet. "You get back to your wife and help her with those kids," snapped Bostin.

Inside of two hours the dead had been buried. Clay Bostin had found a Bible in Dale Roy's saddlebags. He read over the graves, committing the bodies to the sod and the souls to the Lord.

Returning to Rachel, he found the battered girl awake. Mrs. Manor also remained at the girl's side.

"How's she doing?" asked Bostin with interest.

"She's hurt bad," said Rachel heavily. "Are we ready to go?"

Clay nodded. "Let me get a hold of her, I'll carry her to the wagon." Bending over to pick her up, he noticed that the girl had been cleaned up and was wrapped in a different blanket.

The huddled group watched intently as the tall, muscular plainsman carried the young woman to Bucky's wagon and placed her in it gently. He helped Rachel Flanagan climb in and turned toward the buckskin. His eye caught Billy Adams and Dub Smith near the Manor wagon in a heated argument. Martin Manor was trying to break it up.

Bostin moved in and stood between them, facing Smith. From the corner of his eye, he saw Sherry, a smug look on her face.

Smith bolted Bostin with a look of raw hatred.

"I thought I told you to hit the trail, Smith," said Bostin through his teeth.

"You ain't animal enough to turn a man out by hisself with them bloodthirsty Cheyenne on the prowl, are you, Bostin?"

Clay wanted to hit him again. Holding himself in control, he said, "You can stay on *two conditions.*"

"And they are..."

"Number one. You pull your weight around here like everybody else."

"And.. ?"

"You stay completely away from Sherry Manor. I mean it." Bostin's face was like chiseled granite.

Smith glared at him silently, then glanced at Sherry. The girl tilted her head and smiled weakly.

Billy Adams, filled with anger, said, "If he don't, Mister Bostin, I'm gonna break his greasy neck!"

"I'm waiting for your answer, Smith," barked Bostin.

The repulsive hunter let his face relax and said, "Okay, Mister Boss Man. Okay."

"Give me just one excuse, Smith," sliced Bostin, "and Billy won't get a chance at you. I'll feed you to the Hawk. You savvy?"

Before Smith could answer, Cliff Adams, standing to Bostin's left side, said, "You won't need to, Clay. If he causes any more trouble, I'll take care of him myself." Adams's eyes were red with fire.

"Do I have your word on it?" Bostin asked Smith, hovering over him.

"Yeah," he nodded. "Yeah. You have my word."

Turning to the crowd, Clay said, "Let's move out. We've only got three more hours of daylight."

As the crowd dispersed, Billy Adams eyed Dub Smith with a hard look and spat.

Chapter Seven

The last rays of the westering sun set the long, narrow clouds on fire. Within moments, the deep red faded to a pale pink. Daylight contended momentarily in a futile struggle; then succumbed to darkness.

Three campfires cast dancing shadows against the wagons as the weary travelers sat down to eat.

Clay Bostin was standing at the rear of the Manley wagon, looking in. Frieda Manley lit a lantern and looked at Bostin dolefully. "The bullet's got to come out, Mister Bostin. He hasn't a chance if it stays in there."

The tall man took a deep breath and let it out slowly. Tilting his hat to the back of his head, he said, "Mrs. Manley, I've dug bullets out of men before, and I'll do it if you ask me. But I can't guarantee a thing."

Reaching from her seated position in the wagon, Frieda Manley squeezed his forearm. "He'll die for sure if we don't try. Please, Mister Bostin, will you do it?"

Clay looked into her tired, pleading eyes. "Yes, ma'am. If that's what you want."

Word soon spread through the camp of the impending surgery. Clay Bostin ordered water to be boiled. While he waited, he loaded a plate and stood near one of the fires, eating. Presently, a small feminine form moved beside him and a soft voice spoke. "Do you need any help, Mister Bostin? I just heard you're going to be the camp surgeon."

Rachel Flanagan's hair rested casually on her shoulders, shining delectably in the firelight. The tall man eyed her warmly. "Guess I *could* use a good nurse, come to think of it." Running his gaze toward Bucky's wagon, he said, "How's the little lady doing?"

Rachel lifted her shoulders and eased them down with a sigh.

"Hard to tell. She's been awake off and on. Mrs. Manor is with her at the moment. She's lost a lot of blood. Her name is Beth Ann Kiser. She was traveling with her husband. The Cheyennes..." Rachel placed the fingertips of both hands to her temples and closed her eyes. "The Cheyennes...violated...violated her repeatedly...beat her when she...when she screamed." A shudder vibrated Rachel's small frame.

Bostin placed a firm hand on her shoulder. "Get a grip on yourself, Miss Flanagan."

Tears appeared in her eyes. "That other poor girl. After they were through with her, they used a rifle barrel—" Rachel burst into tears. Dropping his plate, the tall plainsman folded her into his arms. Sobbing, she cried, "Oh, Mister Bostin, why do they have to be so barbaric and cruel? Don't those savages have any feelings? How can they be so inhuman? How can they—?" Her words were lost in muffled sobs, buried in Clay Bostin's chest.

As he held the delicate, weeping Rachel Flanagan tightly, Bostin's eyes fell on Dub Smith, who sat on the ground, back against a wagon wheel. The contemptible hide-hunter was eyeing him with heated scorn.

Maude Healy came near and said, "Is she all right, Mister Bostin?"

Clay nodded. "Just tired and a bit frightened, ma'am. The girl we found staked out described some of the Cheyenne brutalities."

"Oh, you poor dear," said Mrs. Healy, patting Rachel's shoulder.

Turning toward the older woman, Rachel sniffed, wiped tears from her eyes, and said, "I'm sorry, Mrs. Healy. I should be comforting *you*. You just buried your husband." Looking up at Clay Bostin, she said, "I'll be all right now, Mister Bostin. I would like to help you with the surgery."

"That's the spirit, honey," said Maude Healy. "Helping others takes your mind off your own problems."

"Find the sharpest knife in the camp and hold the blade in the fire for at least half a minute," Clay said to Rachel. "I'll need soap to scrub my hands."

"I have the soap in my wagon," offered Maude Healy.

"Bucky has a real sharp knife," said Rachel, walking away. "I'll get it."

Clay Bostin moved around the circle toward the Owen wagon. Mrs. Owen was feeding the baby. Harry was eating with the two older children, sitting on the ground. He looked up at the tall wagon-master. "Howdy, Mister Bostin," he said, smiling.

"Harry, have you got any more whiskey hidden in your wagon?" asked Bostin.

Owen's eyes widened. "No, sir," he said emphatically. "Not a drop."

Clay set his eyes on the woman.

"If he does, I don't know where it is," she said, meeting Bostin's gaze.

"I need it for Chester Manley," said Bostin, looking back at Owen. "Gotta dig a bullet out of his chest."

Owen swallowed hard. "Sorry. I ain't got no more."

Clay wheeled and walked to the center of the circle. He noticed Dub Smith limping away from the central fire, carrying a cup of steaming coffee.

"Folks, can I have your attention?" bellowed Bostin. The conversation among the people trailed off and faded into silence. Every eye was fixed on the tall man.

"I need every man in the camp to keep a sharp lookout while I operate on Chester Manley. Black Hawk and his cutthroats are following us. You can't see them, but they're out there. For some reason, he chose to go ahead of us and massacre that small wagon train we found this afternoon. But he's after *us*."

"Why us, more than any other train?" came an unidentified voice from the fringe of the crowd.

"I don't know," replied Bostin, squinting his eyes in the direction of the questioner. "But I *do* know Cheyenne terror tactics. Black Hawk apparently knew about the other wagon train. They were traveling no more than two or three hours ahead of us. I had noticed their tracks earlier. He deliberately wiped them out Cheyenne-style to throw fear and dread into us. The normal thing for Black Hawk to do would have been to attack us again before sundown. Instead, he ran ahead and let us find what you all saw."

"You think they'll come at us at night?" It was Elmer Peabody's voice.

"I'm not sure," answered Bostin. "With most hostiles, you can relax after sundown. They won't attack, for fear of dying at night. Superstition in their religion says to die in battle at night causes the soul to wander alone forever, blind in the darkness. They have a fearsome dread of this fate."

"Well, then, what are we worried about?" chimed in Jack Sutherlin, stepping toward Bostin. "We can all relax and—"

"However, there is one danger," cut in Bostin. "You get a chief who does not hold to their religion...one who can convince the braves that he has power to control things in the spirit world...and you'll have night fighters."

"You have some reason to believe that Black Hawk has shucked the Cheyenne religion?" asked Cliff Adams, who stood near the fire.

"No," replied Clay, "but he's the kind to do it. His braves would ride their ponies over a cliff if Black Hawk told them to. He's almost like a god to them. And he's smart. Plenty smart."

Bostin ran his eyes over the crowd. "One thing we all need to concentrate on, men. When they come at us again, look for Black Hawk and try to kill *him*. If you do the others will scatter like rabbits."

"What does he look like?" asked Jack Sutherlin.

"Rides an albino," replied Bostin. "He's the only one wears a full headdress."

Looking at Cliff Adams, Clay said, "Mister Adams, will you take charge of setting up the watch?"

Adams smiled and nodded. "Sure will."

Scanning the crowd, the tall wagon master said, "I need whiskey for Chester Manley. Anybody got some?"

Several faces turned toward Harry Owen, who was already shaking his head.

"I got some, Clay," said Bucky Wiseman. Chuckling, he said, "Keep it for medicinal purposes." A round of laughter moved through the crowd.

"I need a couple of you men to lift Manley out of the wagon and lay him here by the fire." Instantly, Billy Adams and Martin Manor headed for the Manley wagon. Rachel spread blankets on the ground, next to the fire.

Clay Bostin poured some of the hot water in a shallow pan. Accepting a bar of homemade soap from Maude Healy, he rolled up his sleeves and vigorously washed his hands. Martin Manor and young Adams eased the wounded man onto the blanket. Bostin leaned over Manley, pulled back the torn shirt, removed the compresses, and studied the wound.

Manley was awake and breathing hard. Twice, he coughed and spat blood. Focusing on Clay Bostin's angular face, he said haltingly, "What...what do you think...Bos—Bostin?"

Clay bit his lip, looked up at Frieda Manley, then back at the wounded man. Shaking his head, he said, "The slug is in the upper chest, Manley...I think it punctured your lung."

"I understand," said Manley, nodding slightly. "Just—" He coughed again. Blood appeared at the corners of his mouth. "Just do the best...you can."

Lifting his line of sight, Clay said, "Where's Bucky?"

"Right here, Clay," answered the leather-faced old man. "Here's the whiskey."

Taking the bottle from Wiseman's curled fingers, Bostin said, "Manley, I want you to drink as much of this as you can. Leave me enough to pour in the wound after the slug is out." Twisting off the cap, he lowered the bottle toward Manley's mouth. Hesitating momentarily, he said, "Mrs. Manley, would you sit down here and put his head in your lap?" As she did so, Bostin handed the bottle to her. "Make him drink, will you?"

Clay stood up and removed his hat. Rachel stood by, holding Bucky's knife. "Miss Flanagan," he said, "would you get me some more cloths for compresses? Put them in cold water and stay close. I'll need them as soon as I take out the slug." As she scuttled away, Clay spoke to those women who had gathered around. "Stand back, ladies. I'll do better if nobody looks over my shoulder."

From out on the dark prairie came the lonely howl of a coyote. Clay raised his head, listening. Soon the sound was repeated from the opposite direction. Lifting his voice, Bostin called, "Adams! Keep your eyes peeled! May be Cheyennes!"

"Yeah!" came the answer from the outer fringe of the wagons.

Rachel was quickly back, dropping white cloths in a pail of water. She still held the knife in one hand. Bostin knelt down, eyed the remaining whiskey in the bottle, and said, "Good. I hope it takes effect fast." Setting his eyes on those of Frieda Manley, he said, "Ma'am, I'll do my best, but—"

"That's all I can ask," she cut in. Her eyes were weary. "You go ahead, Mister Bostin."

Rachel knelt beside him, and pivoting the knife handle in her hand, extended it toward him. For a brief moment, their eyes met. She smiled weakly as he took the knife.

Bracing his knees in the soft earth, the tall plainsman took a deep breath and inserted the tip of the blade in the wound. Manley winced, jerked, relaxed. Beads of sweat formed on Manley's brow. He coughed. "Go ahead, Bostin. Get it over with."

Gouging into flesh, the knife produced more blood. Manley screamed, spasmed, and went limp.

"He's unconscious," said Frieda, tears filling her eyes. "Hurry, please. Hurry!"

Chester Manley's breathing grew heavier as Clay Bostin probed for the Cheyenne rifle slug. Several minutes passed. Just as Clay felt metal touch metal, blood gurgled in Manley's throat. His chest rose as he pulled in air, then lowered slowly and stopped, never to rise again.

Frieda Manley muffled a cry with her hand. Clay sat back on his haunches, his face wet with perspiration. His body went numb. The knife fell from his fingers as he stood up. Three women were instantly at Frieda's side, helping her to her feet. Clay Bostin's lip trembled. "I'm sorry, ma'am," he said softly.

"You did all you could," breathed the new widow between sobs.

The disappointed man felt a hand on his arm. Turning, he looked down into the beautiful face of Rachel Flanagan.

"Clay," she said softly. "It was out of your hands from the beginning. The probing may have brought death a little sooner, but Mrs. Manley knows he wouldn't have lived another day."

The tall Bostin bent his head back, straightened his wide shoulders, and stood rigid. Rachel squeezed hard on his arm. "You tried," she said.

Slowly, Bostin relaxed.

"Let me get you some coffee," said Rachel gently. "Why don't you sit down over there by Bucky's wagon?" Ushering him to the spot, she said, "Sit down. I'll be right back."

As Rachel moved toward the fire, she laid a blanket over the body of Chester Manley.

Bostin lowered himself to the cool grass and leaned back against a wagon wheel. Bucky Wiseman materialized from the darkness, coming from outside the wagon circle. Leaning his .50 caliber Sharps against the wagon, he squinted at Bostin and said, "Manley?"

"Dead."

"Aw, too bad," said Bucky mournfully.

"Bucky, will you tell Cliff Adams to have the men spell each other through the night? Every man better get some sleep. Black Hawk may attack at dawn."

"Sure enough, Clay," said Bucky.

"Tell him I'll be on the fourth watch, okay? Right now I feel a little weak in the knees."

"Sure, Clay—"Bucky's words were cut short by loud voices. Bostin was instantly on his feet. Rachel was coming toward him, bearing a steaming cup of coffee. Halting, she looked up at him quizzically.

"Sounds like Billy Adams and that bearded hide-hunter again," said Bostin disgustedly. "I'll be right back."

The noise was coming from between two wagons, the Peabodys' and the Manors'. As Clay approached, young Billy and Dub Smith were standing nose-to-nose, faces red with anger.

"I'm gonna bust your head, Smith!" Billy was shouting.

"If you think you're man enough, hop to it!" screeched Smith.

"Hold it, you two!" bellowed Bostin. "What's going on?"

Without removing his hard gaze from Smith's face, Billy said through his teeth, "He was peekin' into the wagon, tryin' to see Sherry, Mister Bostin."

"You're a liar!" shouted the unshaven hunter.

Billy's fist caught Smith square on the jaw. The force of the punch staggered Smith, who was preparing to return it when Bostin stepped between them.

"All right, that's enough!" said Bostin.

"I was jist doin' guard duty, that's all," said Smith.

"From here on, you work the other side of the circle."

"Okay," said Smith walking away. He gave Billy a hot look and disappeared.

Cliff Adams, standing near, said, "I'm sorry about this, Bostin, but I think Billy is right. I think Smith was playin' peepin' Tom."

"I do, too," said Bostin, "but since I can't prove it, we'll have to let it pass." Looking into Cliff Adams's eyes, he said, "Better pass the word. Women and children stay in the wagons at daylight. If Black Hawk was going to attack tonight, he would have done it just now, when we were occupied with Billy and the hunter. You can bet he's watching us close. Every man is to be awake and ready just before dawn."

"Got it," said Adams.

Bostin returned to Rachel, who sat on the ground near the fire. "I'll take that coffee now," he said, easing down beside her.

As Rachel rose to her knees and poured a fresh cup. Clay asked, "How's Mrs. Manley?"

"As good as can be expected," replied the auburn beauty, handing him the cup.

"Thanks," he said with a smile.

"Mrs. Peabody is with her."

"Good. How's Mrs. Kiser?"

"Not too good. Mrs. Manor says she's afraid the girl has lost too much blood. She's getting weaker."

Clay shook his head and sipped at his coffee.

"You think the Cheyennes will come tonight?" asked Rachel with a quaver in her voice.

"Doubt it. I have a feeling they'll hit us at dawn." Bostin sat quietly and drank the coffee. Rachel placed fresh wood on the fire. The distant yelp and howl of a coyote came from the dark plains. Rachel looked at Bostin. "Cheyennes?"

"Hard to tell."

Silence prevailed for several minutes as both people sat and stared into the fire.

Casually, Rachel broke the silence. "You're not married, Mister Bostin?"

"Nope." Bostin turned to look at her. "I liked it better a little while ago."

Rachel's brow furrowed. Slowly shaking her head, she said, "I guess I'm not following you."

Clay smiled. "A little while ago, you called me *Clay*. Now we're back to *Mister Bostin* again."

Her eyes widened. "Oh? Did I? I'm sorry. I—"

"Don't be," said the lean-bodied man softly. "Now that the formal barrier has been broken, let's leave it that way. Okay?"

Smiling with her lips together, she nodded, then spoke. "On one condition. That works both ways. I'm no longer *Miss Flanagan.*"

"Okay, *Rachel*," said Bostin, the firelight dancing in his eyes. Looking back into the fire, he said, "This young banker you're marrying..."

"Yes?"

"You said you were childhood sweethearts?" Bostin had his eyes fixed on the fire. He could not see Rachel's face.

"Yes," she answered quickly.

"You're not telling me he's the only fella who ever courted you?"

After a brief pause, she said, "I guess you could say that." Before he could probe further, the auburn-haired beauty stood up and stretched her arms. "Guess I better get some sleep, Clay. You'd best do so, too." With that, she was gone.

Chapter Eight

Death hovered in the air, thick and real, almost tangible. Clay Bostin checked the loads in Horace Nething's Winchester. Nething had brought it to him after Rachel Flanagan had gone to bed. With one arm in a sling, Nething would have to use his revolver. Clay was welcome to the rifle.

A hint of gray light appeared on the eastern horizon. The lean and rawboned wagon train leader had not slept. His mind was intermittently filled with Rachel Flanagan and the savages who waited on the prairie.

Bostin could feel it in his bones. Black Hawk was coming at sunrise. The fire was dying. He did not replenish it. Cliff Adams approached.

"Every man is in position, Clay," advised Adams.

"Except me," came a voice from the murky gloom. It was Jeremy Sutherlin. "I want to fight next to you, Mister Bostin."

A smile lined Bostin's face, which Jeremy could not see.

"Good, Jeremy," he said. "Get under Bucky's wagon." Turning toward the dark figure of Cliff Adams, he said, "What about Lon Berry?"

"He seems a bit better," replied Adams. "Talked a little. He's under his wagon, gun ready. The red-headed, bucktoothed hide-hunter is with him."

"Harry Owen?"

"Sober. Ready to fight."

"Billy under your wagon?"

"No. He's covering for the Healy wagon."

"Where's Smith?"

"He's under the Wilson wagon, next to Billy."

"You think that's wise?"

"We're spread thin, Clay. With three men dead, we almost can't close our ranks. Besides, those two will be too busy to fight each other."

Clay glanced at the widening flow of light in the east. "Who's under the Manley wagon?"

"Nobody."

Clay Bostin suddenly realized he did not know where Rachel was sleeping. Mrs. Manor was with Beth Ann Kiser in Bucky's wagon. Bostin wanted to personally guard the wagon that held Rachel Flanagan. Looking at Adams in the dim light, he said, "Did you see which wagon Miss Flanagan went to?"

"No, I didn't," answered Adams. "I grabbed a little sleep. Last time I saw her, she was talkin' to you by the fire."

The tall man stepped toward Bucky Wiseman's wagon, leaned down, and said, "Bucky!"

"Yep," came the hoarse reply.

"Where's Rachel Sleeping?"

"She's with Frieda Manley."

"Thanks," said Bostin. He was relieved. He could station himself under the Manley wagon without being obvious. All empty spots *had* to be filled. Looking toward the form of Jeremy Sutherlin, he said, "Jeremy, you come with me." As the boy scooted backwards and stood to his feet, Clay spoke again to Bucky. "We'll cover the Manley wagon, Bucky."

"Okay," came the reply. The old man paused for a few seconds, then said, "What if she was in Maude Healy's wagon? Would Billy have to move?"

Clay had started to walk away. Stopping, he turned and asked, "What say, Bucky?"

Wiseman cackled. "I was talkin' to meself."

Wordlessly, Clay made his way to the Manley wagon and told Jeremy to crawl underneath.

Cliff Adams was now bellied down under his own wagon. Slowly, Bostin walked the circle, reminding each man to let the Cheyennes come within twenty yards before firing. The eastern sky was turning pink. Scattered clouds took on the same color.

As Clay Bostin studied the brightening plains, he once again sensed the presence of death. The women were feeling it, too. Their voices, coming in depressed tones, filtered through the canvas covers.

The tall wagonmaster made the rounds again, reminding them to lay flat in the wagons when the attack came. Coming finally to Frieda Manley's wagon, he spoke through the canvas. "Mrs. Manley, are you and Rachel all right?"

"Yes!" came the widow's answer.

Suddenly, Rachel's lovely face appeared from the back of the wagon. There was fear in her eyes. "You're sure they're going to come, Clay?"

"Feel it in my bones," he said, nodding. "If it makes you feel any better, I'm going to be under here."

The same strange look he had seen before came into the girl's blue eyes. "Thank you, Clay," she said, trying to smile, and slowly closed the opening.

Bostin waited a minute, letting the memory of that soft, mysterious look in her eyes linger in his mind. Then he moved outside the circle and scanned the horizon. Almost as if it were an omen, the sky turned blood red. The rising sun threw a fan-shaped shaft of light through the broken clouds.

Then they came.

First was the thundering roll of unshod ponies. The sound was coming from two directions, east and west. Bostin twisted around to look beneath the wagons. He could see nothing yet. Jeremy Sutherlin was breathing heavily. In an even tone, Bostin said, "Jeremy. You've used that gun on rabbits and squirrels."

"Y-yessir," said the youth, swallowing hard.

"You do the same thing with Indians. Just sight in on the closest one and squeeze the trigger."

The frightened youth was breathing in short spurts. He was on the verge of panic.

The rumbling sound grew louder.

"We need you, Jeremy," said Clay Bostin, just as twenty-five or thirty Cheyennes, lusting for blood, came into view. Clay knew there would be that many again, coming from the west. Squinting against the blood red sun, he saw the wave of painted ponies begin to shift to and fro like tall grass, swaying with the wind in an open field.

Then came the war cry, as they drew near. A sudden staccato broke loose from the wagon train, and instantly the air was filled with the foul smell of gunpowder. Indians were dropping to the ground, splattered with blood. As Clay Bostin fired the Winchester repeatedly, he heard nothing from Jeremy's gun. The sound of three buffalo guns boomed between the crack of carbines and the roar of Horace Nething's Colt .44.

Clay kept a sharp eye for Black Hawk, but as yet the vicious Cheyenne chief had not appeared.

A bullet kicked up dirt near Jeremy Sutherlin's head. The boy buried his face in his hands, whimpering. Clay sighted in on a screeching savage. The rifle bucked in his hands. The Indian peeled off his horse, hit the ground, and lay still.

From somewhere behind him, Bostin heard a yell of pain. Abruptly an arrow pierced the canvas just over his head. He heard a scream, but there was no way he could check on it now. He prayed silently that it would not be Rachel who was hit.

The whooping, yelling Cheyennes were circling like madmen. Clay assured himself that Black Hawk had come with no less than fifty warriors.

One of the horses hitched to the Manley wagon screamed and fell over dead, an arrow through its neck. The other horses danced with fear, but could not bolt because of the wagon.

Guns continued spitting death. The Cheyennes were paying a heavy price for this attack. Suddenly, they turned and galloped out of rifle range. One of them took a bullet in the back from one of the buffalo guns. He jerked like the backlash of a whip and bounced lifelessly to the sod.

Some of the women began to emerge from the wagons when the firing stopped. Clay Bostin rolled from under the wagon and jumped to his feet. "Get back in the wagons!" he shouted. "The Cheyennes will be back as soon as they regroup!"

The women scurried in quick obedience.

"They didn't come back the last time!" blurted Jack Sutherlin, from under his own prairie schooner.

"Are you blind, Jack?" asked Bostin with irritation. "Last time they rode out of sight and were gone. Take a look out there. You can see them regrouping."

Sutherlin swore and turned around. Bostin cast a quick look toward the milling mass of mounted Cheyennes and stepped to the tail of the Manley wagon. He pulled back the flap. A wave of relief swept over him. Rachel was cradling Frieda Manley's body in her arms. An arrow was sunk deep in the older woman's stomach.

"She's dead, Clay," said the young woman. Bostin was pleased to see that Rachel was in complete control of herself.

"Get down flat," said Clay. "They're coming back."

The silence that hung over the circle of wagons was broken by the sound of galloping horses. Bostin wanted to check for other casualties, but there was no time. He ducked under the wagon. As he reloaded the Winchester, he looked at Jeremy. The boy's eyes were wide, fixed on the charging horde of painted savages. A series of whooping yells pierced the air as the thundering ponies divided and once again formed a circle around the wagons.

Gunsmoke permeated the air. Arrows whistled, bullets whined. On the outer rim of the yapping Cheyennes, Clay Bostin caught a glimpse of the albino horse. On its back was Black Hawk. He was waving a feather-decorated rifle and shouting encouragement to his warriors. There was no way to get a clear shot. The bronze-skinned chief disappeared from Bostin's view.

Suddenly someone behind Clay shouted. He turned to look as a Cheyenne buck entered the wagon circle on foot. Before he could bring the rifle muzzle around, one of the buffalo guns roared and the Indian dropped in a lifeless heap.

Two more savages broke through the barrier, guns blazing. Clay saw Lon Berry whirl and fire. One of the bucks went down. The second one shot Berry, just before Bostin drilled him through the heart. Another Cheyenne was crawling under Lon Berry's wagon when Bostin heard Jeremy Sutherlin scream. Billy Adams was rising to his feet to face the Indian coming under Berry's wagon. Bostin turned his attention to Jeremy.

A Cheyenne was crawling toward the youth, knife poised. Bostin bellied down and fired. The Indian caught Bostin's .44 slug square between the eyes. He died instantly.

An arrow hissed past the tall plainsman's ear, just as one of the buffalo guns boomed amid the smoke inside the circle of wagons. Clay took a quick look, but the smoked was so thick he could see nothing. Apparently Bill Adams had disposed of the Indian.

Turning back to the circling savages, he shot another one off his horse.

Suddenly, the whooping stopped and the painted ponies galloped away. As the smoke cleared, Bostin saw the thundering mass ride into a shallow draw, up over a hill, and disappear.

As he backed out from under the wagon, his eyes fell on the bodies of four Cheyennes. Lon Berry lay dead under his wagon. Cliff Adams was kneeling beside the lifeless form of his son. Mrs. Adams was scrambling from the wagon, screaming, "Billy! Billy! Billy!"

Quickly, Bostin looked into the wagon. "Rachel, you all right?"

The girl with the auburn hair nodded blankly. "Yes."

"Let me help you out," said Clay, reaching toward her.

Placing her hands on his shoulders, she leaned out of the wagon. Bostin eased her to the ground, glancing quickly at the body of Frieda Manley.

Together, Rachel Flanagan and Clay Bostin walked toward the crowd gathering around Billy Adams. Clay saw Dub Smith walk toward Lambert Fielder, limping on the boot with no heel. Fielder had been shot in the left arm and was bleeding.

Cliff Adams knelt beside his dead son, his arm around his grief-stricken wife. Looking up, he said, "They killed him, Clay. Those dirty savages killed him!" Bostin dropped a hand on Adams's shoulder.

Sherry Manor stood over Billy, looking at his inert form. Tears glistened on her cheeks. Adams shot her a heated look. "What are you cryin' about, hussy? You didn't care anything about him."

The girl turned toward her father, who gave her a look of scorn. "Cliff is right. You didn't care anything about that boy." Sherry broke into sobs and ran to Bucky's wagon, where her mother watched from the opening in the canvas.

Jack Sutherlin approached Clay Bostin. "Mrs. Wilson's dead, Bostin. Bullet got her."

The tall man lifted his hat, ran his fingers through his dark hair, and said, "Any others? I mean besides Lon Berry, Frieda Manley, and Billy?"

"Don't think so," replied Sutherlin. Swinging his head back and forth, he said, "Where's Jeremy?" His line of sight fell on the boy, seated on the ground, leaning against a wheel of the Manley wagon. His rifle lay on the ground at his side.

His bulky father strode to him. "How many Cheyennes you kill, Jeremy?" the big man asked.

Jeremy was staring at the ground. He ignored his overbearing father.

"Hey, boy, I asked you a question! I expect an answer!" bellowed Sutherlin.

Silence.

Bending over, the big man picked up the rifle and sniffed the cartridge chamber. His eyes narrowed to angry slits. "You mangy yellowbellied coward," he said breathing each word. "You never even pulled the trigger."

Jeremy stared at the ground, face flushed. Jack Sutherlin dropped the rifle and stormed away.

Bucky Wiseman prodded the corpses of the four dead Indians with the muzzle of his Sharps. "Them's *good* Cheyennes," he said, spitting a brown stream. "This is the one Billy killed, Clay," said the old man to the wagonmaster. The muzzle of his buffalo rifle rested on the chest of the buck Bostin had seen emerge from under Lon Berry's wagon.

"He got Billy, too," added Cliff Adams.

Clay Bostin's gaze fell on the wound in Billy Adams's left side. He eyed the position of the dead Indian.

"Couldn't have been this one that got Billy, Cliff," said Bostin. "Billy was shot from the side."

Adams scanned the area. None of the other dead Indians within the circle were in position to have shot him from that angle.

Bostin knelt down and examined Billy's gunshot. The bullet had entered his left side from below where Billy stood. It was angled upward.

Clay stood up, his face hard. His eyes flashed with fire. "Cliff, I would like your permission to remove the slug from Billy's body."

Mrs. Adams furrowed her brow. "What for, Mister Bostin?"

"What are you thinking, Clay?" asked Cliff Adams.

"I got a feeling it's a fifty caliber slug. The Cheyennes don't have buffalo guns."

Cliff Adams's jaw slackened. His face lost its color. "You don't mean that filthy hide-hunter—"

"Don't jump yet," butted in Bostin. "Get a grip on yourself."

"If he—"

"Cliff," said Clay, "do I have your permission?"

Adams looked at his wife. Tearfully, she nodded.

"Go ahead," said Adams.

"Cliff, will you do me a favor?" asked Bostin.

"Sure."

"Take your wife to the wagon. Then check on everybody. Let me know on the casualties."

"Okay."

"Would you have a couple of the men make sure all those Indians lying out there are dead? Let me know how many we killed."

Nodding, Adams put his arm around his wife and led her away.

Clay Bostin could hear a woman sobbing as he turned to Bucky and said, "Could I use your knife again?"

"Sure," said Bucky. "I'll go get it."

Looking down at Rachel, Bostin said, "Would you see who's crying? Let me know, please, if it's serious?"

Clay knew that the best thing for Rachel was to keep her occupied. Less time to think about future Cheyenne attacks.

As Rachel walked away, Bucky returned with the knife. Kneeling down, Bostin said, "Bucky would you hold him on his side for me, so I can dig out the slug?"

Bucky complied immediately. Within three minutes, Bostin stood up, a bloody lead slug in his hand. "Take a look, Bucky," he said, with a note of anger.

The old man breathed a low whistle. "Fifty caliber. That ain't no Cheyenne bullet, Clay."

Bostin was washing his hands when Rachel Flanagan returned. "It was Esther Owen, Clay," she said in a sorrowful tone. "The oldest boy is dead. Bullet in the head."

The tall man shook his head grimly.

Cliff Adams approached. "Five dead, Clay," he said. "Mrs. Wilson, Tommy Owen, Frieda Manley, Lon Berry...and...and Billy."

"*Six.*" It was the voice of Mrs. Manor. The group turned to face her.

"Oh, no," said Rachel, twisting her face.

"Beth Ann died just before dawn, Mister Bostin," said Mrs. Manor, her face pinched. "Didn't see any reason to tell you before the attack."

Sherry Manor stood silently beside her mother.

Mary Lou Adams had rejoined her husband. "What about the bullet, Clifford?" she asked in a half whisper.

"Just a minute, honey. I've got to tell him about the wounded." Facing the tall, rawboned wagonmaster, he said, "Elmer Peabody took an arrow in his hip, Clay. Wasn't deep. His wife has already pulled it out. She's dressing the wound now. Fielder got it in his left arm. Bullet went clear through. Smith's got Maude Healy wrapping it up."

Adams stepped closer to Bostin. In a subdued tone, he spoke tight-lipped. "Now what about the slug?"

Bostin was about to answer when Bucky Wiseman's crackled voice bit the air.

"Clay! Lookit what we got!"

Bostin wheeled. A woman gasped. Jack Sutherlin and Wiseman had a Cheyenne brave between them. The Indian was limping on a bloody leg.

Chapter Nine

Esther Owen's baby wailed loudly from inside the wagon as the group of travelers fixed their eyes on the Cheyenne brave. There was a bullet in the Indian's leg, but his stolid face revealed no pain. Blood was running into the rawhide-soled knee-length moccasin. As the two men halted him in front of Clay Bostin, Rachel eyed the white strip of paint which ran cheek-to-cheek just beneath the savage's dark eyes. A quivering sensation ran through her body. Bostin felt her fingernails dig into his arm.

Speaking in the Cheyenne tongue, Bostin said, "My name is Clay Bostin. What's yours?"

The Indian bolted him with a hard look and said nothing. Jack Sutherlin, who held one arm, jerked it violently and shouted, "Answer the man!"

The young buck gave Sutherlin the same look he had give Bostin.

"You speak up or I'll kill you!" grated Sutherlin, jaws clenched.

"Hold it, Jack," cut in Bostin. "Those tactics will never work. You can't frighten him." Suddenly the Indian's head flopped back, his eyes rolled and he slumped heavily in the hands of Sutherlin and Wiseman.

"He's passed out," observed the lean wagon train leader. "Lay him down. I'll have to get that bullet out of his leg."

"Wait a minute, Clay," said Cliff Adams. "Why waste your time on this brute savage who just tried to kill us?"

"That's my sentiments, too," said Jack Sutherlin. "Let the stinkin' animal bleed to death."

"I agree!" came the voice of Dub Smith. "He sure wouldn't waste effort if it was one of us in *his* hands. He'd scalp us and let us die!"

Clay Bostin looked hard into the eyes of each man. "If we do it like he'd do it, then the very thing we despise in him is in our-selves."

"That's keerect, Clay," spoke up Bucky Wiseman. Looking at Sutherlin, Adams, and Smith, he added, "Now you fellers tell Clay he's wrong." Waiting for an answer which did not come, the old man said, "Here's my knife again, Clay. Dig that bullet out."

Looking at Sutherlin, Bostin said, "Get a burial detail together, Jack. We'll need six graves.

"I'll dig Billy's myself," put in Cliff Adams.

"I'll start a fire so you can sterilize the knife," said Rachel.

As the girl walked away and the circle of people dispersed, Adams confronted Bostin. "The bullet, Clay. What caliber was it?"

The tall man bit his lip. "Fifty caliber," he said solemnly.

Adams wheeled, face florid, and charged toward Dub Smith, cursing the hide-hunter vehemently. The latter had just palmed a shovel. He swung it at Adams savagely. Adams ducked and slammed a fist into Smith's nose. Smith was already off balance because of the boot heel missing. He hit the ground hard.

The furious father pounced on the hide-hunter like a ferocious wild beast. They rolled over and over, fists flailing.

The crowd gathered, watching the fight intensely. Jack Sutherlin looked across the circle at Clay Bostin. "You gonna stop it?"

Bostin shook his head. "Let Cliff get it out of his system. He'll be easier to handle, then."

The two men were on their feet, sucking hard for air. Adams backed up a few paces, then charged Smith like a maddened bull. "You killed my son!" he yelled.

Cliff struck him with his shoulder. Breath whooshed from the hide-hunter's mouth. Adams landed on top of him. His fist landed squarely on Smith's nose. Blood spurted, showering Adams.

Smith spat blood and struggled to free himself from Cliff's weight. It was to no avail. Another punch smashed Smith's mouth, splitting his upper lip.

Mary Lou Adams was screaming at her husband to stop. For a brief moment, he put his attention on her. When he did, the hide-hunter, fighting like a cornered beast, clawed at Adams' eyes. The two men rolled over and over. The raging Cliff Adams struck Smith again and again. Adams gained his feet and stood up, shoulders stooped, fists clenched. "Get up!" he rasped, sucking air.

Smith rolled to his haunches, wiping blood from his battered mouth. "I didn't kill your son," he said, blood bubbling in his nose. "The Cheyennes did. I was fightin' 'em. Just like the rest of you."

"You're a filthy liar!" yelled Adams. Running toward the bloody hide-hunter, who was now on his knees, he kicked him savagely in the face. Smith keeled over and lay still. He was out cold. Before Clay Bostin could get to him, Adams placed a hard kick in Smith's rib cage.

"That's enough, Cliff," said Bostin loudly, pulling him away.

"He has to died, Bostin!" Adams shouted, struggling against Clay Bostin's steel grip. "He killed Billy!"

"Get a hold of yourself, Cliff. You're acting like a madman," Clay said, shaking him by the shoulders.

His face set in hard lines, Cliff Adams walked stifflegged to his wagon and pulled out a shovel. Bostin eyed the others and said, "Better get to digging the graves. We've got to keep moving toward North Platte."

Jack Sutherlin, shovel in hand, paused beside the wagonmaster and spoke gruffly. "Cliff's right, Bostin. Smith needs to be strung up."

Bostin bolted him with a cold stare. "Don't you start that kind of stuff, Sutherlin," he said. "If Smith is hung, it'll be at the hands of the law, not a lynch mob."

Sutherlin looked callously into Bostin's eyes for a long moment, turned, and walked away.

Bostin cast a glance at Dub Smith, who was coming to, attended by Lambert Fielder. Rachel waited for him beside the prostrate Indian, Bucky's knife in hand.

"It's sterilized, Clay," she said, trying to smile. "The water is almost hot and I have some cloths here for bandages."

"Thank you," said the lean plainsman. "You're gonna make that banker fella—what's his name?"

"Alvin Penell," she answered quietly.

"Penell," Clay said, nodding. "You're gonna make him a mighty good wife." Bostin was smiling when he said it, but it was a façade. He knew in his heart that his greatest desire was to have this Irish lassie for himself.

Dark clouds were gathering in the north as Rachel Flanagan wrapped the Indian's leg, pulling the dressing tight to stop the bleeding. Enough of Bucky's whiskey remained to pour in the wound. The young buck was still unconscious.

"That's all we can do, Clay," said Rachel, standing to her feet.

"I hope he comes out of it," Bostin said thoughtfully. "I would like to talk to him. He could tell me what triggered this uprising."

It was just shy of noon as the survivors gathered around the six graves. The entire sky was dark with heavy clouds. The wind swept in from the prairie with an ominous moan, rustling the pages of the Bible Clay Bostin held in his hands. Stiff gusts ruffled the dark locks on Bostin's hatless head.

While their towering leader read words from the sacred pages, the huddled group listened quietly.

Rachel Flanagan stood just to Bostin's right side, her eyes resting on his angular face. She had her arm around Esther Owen's shoulder. Harry stood on his wife's other side, holding the baby. The remaining Owen boy stood in front of his mother, sobbing openly.

Dull rumbles of thunder warned of the approaching storm. Lightning flared on the distant northern horizon.

Cliff Adams stood over Billy's grave, a seething hatred for Dub Smith boiling like volcanic brimstone within him. One arm held his brokenhearted wife while the other engulfed Billy's weeping sisters.

Clay Bostin's eye caught Dub Smith on the fringe of the crowd, his face a battered mess. The man with too many teeth for his mouth stood beside him.

Jeremy Sutherlin was pressed between Horace Nething and his wife, opposite his scowling father and pinch-faced mother. Mrs. Peabody had left her wounded husband in the wagon to stand next to Maude Healy. Martin Manor and his wife stood next to the Sutherlins. Bucky Wiseman stood a pace or two from Smith and Fielder, casting a glance now and then toward the limp form of the Cheyenne warrior lying inside the wagon circle.

Aloof and apart from the group stood Sherry Manor, face ashen gray, head hung low. Clay Bostin thought she looked smaller than usual. Her long blond tresses whipped loosely in the wind.

The rumbles were growing louder and more frequent when Clay Bostin finished and said, "Let's prepare to move out. We'll leave the Berry, Wilson, and Manley wagons behind. We'll put the horses on lead ropes and take them with us. Take all the food, guns, ammunition, and other useful items out of those three wagons and disperse them among you. Let's pull out in half an hour."

Slowly, the frightened and wary travelers walked back to the wagons. Clay Bostin stepped beside Martin Manor and said, "Did Dale Roy have you even out the ammunition among the wagons?"

"No," replied Manor.

"I guess he forgot," said Bostin. "We better do it by morning. We're lucky Black Hawk hasn't used fire arrows on us yet. If he plants one in your wagon, we'll be out of ammunition in a hurry."

Manor nodded his head in agreement.

The half hour passed quickly. Clay Bostin had directed Jeremy Sutherlin to drive the Peabody wagon, freeing Mrs. Peabody to remain in the back with her wounded husband. Maude Healy would drive her own. Lambert Fielders' arm was hurting him severely. He would ride in the back of the Healy wagon, along with the wounded and yet unconscious Cheyenne.

There remained one item yet to handle. Dub Smith. The battered hide-hunter stood next to the Healy wagon, talking to Lambert Fielder. The buffalo gun was in his right hand. Bostin approached from the blind side, his Colt .45 drawn and pointed at Smith. "I'll take the gun, Smith," Bostin said evenly. The shorter man started to argue but changed his mind and handed Clay the Sharps. The look in Bostin's eyes told Smith the tall man was dead serious.

"Bostin, you can't disarm a man in hostile country," Smith protested.

Jack Sutherlin and Cliff Adams moved near.

Clay Bostin said, "Cheyennes don't have nor use fifty caliber weapons, Smith."

"So what?" lashed the hide-hunter.

"Billy Adams was killed with a fifty caliber slug."

Smith cursed. "Now, jist how do you know that?"

Slipping the lead slug from his shirt picket, Bostin said, "I dug this out of him."

Sutherlin and Adams were now standing close.

Smith cursed again. "How do you know it's mine? Fielder has a Sharps...and...and so does that dried up little Bucky dude!" Sweat was forming on Smith's brow.

"Both of them were on the other side of the circle," said Cliff Adams heatedly.

"Now, look here," said Smith, his battered face losing its color, "you can't prove nuthin'!"

"Which side of Billy were you on during the attack?" Bostin asked, eyes hard.

"I wuz...uh...on his *right* s-side," stammered Smith. His eyes widened. "Yeah! His right side...and he was shot in the *left* side. You s-see! I couldn't have done it!"

"You shot him when he stood up to face that Indian he killed," said Bostin. "You were under the wagon. His left side was toward you. The bullet entered his body at a sharp upward angle."

Dub Smith's eyes held Bostin's for a brief moment, then shot to Cliff Adams. He had no more to say. He was caught and he knew it.

"It's murder, Clay," said Adams, his face red. The veins stood out on his neck and forehead. "He has to hang."

"That's right, Bostin!" said Jack Sutherlin.

Horace Nething, Martin Manor, and Harry Owen had joined the group. Lightning ripped across the sky and thunder boomed.

Martin Manor lifted his voice above the wind and thunder. "If he's guilty, we oughtta string him up to the next tree we come to!"

Nething and Owen voiced agreement.

Terror, like an icy hand, closed around Dub Smith's heart. "Y-you need me!" he screamed. "You need every man with a gun you c-can get!"

"We turn you loose with a gun, you'll kill us before the Indians do!" shouted Jack Sutherlin. Setting his eyes on the wagon leader, he said, "I've got a rope, Bostin. There'll be a tree down the trail. When we get to it, *he hangs!*"

Rachel Flanagan was watching the scene from the seat and stepped up beside Bostin.

"You men aren't judge and jury," Bostin said, tightlipped.

"He's guilty, Clay...and you know it!" hissed Adams.

"In a civilized society, he still has a right to a legal trial," retorted Bostin. "I know how you feel, Cliff. I'm mighty sorry about Billy. But you can't take the law in your own hands. I promise you. When we get to Fort Laramie, I'll turn him over to the law. He'll hang, but let it be done within the confines of the law."

"This wagon train is a unit of society, just like a town," reasoned Adams. "This murderer deserves to die!" Adam's eyes were wild.

"You men asked Clay to lead this train," cut in Bucky Wiseman. "He's doin' the job, an' now you want to take over. I wouldn't blame him if he jist clumb on that buckskin horse and told you to tough it out."

"I wonder how you'd feel if it was *your* son this filthy murderer had killed, Bucky," said Horace Nething.

"Right's right and wrong's wrong," said the old man sharply.

"I agree, Bucky," said Cliff Adams. "He killed my son and it's right that he should die."

"Clay ain't arguin' that, Cliff. All he's sayin' is he oughtta be executed by the law."

Cold fear gripped Dub Smith. His eyes followed from face to face as the conversation progressed.

"When we get to the first tree, Bostin, you'd better just back off. We're havin' us a necktie party," said Jack Sutherlin. The big man's face was livid with rage.

Lightning crackled directly overhead. As thunder retaliated, Dub Smith looked at Clay Bostin pleadingly. "You can't let 'em do it, Bostin!" he cried. "You gotta protect me!"

"You get in the back of Bucky's wagon, Smith," commanded Bostin.

The frightened buffalo hunter stood frozen in his tracks.

"Go on," said Bostin, "before I just walk away and let 'em have you."

Smith turned and ran to Bucky's wagon.

Bostin said, "Bucky, you got some rope?"

"Shore do, Clay."

"Climb in there and tie him up good. I'm going to deliver him to the U.S. marshal at Fort Laramie."

"Consider it done," said Bucky, walking away. He spit a stream of tobacco juice and climbed in the wagon.

Bostin fixed his gaze, cold and hard, on Jack Sutherlin. Determination was raw in the tall man's voice. "I want him hanging by his neck as much as you do, Jack. Almost as much as Cliff does. But we are not savages. He'll hang by due process of law. If you try to take it in your own hands, you'll have to go through me."

Bostin's eyes were black and piercing. He looked from man to man. "Understood?"

Sutherlin and Adams looked at each other blankly. Adams turned to Bostin. "Okay, Clay. We'll leave it to the law. I know you mean to keep your word." Looking at the others, he said, "Let's go, boys. We gotta make it to North Platte by day after tomorrow."

Jack Sutherlin shot Bostin a cold look and walked away.

Cliff Adams offered the rawboned wagonmaster his hand. "Sorry, Clay. It's just that...well, you know. Billy—"

"I understand, Cliff," Clay said.

"You're doin' a good job, Bostin," said Horace Nething with a smile.

Martin Manor's face was drawn and sober. "None of this would have happened, Clay," he said, "if my daughter hadn't tormented Billy by playin' up to that filthy hunter." Pivoting, Manor headed for his wagon. Sherry was looking at him through the opening in the back. Stopping in his tracks, he pointed an angry, accusing finger at the girl. "It's *your* fault, you little witch! If it wasn't for you, Billy would still be alive!"

Manor's face was hot with rage. "It oughtta be *you* lyin' back there beneath the sod, instead of Billy! And right now, I wish it was."

Mrs. Manor, inside the wagon out of sight, burst into tears.

Sherry's insides turned to ice and her body trembled violently. Manor climbed onto the wagon seat and started the horses moving.

Clay Bostin swung into the saddle, checked the horses on the lead rope, which was tied to the last wagon, and trotted up beside Rachel Flanagan. As she looked into his eyes from the jostling seat, he caught a glimpse of that same nameless something.

"You've guided a lot of trains, Clay. Have you ever had a situation like this before?"

"I've had some sticky ones, but never one quite like this," he answered, smiling.

A vivid streak of lightning slashed across the black sky. Thunder hammered violently, shaking the prairie with resounding echoes.

Then the rain came.

Chapter Ten

Darkness came early with the sky heavy-laden. The rain fell in torrents.

The eight wagons formed a circle. The evening meal was cold jerky, cold beans, bread, and water.

Clay Bostin transferred Lambert Fielder to Horace Nething's wagon, while he sat in the back of Maude Healy's with the wounded Indian. Rachel was with the Manors. Bucky sat in his own wagon with Dub Smith.

The Cheyenne was conscious. He sat silently and studied the angular face of Clay Bostin in the light of the lantern. The wind-driven rain came with a rippling onslaught upon the canvas cover of the wagon. Periodically, the entire inside of the prairie schooner was illuminated by flashes of lightning.

Speaking in the Cheyenne tongue, Clay Bostin said to the Indian, "I hope your leg feels better by now."

The swarthy face of the young brave was a hard mask of animosity. His dark eyes bore hard at the white man.

"I still don't know your name."

Silence.

"I mean you no harm, friend," said Bostin with a warm smile. "I was raised among your people up in Wyoming Territory. That's why I know your language."

Silence.

"I understand your loathing for the whites. They have forced you off your land, slaughtered your buffalo, robbed you blind, and made treaties only to break them."

The Cheyenne blinked. It wasn't much, but Clay read in it a slight hint of progress.

"My father," said Bostin "is the Indian agent at Fort Laramie. He and Running Horse were friends. I, too, am a friend to the

Cheyenne. I have only fought your people when they attacked me. Black Hawk staked me out and left me for dead thirty miles back. I had given him no reason. The people in this wagon train do not want to fight Black Hawk. We bear no ill will toward the Cheyenne. We want to live in peace."

The Indian stared hard at Bostin. "White Eyes lie!"

"What do you mean?"

"You have white men in wagon train who molest Cheyenne girl while she bathe alone in river."

"This is not true," Clay insisted. "We've never been near one of your camps or villages. It had to have been some other train."

"Black Hawk say *this* train."

"He's mistaken. None of the men in this train have ever left—" Suddenly, Bostin thought of Smith and Fielder.

"Do you know how many attacked the girl?"

"No. Black Hawk knows."

"Did the girl describe them?"

"Don't know. You need to talk to Black Hawk."

"I would welcome that opportunity."

"You let me go...maybe he come for powwow."

"I'm not holding you—What's your name?"

"Lone Elk."

"I'm not holding you, Lone Elk. You're not a prisoner. I took the bullet out of your leg. That bandage was put on you by one of our women. We could have let you bleed to death."

Lone Elk nodded.

"You're free to go anytime you want."

Lightning flared with an eerie sulphurous light. A thunderbolt followed that shook the wagon. The lantern flickered as the wind and rain hammered against the canvas covering.

Lone Elk looked at his bandaged leg. "I not get very far on this."

"I'll take you to your camp if you wish. How far is it?"

"Not far. 'Bout ten mile southeast."

"Think you can sit a horse?"

Lone Elk nodded.

"Good," said Bostin, smiling. "We'll go in the morning."

"You cannot enter camp," said Lone Elk evenly. "You take me close. I go rest of way alone. I tell Black Hawk you want powwow."

"That's fine," said Clay. "Now, you get some rest. I'll see you in the morning."

Pulling his hat low, the lean Bostin slipped through the opening and stepped to the wet ground. The wind flopped his hat brim as the rain pelted his face. Running to Bucky's wagon, he yelled that he was coming in and plunged inside.

Lightning flashed. Thunder boomed.

"How's the Indian?" asked Bucky, rolling the plug of tobacco from one side of his mouth to the other.

"He's gonna be okay," Bostin replied.

Dub Smith's face had swollen. He looked especially gruesome by lantern light. Clay Bostin fixed his dark eyes on Smith. "Did you and Fielder molest a Cheyenne girl?"

The hide-hunter's eyes widened. "Why you askin' that?"

"I asked the first question," rasped Bostin, staring hard.

"No, we never touched no Indian girl." Smith's eyes were cold, passionless. "What are you gittin' at?"

"Lone Elk says there are men riding this wagon train who caught a Cheyenne girl bathing alone in a river where his people were camped...and molested her."

Fire flashed in Smith's eyes. He swore vehemently.

"Fielder and me ain't the only males in this train. Why you pickin' on us?"

Bostin looked at Smith with disgust. Turning his gaze to Bucky, he said, "See that he's uncomfortable for the night."

Wiseman smiled, exposing the gap in his upper teeth.

Bostin slid out of the wagon and was gone. Almost blinded by the driving rain, he groped his way to the Nething wagon. "Horace!" he called loudly, "I'm coming in!" The flap came open and he dived in.

"Doesn't look like it's letting up," Nething said to Clay.

The latter wiped rain from his face, removed his hat, and shook water against the canvas. "I'm beginning to know how Noah felt," said Clay idly.

Mrs. Nething sat by the lantern, huddled in a blanket. Clay eyed her pleasantly and said, "Sorry we can't build you a fire, ma'am."

The lady shrugged her shoulders morosely.

Turning his attention to Lambert Fielder, Bostin said, "Fielder, I want to ask you something."

The redheaded buffalo hunter lifted his eyes to meet Bostin's.

"Before we picked you and Smith up, did you two go near any of the Cheyenne camps?"

A visible tensing washed over Fielder. He tried to hide it, holding his face rigid. "No. Why?"

"The Cheyenne brave tells me that Black Hawk is after this train because there are men riding it who attacked and violated a Cheyenne girl. She was bathing alone in a river near their camp."

Shaking his tousled head, he said defensively, "Why do you single us out? Have you questioned any of the other men in the train?"

Ignoring Fielder's question, Clay said weightily, "If you're lying to me, mister, you're in trouble."

"I ain't lyin'!" snapped Fielder.

Looking at Horace Nething, Bostin said, "Good night, Horace. See you in the morning." Then, to the woman, "Good night, ma'am." Donning his hat, he melted into the cold, wet night.

Leaning against the wind, the rawboned man made his way toward Martin Manor's wagon. Approaching the rear, he called out, "Martin! I'm coming in!" The flap opened, Rachel Flanagan's face appeared, and Bostin plunged inside.

Rachel pulled the flap shut as Clay hunkered down. His eyes lined immediately on the pale face of Sherry Manor. She sat in a far corner of the wagon, staring disconsolately at the floor. Mrs. Manor looked weary, with eyes too old and lips too thin for a woman just past thirty.

"How's the Indian?" asked lovely Rachel.

"I think he'll be all right," answered Clay, smiling.

"What are you going to do with him?" asked Martin Manor stiffly.

"I'm taking him back to his camp in the morning," said Bostin.

"You're *what*?"

"I'm returning him to Black Hawk."

"What for? We oughta string him up by his toenails!"

"Listen, Martin. You're not thinking. You may not believe it, but Indians are human."

Manor swore.

"If I take Lone Elk back to his people, bandaged and fed maybe I can get a powwow with the Hawk. There might be some way to appease his anger and get him to let us go, without any more attacks."

Manor's eyes softened. "I'm sorry, Clay. You're right. My temper's been on edge lately. Sometimes I speak before I think."

"Like what you said to Sherry today," snapped Mrs. Manor.

The man turned his eyes on his wife and gritted his teeth. "I meant every word I said to her," he hissed.

Sherry's stare never altered.

"Sounds like it's going to rain all night," said Rachel.

"I expect to feel the wagon start to float any minute," Clay chuckled, trying to ease the tension. His eyes were fixed on Rachel's lovely features. A warmth filled his breast. Clay Bostin was in love with this captivating woman. He reprimanded himself for letting it happen. She was promised to Alvin somebody in San Francisco. He had no right to want her for himself.

She will never know how you feel about her, Clay told himself. He had his pride. Rachel was in love with another man. He would only cheapen himself in her sight, and his own, by revealing his love for her.

Every turn of the wagon wheels took Rachel closer to the man in San Francisco. The dawn of each new day brought the dreaded moment closer when Clay Bostin would have to see her for the last time. He shook his head, as if to discard the ugly thought.

"Are you cold, Clay?" asked Rachel.

"Not really," the lantern-jawed man answered. "Just shaking my cobwebs loose." He raised himself slightly. "Well, guess I'll turn in for the night."

"Where are you sleeping?" Rachel asked.

"In the Healy wagon with Lone Elk," Clay answered. "Mrs. Healy is bedded down with the Peabody's." Pulling back the flap, he looked toward the somber members of the Manor family. Suddenly he felt sorry for Sherry.

Closing the flap again, he said, "Sherry."

The girl's countenance remained stonelike.

"Sherry," said Clay softly. "We all make mistakes. We're human. So you made a mistake in your relationship with Billy. We're going to get through all of this. You've got your whole life ahead of you. You've got a great future. Don't throw it away by punishing yourself.

Out there in Oregon somewhere, there's a fine young man just waiting for you to walk into his life. Why don't you pull yourself out of it, now and—"

"I'll handle Sherry, Clay," broke in Manor. "You haven't lived with her. You don't know—"

"I'm not trying to interfere," said Bostin. "I'm only trying to help your daughter."

"Good night," said Manor firmly.

"We're all on edge, Mister Bostin," said Mrs. Manor apologetically. "Please excuse my husband's manners."

"Sure ma'am. I understand. Good night." With that, Clay opened the flap and stepped into the rain. As it pelted his face, Rachel paused in the opening.

"Goodnight, Clay," she said. Her eyes were soft and warm.

"Goodnight, Irish lass," he said, and dissolved into the darkness.

The rain had stopped when Clay Bostin opened his eyes. A dull light illuminated the canvas covering of Maude Healy's wagon. Lone Elk was sleeping soundly.

Quietly, Clay pulled on his boots, made sure the Colt .45 was in its holster, donned his hat, and stepped out into the chill dawn. The sky was clear.

Making his way to the side of the wagon, he lifted a short-handled pan from a peg and dipped it into the water barrel which hung on the side. Balancing the pan on the wheel, he splashed cold water in his face. His hands brushed the prickly stubble on his chin. It was then that he remembered that a razor had not touched his face in three days.

Movement caught the corner of his eye. It was Bucky. He was pulling dry wood from his wagon, preparing to build a fire. "'Mornin', Bucky," said Bostin, approaching the small-framed man.

"Has been since just after midnight," said the old man with a furtive grin.

"Aren't you ever serious?" asked Clay, showing his teeth.

"Not too often, son. Don't pay to be." A sly look captured his eyes. "*You* sure are, though."

"What's that?"

"Serious."

"I have to be. I've got to get these people through to Fort Laramie."

"That ain't whut I'm referrin' to."

"Bucky, what are you talking about?"

"Not *whut*, son. *Who*."

"You're talking in riddles."

"I'm talkin' about that young lady with the deep red hair."

Through the gray gloom of early dawn, Wiseman could see Bostin's face redden.

The old man stepped close and looked the tall plainsman in the eye. "It's written all over yuh, Clay. There's big ole stars leap in your eyes whenever you look at her."

Bostin bit down on his lip. "Bucky, sometimes I wonder about you," said Clay, ambling toward the Adams wagon.

Cliff Adams was just sliding out of the vehicle when Bostin approached. "Mornin', Clay," he said sleepily.

"Mornin', Cliff," replied Bostin. "Better rouse the men. Black Hawk may have picked up his dead and counted the graves we left by now. Six graves may give him incentive to hit us again at sunup."

"You're the doctor," Adams said dryly.

Bostin could sense the resentment in Cliff's voice. His heart went out to the man. Losing a son like Billy would be a real tragedy. Natural instinct would make a man want to take out instant vengeance on his killer. But it just couldn't be. Law and order was becoming a part of this raw country, and it must be upheld.

Sunrise found eight men lying in the wet grass, one under each wagon. Elmer Peabody was incapable of leaving his wagon. His wounded hip was badly swollen and his body was hot with fever. Jeremy Sutherlin was absent, having been ordered by his father to stay in the wagon. Dub Smith remained incarcerated.

Sutherlin lay adjacent to Clay Bostin. The latter turned and said, "Jack, how many dead Cheyennes did you count after the attack yesterday?"

"Sixteen," came the flat answer. Sutherlin paused for a moment, then said, "Billy Adams was killed too, Bostin. By a scaly snake in the grass."

"Don't start that again," rasped Bostin.

Silence prevailed through the camp, except for the cry of the Owen baby.

When the sun lifted its lower rim from the horizon, Clay stood up and said, "Looks like a calm morning, men. Couple of you keep watch. Rest of you build another fire."

Bucky's fire was crackling and blazing good. The gray smoke sifted slowly toward the fresh, clean sky. The early morning sun reflected brightly in numberless tiny pools of water, which were scattered across the rolling prairie.

The women soon had the air filled with good smells. Clay Bostin ate breakfast with Lone Elk, who continually cast a suspicious eye about the camp while he ate. Rachel changed the dressing on the Cheyenne's leg and pronounced the wound in improved condition. Being that close to the hostile left her a little unnerved.

The hardy plainsman saddled the big buckskin and helped Lone Elk into the saddle. Rachel Flanagan stood near. Next to her was Bucky Wiseman. Next to him stood Sutherlin, Manor, and Adams.

Bostin eyed the three and said, "Get the train moving, fellas. I'll catch up to you. Lone Elk tells me the Cheyenne war party is camped about ten miles southeast of here. I'll take him close enough to hobble into camp and head back for the trail."

The three men nodded in agreement.

"I'm holding you three responsible to see that nothing happens to Smith," said Bostin, a slight edge to his voice.

Again, they nodded.

The lanky man stepped toward the horse. Almost without thinking, Rachel reached out and touched his arm. A twinkle struck Bucky's eye.

"Clay, you be careful," she said softly.

"I'll catch up to you," said Clay, stepping in the stirrup and swinging himself to a seated position behind the saddle. Reaching around the sober Cheyenne, he took the reins and spurred the horse.

Instantly, the three men scattered and Bucky began checking the harness on his team.

Rachel Flanagan, auburn hair glistening in the Nebraska sun, fixed her eyes on the buckskin. Slowly, she moved around the wagon, to keep the riders in view. Bucky eyed her, but busied himself, feigning ignorance.

The object of her attention was a small black dot on the horizon when the leathered old man said, "Time to go, honey." He was standing next to the wheel on the driver's side. Rachel turned. "Here, let me help you up on this side. You can just scotch across the seat."

She gave him her hand, stepped on a spoke, and was instantly in the seat. Pausing momentarily, she cast her gaze to the southeast. The small black dot was gone.

Chapter Eleven

Time dragged slowly as the wagons moved westward. A cool breeze was blowing out of the north. Meadowlarks and prairie dogs played propitiously in the shiny wet grass.

Bucky Wiseman swept the country with narrowed eyes. Periodically, he stood up and looked to the rear and was pleased to catch sight of other drivers doing the same thing. They missed Clay Bostin scurrying back and forth on the buckskin.

Rachel Flanagan rode quietly, eyes straight forward. Over an hour had passed since she had said a word. Her body swayed with the motion of the wagon. Her mind was far away. Bucky squinted at the freshly scrubbed face.

A tight grin tugged at the old man's mouth. "He'll be back, honey."

The sound of Bucky's high-pitched, crackly voice penetrated the beautiful lady's world of thought. "What's that, Bucky?" she asked, setting her deep blue eyes on him.

"I said he'll be back."

"Clay?"

"Yes. Clay."

"It's gonna bust him to pieces to give you up at Fort Laramie," Wiseman said, watching her from the corner of his eye.

"What do you mean?" asked Rachel, eyes glued once again on the prairie ahead. "He has led a lot of wagon trains, seen a lot of people for the last time."

Bucky's face took the form of a dried prune. "Rachel May Flanagan! That young man is head over heels about you."

Twisting in the seat, she faced the old man and said, "Bucky Wiseman, you are *wrong!*"

"Oh, yeah?"

"Yes!"

"Think so, huh?"

"I *know* so!"

"Oh, yeah?"

"Yes! It's Rachel Marie Flanagan!"

Bucky laughed, slapped his leg and spit tobacco. "That's a good un, honey." He paused a moment. "Now, back to Clay Bostin..."

"Look and see if he's coming," she said

Wiseman stood up, looked back, squinting against the sun. Taking a long look, he sat down again. "No sign of him. No sign of whooping Indians, either."

Bucky made no effort to pick up the unfinished conversation. Rachel thought she had successfully diverted the subject. Both rode silently until the wagon topped a hill and a swollen, turbid river came into view.

"Looks like we got a decision to make, kid," said the weather-worn man.

"What do you mean?" asked Rachel, craning her neck to view the river.

"As fast as that water is movin', it could wash away these wagons. It's going to take an experienced eye to decide if we can make it. The rain last night has really deepened it. Those rapids look treacherous. Listen to it roar."

As the river drew slowly closer, Bucky said, "Rachel, I don't mean to be a nosy old duffer, but I wanna ast yuh a serious personal-like question."

Rachel cast him a quizzical look. "Go ahead."

"Do you love this Alvin Pennock fella?"

"Penell, Bucky," she corrected him. "Alvin Penell."

"Yeah. Penell. Do you love him?"

The auburn beauty shifted her position in the seat. No answer came.

"Do you?" pressed Bucky.

Rachel cleared her throat. "Why, yes, Bucky. Of course I do. Alvin and I have loved each other since we were children."

The roar of the river was growing louder.

"Let me rephrase my question, honey," the old man said, raising his voice above the roar. "Are you *in* love with Alvin?"

The girl's face flushed.

"I can see you lovin' him like your big brother...but are you really *in* love with him? The *marryin'* kind of love?"

Rachel's mouth formed a word, but suddenly Cliff Adams's wagon pulled alongside and Adams yelled, "What do you think, Bucky? Can we make it across?"

Wiseman tightened the reins and pulled the wagon to a halt. "Looks questionable, Cliff!" the old man yelled.

Martin Manor drew up his wagon on the other side. "We can make it, men!" he bellowed. "Let's get moving!"

"We better climb down and talk it over," retorted Bucky.

Within two minutes, the men of the wagon train stood together on the bank of the surging river.

"I think we'd better wait for Clay," Bucky said emphatically. "He's made this trip many times. He'll know whether we should try it or not."

"What if he doesn't come back?" threw in Martin Manor. "That Cheyenne may have led him into a redskin trap."

"Clay'll be back," argued Bucky.

"We need to keep moving," said Jack Sutherlin. "The quicker we reach North Platte, the better chance we have of getting cavalry protection."

"If we get washed down the river, we won't be going east, Sutherlin," disputed Bucky. "We'll be going south. Yuh can't get to North Platte by goin' south!"

"I don't think it's very deep," countered Sutherlin. "I say let's cross it. I'd rather face the river than those bloodthirsty savages!"

"I agree!" exclaimed Martin Manor.

"Let's go!" shouted Cliff Adams.

Horace Nething and Harry Owen agreed.

"You going with us, Bucky?" chided Manor.

"Don't leave a sensible gent much choice, do yuh? Me and the Irish lass can't stand off them painted, yappin' Cheyennes by ourselves! Long as we're goin', we'll go first!"

The old man was swearing under his breath as he climbed into the seat.

"Are we going to try it, Bucky?" shouted Rachel.

"Dadblamed idiots won't listen to reason, honey. They'd leave us behind if we don't cross, too. So we're goin' first! Might as well git it over with!" Snapping the reins and shouting at the team, the silver-haired Wiseman moved down the bank.

Rachel's face took on an unpleasant look.

"Hang on, little gal!" Bucky shouted. "Here we go!"

The Flanagan girl's knuckles matched the pallor of her face as she gripped the edge of the wagon seat.

At first the two horses balked, as their front legs felt the swiftness of the current.

"Hyah! Hyah!" screamed the old man, popping the reins. The frightened horses lunged forward, straining into the harness. Wiseman's face was pinched tight, while Rachel's remained pale and slack.

Suddenly, the wheels quit turning and the wagon swayed recklessly. It was floating and being carried downstream by the swift current. The gallant horses held their heads high and paddled furiously. By the time the wagon had traveled fifty yards downstream, their hooves struck solid footing and quickly the Wiseman vehicle was rolling up the bank.

Dub Smith was shouting something from the back that neither Bucky nor Rachel could understand. Wiseman guided the dripping wagon up the riverbank and stopped slightly downstream from where the other wagons would enter on the opposite side.

Reaching inside the bed, he lifted out a large coil of rope, jumped to the ground, and tied one end of the rope to the axle of the wagon. Waving the coil, he signaled to the others that he would toss each driver the rope. Using hand signals, he told them to tie it securely to their wagon. This would keep them from floating helplessly downstream. The men on the opposite bank nodded that they understood.

The second prairie schooner to enter the river was that of Cliff Adams. It began to float to almost the same spot Bucky's had. The lithe oldster stood on the bank, swung the coiled rope circular fashion over his head, and leading the wagon slightly, flung it into Cliff's waiting hands. He hastily secured it to the metal brace that held the seat to the bed. The slack rope quickly tightened. Bucky's wagon quivered slightly. Within minutes, the Adams wagon was safe on the west bank.

Dub Smith was hollering from inside Bucky's wagon, but no

one paid any attention. Rachel had left the wagon and was positioned behind Wiseman, watching him adeptly handle the rope.

Parking his prairie schooner above the riverbank on the sod, Cliff Adams descended the bank to stand beside Bucky.

The river was a murky brown color. Even the foam caused by the rapids had a tan cast. Broken tree limbs, bushes, logs, and other debris bobbed and weaved in the water. The loud rumbling sound of the turbulent river made it difficult to hear one another's words.

Cliff shouted something Bucky could not understand. The old man's attention was on Horace Nething's wagon, which was descending the bank on the other side. Glancing at Adams, he pointed to his ears and shook his head.

Cupping his hands around his mouth, Adams shouted, "The heaviest wagon is Manor's! Has most of the ammunition! It'll be the toughest to get across!"

"We'll hold it till last!" screamed the leather-faced old man. "Can you get the idea across to 'em?"

Cliff nodded, walked closer to the water's edge, and started making hand signals to those on the other bank. It took several minutes, but finally those on the other side signaled that they understood.

The Nething wagon reached the swift water. The team fought their bits as Horace Nething snapped the reins with his good arm. The other was still carried in a sling. The terrified horses, eyes wild, eased into the water. Nething shouted, but the animals couldn't hear him.

The front wheels slipped over the edge and hit bottom. Having little momentum, they lodged in the mud. Nething popped the reins, lashed the horses' rumps with the loose ends, and swore savagely.

Martin Manor, Jack Sutherlin, Jeremy Sutherlin, Harry Owen, and Lambert Fielder ran toward the helpless vehicle. The elder Sutherlin and Martin Manor stepped into the water and, one on each side and gripped spokes, tried to free the wheels. Jeremy waded in to aid Manor, and Owen joined big Jack. Fielder put his shoulder to a rear wheel but could help little because of his wounded arm.

Bucky and Cliff Adams watched helplessly from the opposite bank.

Cupping his hands again, the younger man said, "If we could throw a rope to them, we could tie it to our wagons and pull from over here!"

"Too far!" bellowed Bucky. "Even if we had enough rope, it's at least a hundred feet across. No way to toss a rope that far!"

The women were now leaving their wagons and joining Fielder at the rear wheels. As Esther Owen stepped to the ground, ten-year-old Bobby followed.

"No, Bobby," commanded his mother. "You stay in the wagon with the baby."

With a sour look wrenching his face, the boy complied.

Soon the determined travelers had the Nething wagon rocking to and fro. Abruptly, it eased from the ruts and slipped into the river. Floating freely, it headed downstream. Bucky flung the rope toward Horace Nething. Mrs. Nething grabbed it and tied it securely.

Cliff Adams laid hold on the rope behind Bucky, trying to cushion the jolt against the axle of the Wiseman wagon. The rope rose out of the murky water, stiffened to full length, and held. Nething's wagon fishtailed a little, but soon his team found footing and pulled the schooner ashore.

"What about the horses on the lead rope?" Cliff Adams shouted.

"We'll have to turn 'em loose. Don't think we could get 'em across," answered Wiseman.

As Horace Nething halted his wagon on higher ground beside the Adams wagon, he dropped to the ground and ran to Wiseman and Adams. Laboring to make themselves heard, they discussed the problem of getting the last wagon loose if it bogged down. All the muscle would be on the opposite bank.

"We know now we have to hit the water with plenty of momentum," said Nething. "Martin will have it rolling good before the wheels touch the water"

Mary Lou Adams and her two girls, along with Mrs. Nething, joined Rachel Flanagan. Together, they watched Maude Healy draw her team to the crest of the rise, just above the sloping bank. Sutherlin and Manor were giving the heavyset woman final instructions. The redheaded hide-hunter sat on the seat beside her, holding his bandaged arm.

Mrs. Healy nodded. Sutherlin and Manor stepped aside.

Bellowing like a man, she slapped the reins to the horses' rumps. The startled animals lunged down the slope and were instantly treading water. Bucky tossed the rope. Mrs. Healy secured it. People on both banks cheered as the rope stiffened and the Healy wagon rolled onto solid ground.

Jack Sutherlin guided his wagon to where Maude Healy's had stood moments earlier. Mrs. Sutherlin sat stiff-backed and pale next to him.

On the opposite bank, Bucky had re-coiled the rope and waved that he was ready.

"Hyah!" roared Sutherlin, stinging his horses hard.

The wagon made a big wave of its own when it struck the water. The horses, water over their backs, pointed their noses toward the sky and worked against the current. Bucky's rope whistled through the air. Sutherlin tagged it, and knotted it quickly to the seat brace. The wagon rocked like a boat, then settled down as the horses reached solid footing.

Water gushed from between the wooden seams as Sutherlin guided the wagon up the slope.

Next in line was Harry Owen. Lined up directly behind Owen's wagon was Elmer Peabody's. Peabody lay semiconscious in the back. His wife was beside him. In the driver's seat was Jeremy Sutherlin.

Jeremy watched the wagon in front of him draw to the crest. Bobby Owen was positioned at the tailgate, leaning precariously over the edge. As the Owen wagon lurched forward, Jeremy shouted at Bobby to get clear inside, but the roar of the river drowned out his voice.

Owen's wagon met the water properly, but when it started to float, something heavy inside shifted and it lurched heavily to one side. The swift current hit it full force, causing a severe fishtail. The heavy jolt broke Bobby's grip on the tailgate and he flopped into the water.

No one on the west bank was aware that Bobby was in the swirling waters. Martin Manor was busy checking his wagon on the east bank. His back was to the river. Mrs. Manor was conversing with her husband. Sherry sat in the middle of the seat next to her mother, staring blankly at the floorboards.

A cold chill washed over Jeremy Sutherlin, followed by a tingling prickly sensation, when he saw Bobby plunge out of sight. He leaped off the wagon and ran along the bank, watching for the boy's head to bob up.

On the other bank, Jack Sutherlin spied Jeremy and swore. "What's that dumb-fool kid doin'?" he bellowed.

All eyes were instantly on Jeremy, who was running frantically on the bank. Suddenly Bobby's head appeared. The current swirled him around and around. His hands were raised above his head in frenzied terror. Jeremy was about thirty feet ahead of him and dived into the angry waters.

On the floating, lurching wagon, Esther Owen was screaming Bobby's name. Harry dared not look downstream, as Bucky was throwing him the rope. The wagon was leaning dangerously.

Cliff Adams bolted down the riverbank, followed by Horace Nething and Jack Sutherlin.

Jeremy's head appeared. The muddy water had kept him from seeing beneath the surface. He had missed Bobby. Fighting the swift current, he looked right and left. Suddenly, he spotted two hands protruding from the whirling mass. The three men watched Jeremy disappear. Bobby's hands were no longer visible.

Abruptly, out in the middle of the river, Jeremy bobbed to the surface. For a brief moment the three men saw that he had the boy in his arms. Bobby was limp. The gallant youth was laboring desperately to bring him to shore. His strength was ebbing.

Cliff Adams pulled off his boots, dropped his gunbelt, and plunged in. The two boys spun as if they were in a whirlpool, then dropped out of sight.

Adams fought the rapids until his strength was gone and crawled listlessly onto the west bank. As he flopped down, gasping for breath, Nething and Sutherlin lifted him to his feet. The frantic parents of Bobby Owen came on the run, preceded a few steps by Mrs. Sutherlin.

The latter was screaming, "Jack! Go after him! Go after him!"

Grasping her shoulders and swinging her around to face him, he yelled, "It's too late, Helen! It's too late! He's gone!"

Esther Owen angled down the bank at the point the boys were last seen, intending to jump in. Harry wrapped both arms around her, holding her tight.

"Let me go!" she screamed. "Let me go!"

"It's no good honey," shouted Owen. "They're gone!"

The bodies of Bobby Owen and Jeremy Sutherlin were never seen again.

The mothers, attended by their husbands, returned to their wagons, stunned and shocked. Rachel Flanagan and Cora Nething attempted to comfort them. Mary Lou Adams returned to her wagon to fetch dry clothing for her husband. His body trembled as his teeth chattered in the breeze.

As she emerged from the wagon with his clothes, he said, "Hold those till I get back. Somebody's got to bring the Peabodys across. I'll swim over and bring them, then change."

Mrs. Adams started to protest, but Cliff was already walking down the slope toward Bucky.

The old man patted Cliff Adam's back. "Was a mighty decent thing you did, Cliff!" voiced Bucky loudly.

Adams smiled and looked across the river. Mrs. Peabody was now in the seat of her wagon, conversing with Martin Manor, who stood on the ground. Apparently she was preparing to make an attempt at crossing the river. Adams waved his arms until he caught their attention. He gestured his intentions until they nodded acknowledgment.

"Maybe you better not try it, son!" yelled Bucky. "You may not make it!"

"You just get your rope ready!" hollered Adams.

Running upstream along the bank, he dived in. Dodging debris and fighting the current, he made it to the other bank.

Another fifteen minutes found the Peabody wagon safe on the other side.

Martin Manor labored for some time to get the spare horses in the river, but to no avail. The frightened animals would not go near the violent water.

Bucky waved from the other side for Manor to turn them loose and let them go. Removing their bridles, he set them free to roam the prairie.

Climbing into the seat, Manor said, "Hang on, girls. We've got to hit the water hard so we don't bog down."

Mrs. Manor gripped the seat and clenched her teeth. Sherry

showed no interest and no emotion concerning the impending danger.

As Martin Manor walloped the horses and plunged the heavily loaded wagon into the angry waters, a lone rider topped the rise where Bucky Wiseman first spotted the swollen river.

Chapter Twelve

Clay Bostin studied the scene for a moment, then spurred the gelding to a full gallop. Martin Manor had driven into the thundering rapids not noticing a reeling, swift-floating mass of debris, which was now bearing down on his red-wheeled wagon. The extra-heavy load caused the vehicle to settle deep in the water.

Just ahead of the menacing mass was a whole tree. The jagged edge of the trunk was headed for the side of the half-submerged wagon. People on the other bank were waving their arms frantically. Manor looked upstream just as the gigantic tree slammed into the wagon. Wood splintered, scattering bits and pieces into the brown water. The wagon listed severely and swung with the current. Mrs. Manor's scream could be heard above the rumbling din as the great mass of debris struck the two horses, twisted slightly, and overturned the listing wagon.

Clay Bostin was peeling off boots and sidearm as all three Manors disappeared into the churning waters. Leaving his hat on the pommel of the saddle, he charged down the bank and plunged in. Bobbing up, he saw Sherry appear for a moment and then vanish under a cluster of floating bushes. Dodging an onrush of driftwood, he swam toward the girl. It was evident she was making no attempt to save herself.

From the bank, Rachel Flanagan welded her gaze on Clay Bostin as he fought the rapids, straining to reach Sherry Manor.

The horses were helplessly pinned under the heavy mass of debris. Their flailing legs soon went limp. The tongue and double-tree broke loose from the battered schooner. All the contents of the wagon were dumped into the angry waters and soon disappeared.

Martin Manor bobbed to the surface, his terrified wife in his arms. Bucky tossed his rope to Manor and began pulling them to shore.

Sherry appeared again thirty yards downstream. Some of the horrified travelers were running along the bank. Others were giving aid to the Manors. Ahead of the group running the bank was Rachel Flanagan. She watched Sherry appear at the surface briefly, then go down. Clay had come up at the same time, spotted her, and disappeared.

Cliff Adams dashed past Rachel and dived in where Clay was last seen. Adams quickly surfaced, looking right and left. Neither Bostin nor Sherry was in sight.

Several moments passed. Adams searched frantically. Clay and Sherry were gone. Rachel paced the grassy bank. Her throat was tight, almost choking her. She felt a clutching against her backbone, as if some unseen hand were squeezing it with icy fingers.

Words audibly escaped her lips. "Oh, dear God, no!"

Suddenly, seventy-five or eighty yards father downstream, Clay's dark head emerged. He was next to the bank. The matted blond locks of sherry Manor stood out in contrast, as he held her limp form in his arms. Cliff Adams reached them first, steadying Bostin as he carried the girl to level ground.

Rachel breathed a word of thanks as she ran toward them.

Immediately, Clay Bostin laid the girl facedown and began pressing on her back while squeezing her rib cage.

"Work her arms up and down!" said Clay to Adams, panting and gasping for breath.

Water spurted from Sherry's nose and mouth as Bostin worked frantically. Rachel stood over him, watching. For a brief moment, Clay lifted his eyes toward her and smiled weakly.

The crowd had gathered, watching hopefully. Moments passed. Mrs. Manor, dripping wet, elbowed her way through the crowd. Kneeling beside her daughter, she looked at Bostin. "Is she—?"

"She's alive, ma'am," said Clay calmly.

At that moment, Sherry coughed and opened her eyes. Mrs. Manor broke into tears. As the girl continued to cough, Bostin helped her stand. Her breathing improved. After a few moments, Clay released Sherry to the arms of her teary-eyed mother.

"How can I thank you, Mister Bostin?" blurted Mrs. Manor.

"No need, ma'am," replied the tall man, smiling.

Martin Manor stood on the fringe of the crowd, making no attempt to approach his daughter. The mother, arm about her child, led her to Manor. His face was stolid, lined with contempt.

"Your daughter almost drowned, Martin," said his wife, lips pulled tight.

Manor stood, face hard, and said nothing.

Sherry eyed him blankly. "He said he wanted me dead, Mother. Look at him. He's sorry Mister Bostin saved me."

Manor looked at the girl with passionless eyes.

Sherry's lips trembled. "Well, Daddy, I'm sorry, too. Believe me, after the way I acted and caused Billy's death, I deserve to die. Maybe you'll get your wish yet."

Manor did not move. His expression did not change.

Turning toward Clay Bostin, Sherry said, "Mister Bostin, I deeply appreciate you risking your life to save me, but I'm not worth it."

Manor's wife eyed her husband with livid scorn. "Can't you see she's sorry for what she's done, Martin? Can't you find it in your heart to forgive her? *She's your own flesh and blood!*"

"Don't remind me," said Manor through his teeth.

Embarrassed by the scene, the others began walking back toward the wagons.

Vida Manor, still holding her daughter with one arm, looked him straight in the eye and said, "I'm a lady, Martin Manor, which prevents me from calling you what you are. However, I'll say this. When a man is born into this world without a legitimate father, he has no control over what he is. But you...*you're a self-made man!*"

Martin Manor stood like a statue as the mother and daughter walked slowly toward the wagons. Up ahead, Clay Bostin was flanked by Rachel Flanagan and Bucky Wiseman. Leaving the troublesome family scene, they walked silently behind the rest of the group.

Rachel broke the silence. "Clay, Jeremy Sutherlin is dead."

Bostin's head snapped around, unbelief in his eyes. "Dead?"

"Yes. Bobby Owen fell into the river when their wagon was crossing. Jeremy went in after him. They both drowned. Their bodies never surfaced."

Bostin's shoulders slumped. "Didn't someone try to help?"

"It all happened so fast, Clay. Cliff tried when he saw what was happening, but it was too late."

Bostin shook his head. "And Jack called him a coward."

"You're wet," observed the auburn-haired lady. "We'd better find you some dry clothes."

"Gotta go after my horse first," said Bostin, pointing across the river. The big buckskin stood patiently where his rider had left him. "Before I do it, I want to offer my condolences to the Sutherlins and the Owens."

The Owens were sitting inside their wagon. Both were weeping. Mrs. Owen held the baby.

Stepping to the rear of the wagon, the rawboned man said, "Harry...Mrs. Owen...I'm sorry about your boy. I know you're still grieving over Tommy. I know there's nothing I can say that will take away your sorrow, but please know that I feel your grief with you."

Esther could not speak. Tears spilled from her eyes as she nodded toward Clay Bostin, acknowledging his words.

Harry sniffed, ran his sleeve under his nose, and said, "Thanks, Clay."

Rachel was at Bostin's side as he turned and moved toward the Sutherlin wagon. Mrs. Sutherlin sat inside, silent tears washing her cheeks. The hulky father of Jeremy Sutherlin sat on the tailgate, his face buried in his hands. He looked up as Bostin approached.

"Folks, I want to tell you how sorry I am about Jeremy. He was one fine boy," said Clay in a tender tone.

Mrs. Sutherlin drew a deep breath. With shaky voice, she said, "None of us knew what a brave boy he was, Mister Bostin."

"That was an unselfish and courageous thing that he did, ma'am. He died a heroic death."

Sutherlin's face was ashen gray. There was a pinched, white ring around his mouth. "How could I have been so wrong, Bostin?" he asked hoarsely. "How could I have been so wrong?"

"Anybody could have made the same mistake, Jack," replied Clay. "Please accept my condolences."

"What about Black Hawk?" queried Sutherlin.

"I'll explain it to the whole group in a little while, Jack. Right now, I've gotta go get my horse."

Three quarters of an hour later, Clay Bostin emerged from the back of Bucky Wiseman's wagon, dressed in dry clothes. Gathering the dejected and wary travelers around him, he eyed Martin Manor standing aloof from the group, his face gray and sullen. Dub Smith, having been allowed out of the wagon, sat morosely on the riverbank.

Asking no one in particular, Bostin said, "What about Elmer Peabody?"

"He's getting worse, Clay," said Rachel Flanagan advisedly. "Mrs. Peabody is staying with him."

Bostin nodded. Scanning the somber faces about him, he said, "The Cheyennes are moving their camp this way. I didn't get close enough to see it. Lone Elk insisted on walking in from a spot where I couldn't get a view of the camp. He felt certain that he could talk Black Hawk into coming for a powwow, once the chief learns how we treated him. Only thing we can do now is wait and see."

"You know Black Hawk, Clay," said Cliff Adams. "What do you think?"

"I can only guess," replied the man with the angular face. "I think we'll get our powwow. We'll take no chances, though. We will travel as usual. Guns ready; prepared at all times to form a quick circle."

Casting his glance at Martin Manor, Bostin said, "Martin, did you disperse the ammunition among the wagons?"

Manor's colorless lips pulled hard against his teeth. "No. It slipped my mind."

Bostin looked at the ground, removed his hat, and ran his fingers through his hair. Setting his eyes on Cliff Adams, he said, "Before we move on, Cliff, will you check with each wagon and let me know what ammunition we have left?"

Adams nodded.

"Okay, folks," said Bostin, "let's pull out in about twenty minutes. Without the ammunition in Manor's wagon, we need to get to North Platte all the faster."

The sun was midway in the afternoon sky as the seven wagons in the dwindling train pulled away from the raging river which had claimed two lives. Martin Manor drove the Peabody wagon. Vida Manor rode with the Nethings, Sherry in the Adams wagon. Lambert Fielder rode with Maude Healy. Dub Smith remained in the back of Bucky's wagon. The rest of the day was uneventful, which in light of the recent tragedies was a blessing.

Night fell. The stars twinkled in the moonless sky. Coyotes howled.

Clay Bostin sat by the single fire, talking to Cliff Adams, as the weary travelers settled down for the night. The two men soberly discussed the low supply of ammunition.

"We better pray your powwow with Black Hawk works," said Adams worriedly. "About one more attack like the other two and we'll have to throw rocks at 'em. Ammunition is mighty low."

"If we can move steadily, I figure we can reach North Platte by noon, day after tomorrow," said Bostin.

The two men talked for a while longer, then Adams said, "Well, I better get some shut-eye. My time to go on watch at midnight."

"G'night," said Bostin.

"G'night," returned Adams, and filtered into the darkness.

Clay sat alone, watching the dancing flames. He thought of Elmer Peabody. If the man could hold on another day and a half, he would be under the care of the doctor in North Platte.

Ironically, Bostin's thoughts turned to Rachel, when a soft, rustling sound met his ears. Turning slightly, he saw her appear out of the shadows. She was stunningly feminine in a long, flowing robe.

"You oughtta be asleep, little lady," he said softly.

"I won't stay but a minute, Clay," she responded. "I just wanted to tell you that I think it was a marvelous thing that you did today." She eased down slowly beside him.

"Going in after Sherry?" he asked, fixing his gaze on her comely features. The firelight reflected alluringly in her eyes.

"Yes. You could have drowned." A touch of fear appeared on her face. "I thought for a moment you had. You were out of sight for a long time."

"She fought me for a while. Not in panic, but in determination. The girl wanted to die, Rachel."

"I gathered that," she said, nodding.

The two sat quietly for a long moment, staring into the fire. Clay wanted to look at Rachel, let his eyes drink her beauty, but it would be utterly obvious. It was enough just to have her near him. He would treasure every golden moment of her presence. A coldness came over him as he thought of the awful day that was coming, when he must say good-bye forever. Instead of her warm and enchanting presence he would have only a haunting memory.

As the Irish beauty watched the flames consume the logs, she wrestled inwardly with the fire which tortured her heart. Rachel Flanagan was in love with this tall, rugged man of the plains. Bucky Wiseman's brazen question had settled all doubt. The weather-worn old scalawag was right. She loved Alvin Penell as a big brother. Until she had fallen in love with Clay Bostin, she never knew her true feelings for Alvin.

But now what? Miss Rachel Flanagan had promised to become Mrs. Alvin Penell. In spite of the heat from the fire, a cold shudder shook her body. Marrying Alvin was out of the question. Even if Clay did not want her, she could never marry Alvin. But what would Clay think of her? If she suddenly announced that she was jilting the man who waited for her in San Francisco, she would appear cheap and despicable in his sight.

Rachel thought of the predicament of the wagon train. Blood-hungry, hostile Cheyennes tracked them like wild beasts. Chances were, they would never make it to Fort Laramie. North Platte was a slim hope. If there was no cavalry there, they would have to strike out for Wyoming territory alone.

Would Clay be able to ward off more attacks by the Cheyennes by meeting with Black Hawk? Something inside her told Rachel the powwow would not work. Another chill washed over her.

Clay saw the girl quiver from the corner of his eye. Turning, he said, "This night air will give you pneumonia, little lady. You'd better head for the sack and get covered up."

"Guess so," said Rachel, stirring herself.

Bostin jumped to his feet and offered his hand. As his strong hand hoisted her up, their eyes met.

The tall man caught the nameless something in her eyes again. Every fiber in his system yearned for her. He wanted to take her in his arms, hold her...tell her of the love that enflamed his aching heart. But it could not be. She belonged to another man.

Clay Bostin relieved Cliff Adams at four o'clock. He had not slept.

Shortly, the eastern horizon broke into a dull gray. A few

low-lying vapors took on the same hue, gradually transformed into obscure orange-red puffs, then slowly evolved into cotton-white clouds. The danger of a sunrise attack was gone, and the ring of wagons became a hive of activity.

By six thirty, wheels turned to the sound of axles creaking in dry sockets and the worried emigrants moved westward once again.

Clay Bostin moved up and down the line astride the magnificent buckskin. Man and horse moved together as if they were one body. The sun was warm, but a cool breeze blew. It was early June, but summer would be late in coming to the plains this year.

The tall rider galloped ahead of the train for about a mile, scanning the country. From the seat of the lead wagon, Rachel Flanagan pinned her gaze on horse and rider. Trotting the gelding crisscross on the trail, Clay rode back toward the wagons, studying the land eastward. As he drew near, Rachel stared into his bronzed, handsome face. The jagged scar on his left cheek seemed illuminated by the morning sun. The Irish lass told herself she would love this man if he was nothing but scars.

The day passed slowly. Anxious eyes from seven rattling wagons watched for an appearance of painted ponies, hoping against thoughts of despair that Black Hawk would appear for a peaceable confrontation with their stalwart leader.

As the sun lowered amid flaming purple clouds, the wagons formed their familiar circle and ground to a halt. A bubbling brook sang nearby, providing fresh water for the barrels and a welcome drink for the weary animals which pulled the wagons.

Clay Bostin had unsaddled the big buckskin and stood holding the reins while the gelding sucked water. The top rim of the sun was visible on the western horizon, beneath a collection of long-fingered clouds, casting an orange radiance over the rolling country. Suddenly, on the crest of a low hill to the south, he saw the grotesque silhouette of a band of Indians against the lowering sky. The colorful headdress of Black Hawk stood out strikingly in the last rays of the sun, contrasting more than ever with the pale horse upon which he sat.

The savage chief had already demonstrated that he would not attack at night. No one ever saw an Indian unless he wanted them to. Was this appearance to announce a sunrise attack? A vile scheme to frighten the dwindling travelers into sleeplessness? Or was it a subtle hint of a powwow which would be offered at the birth of a new day? Tomorrow would tell.

Chapter Thirteen

Morning came with a thick mist hovering ghostlike over the surface of the prairie. The air was cold and humid. There was no breeze.

Having missed sleeping the night before, Clay Bostin slept the night through, but was awake at dawn. No one in the camp besides himself had seen Black Hawk and his warriors at sundown. He had decided that telling them last night would only rob them of much needed sleep. A few moments before sunrise would be soon enough.

Horace Nething had taken the last watch in Bostin's place. Clay strolled to the outer fringe of the wagon circle and approached Nething, who was peering suspiciously into the heavy mist, gun ready.

"Hear something?" asked Bostin.

"Not sure," answered the man, rubbing his eyes. "Thought so for a moment."

"They're close," said Clay flatly.

"Yeah?"

"Mm-hmm. I saw about sixty of 'em on a ridge about half a mile south at sundown yesterday."

"They let you see 'em?" asked Nething in amazement.

"Yes. I'm not sure whether it was fear tactics or Black Hawk's way of telling us he's coming for a powwow this morning."

"Think he'll wait for this mist to clear up?"

"To attack...or powwow?"

"Either."

"I would say so. Redskin eyes can't see to shoot through this stuff any better than we can. If it's a powwow, the Hawk will come waving a white flag. He'll want us to see it at a good distance. I'm sure he'll wait till this stuff is gone."

The lean-bodied wagonmaster turned to reenter the circle.

Pausing, he said, "You keep your eyes peeled just the same."

"Don't worry," replied Nething, waving his revolver.

Bucky Wiseman had a fire started and was placing a coffeepot over the flames as Clay moved in.

"Think I'll heat some water and shave," said the tall man.

Wiseman rubbed his own stubble and said, "Think I'll shave, too, Clay. Rachel will probably want to kiss me when she gets up." Cackling, he added, "I wouldn't wanna scratch thet purty face o' hers."

Bostin gave him a dry look.

"Jealous, eh?" continued the old man. "Well, if you were a towering five-foot-six-inch handsome dog like me, an' had a hunnerd an' twenty-eight pound he-man physique like mine, she might give *you* a second look."

Bostin chuckled. "With an irresistible prince like you around, it's a wonder the women don't stampede themselves to death."

Bucky stepped closer, lowered his voice, and said, "Seriously, young feller, when air yuh gonna take that sweet lassie into yore brawny arms and tell her how yuh feel?"

"Mister Wiseman, what makes you think I feel something?" asked Bostin.

Bucky spit a stream into the fire. "Who do yuh think yore kiddin'? It sticks out all over yuh like spines on a shiverin' porkypine!"

"Buck, ole boy," said Clay in a hushed tone, "She's engaged to a man in San Francisco."

"But she ain't in love with him." Bucky's words came so fast, they were almost run together.

Bostin's heart bounced to his throat. "She tell you that?"

"Not in so many words, but I ast 'er an' she hesitated real peekyulyar-like."

"What did she say?"

"She said she loved him. And I ast her if she wuz *in* love with him, or wuz it sorta like lovin' yore big brother. She didn't gita chance to answer me, Clay, but I seen the look in her purty blue eyes. Old Bucky had done hit the nail square on the head. I—"

The old man was interrupted by the appearance of Cliff Adams, coming from his wagon. Rubbing his eyes, Adams yawned and bade the two men good morning. Clay told Adams and Wiseman about the appearance of the Cheyennes at sundown. Before breakfast he told it to the entire camp.

During Bostin's rehearsal of the incident, Dub Smith sat, hands tied, next to Lambert Fielder. Smith whispered steadily to his red-headed friend. Cliff Adams, eyes full of hate, moved toward them and said, "Smith, will you shut up? You're disturbing Mister Bostin."

Smith glared at him hard and closed his mouth.

It was after ten o'clock before the heavy sky commenced to break up. Patches of blue began to appear. Soon the yellow sunlight blanketed the Nebraska prairie and a light wind came up, swirling the thinning vapors about. Within half an hour the mist was gone.

Clay Bostin had every man in the camp watching for Black Hawk while he visited the Peabody wagon.

Mrs. Peabody sat next to her husband in the back of the prairie schooner, bathing his fevered brow with a wet cloth. Leaning his head inside at the tailgate, Bostin said, "How's he doing, ma'am?"

The woman's face was pale. Dark circles surrounded her tired eyes. "Not good, Mister Bostin," she answered dejectedly. "The wound is badly infected. The hip is swollen terribly."

"No telling what was on that Cheyenne arrow," said Bostin.

Elmer Peabody lay on his back, staring blankly at the bowed ribs of the wagon over which the canvas was stretched.

"Are you in a lot of pain?" Clay asked him.

Peabody rolled his languid eyes and fixed his gaze on the dark, angular face of Clay Bostin. He stared emptily for a moment. Working his mouth with effort, he whispered, "Much pain. Yes. Much pain."

"We're going to have you in North Platte by tomorrow after-noon, Mister Peabody. There's a doctor there. He'll fix you up."

As he turned from the wagon, Clay observed Dub Smith pacing inside the ring, limping on his heelless boot. Lambert Fielder was just retreating from Smith, a guilty look riding his face.

Walking the outer circle, Clay learned that nothing had moved on the prairie. Lifting his voice, he said, "All right! We'll move out in ten minutes!"

The tall man made his way to the buckskin, which was staked out by the stream. The gelding was quickly saddled. As Bostin tightened the cinch, a cold voice spoke behind him.

"Git yore hands up, Bostin!"

Clay turned slowly to face Lambert Fielder, who held a Winchester lined on his chest.

Lifting his hands, Bostin said, "What's goin' on, Fielder?"

"Me an' my pard are lightin' a shuck outta here, and we're takin' yore hoss, thet's whut!"

"You won't get two miles," iced Bostin. "Black Hawk will chop you into dog meat."

"You jist move into the camp and tell 'em to untie Smith," rasped Fielder, teeth clenched. As Clay moved by him, Fielder lifted the Colt .45 from his holster and stuck it under his own belt. "You do whut I tell yuh, mister, or they'll bury you before sundown. Now, git."

Bostin entered the circle, passing between the Wiseman and Sutherlin wagons. Rachel Flanagan, inside the Wiseman wagon, saw Fielder following Bostin, holding the muzzle on his spine.

"Everybody gather out here!" bellowed Fielder. *"Right now!"* His eyes were wild, face flushed. Stopping just inside the circle, he shouted, "Come on, right now! Anybody tries anything, Bostin gits a lead backbone!"

Cliff Adams straightened up from his work on a doubletree. Harry Owen froze with a dipper of water at his mouth. Jack Sutherlin had just lifted his wife to the wagon seat. He turned and scowled.

Slowly, the group gathered in front of Bostin and Fielder. Dub Smith limped toward Fielder, a wide, evil grin curling his mouth.

"Tell somebody to untie my pard," Fielder said to Bostin, nudging his back with the rifle muzzle.

"Better untie him, Bucky," Clay said reluctantly.

As Bucky Wiseman released the rope which laced the wrists of Dub Smith, he said, "You two will be buzzard rations. The Cheyennes will see to that."

Ignoring the old man, Smith stepped to Fielder and said, "Gimme the rifle. Pistol, too."

Like a well-trained hound dog, the redheaded man obeyed. Smith held the Winchester on Fielder, whose eyes bulged, and said, "Git over there with the rest of 'em!"

Fielder stumbled next to Clay Bostin, confusion on his countenance. "Dub, what the—?"

"Shuddup! I'm goin' alone. Birdhead like you would slow me down."

Lambert Fielder pouted like a disappointed child. Smith sneered triumphantly and said, "Now, folks, I'm takin' Bostin's horse. Anybody sticks his head outside these wagons will git it blown off!"

Slowly, Smith stepped backward between the Wiseman and Sutherlin wagons, a cynical sneer on his bearded face. Suddenly, the sneer vanished as he felt a cold muzzle on the back of his neck and heard the double click of a hammer being thumbed back. Smith froze as Rachel spoke from the back of Bucky's wagon. There was a threatening tone in her voice.

"Drop it, mister, or I'll ventilate your dirty buzzard neck!"

The rifle slipped from Smith's fingers and clattered to the ground.

"The pistol, too, buzzard face!" grated the Irish lassie.

Smith slipped Clay Bostin's revolver from under his belt and let it drop. Instantly, Bostin had both guns in hand. Smith's face grew sullen as Bostin told Bucky to tie his hands again and called for Cliff Adams to tie up Fielder.

The crowd relaxed as Clay moved to the wagon and looked up at Rachel. She was holding the empty Spencer rifle which Black Hawk had used in staking him out. When she smiled down at him the tall man burst into laughter. Every eye turned toward him. No one had laughed for some time in the wagon train.

"Hey, folks," Clay said, laughing, "Rachel took Smith with an empty gun!"

Dub Smith shot a surprised glance at Rachel. His mouth dropped open. Laughter burst out through the crowd.

Rachel laid the rifle down. Clay reached for her and, grasping the slender waist, lowered her earthward. Holding her feet about twelve inches from the ground, he looked her straight in the eye and said, "Think I'll turn you loose on Black Hawk. I didn't know you could be so touchy!"

"That vulture got my Irish up," she said heatedly.

"What would you have done if he'd called your bluff?"

"I don't know. I was leaning heavy that he wanted to live pretty bad."

Still holding her at eye level, he said, "Sure hope you never get your Irish up at me!"

Rachel saw the crowd looking on. Becoming a little embarrassed, she said, "I will, if you don't put me down."

Lowering her quickly, he said, "Yes, ma'am!"

While Rachel smoothed her ruffled hair, Bostin gave orders that Smith and Fielder were to ride in separate wagons and stay apart at all times.

Cliff Adams walked swiftly to Bostin and said, "We can cure that one easy, Clay. Let's hang Smith."

"Best words I've heard all day," chimed in Jack Sutherlin, who stood near.

"Yeah, Clay," added Horace Nething. "If he gets loose again, he'll prob'ly start killin' all of us. I say Billy Adams's killer oughtta hang!"

Others voiced their agreement, including most of the women.

"I'm turning Smith over to the law at North Platte," Bostin said. "His partner, too."

"I ain't his pardner no more!" spoke up the bucktoothed Fielder. "He wuz gonna run off an' leave me. I ain't his pardner no more. I hate his guts!"

"You didn't mind throwing a gun on me," lashed Clay Bostin. "You're gonna face the law as his accomplice."

"The law will just term 'em loose, Bostin!" said Cliff Adams, anger in his eyes. "If Smith hangs, that'll stop him from killing somebody else's son!"

Clay Bostin squared his shoulders and set his jaw. "I thought we settled this once. If folks like us start hanging people, there *is* no law."

"He almost got away," cut in Jack Sutherlin. "If it hadn't been for Rachel, he would've!"

"He wouldn't have gotten far, Jack," said the rawboned man. "The Cheyennes are killing every white man in sight. I guarantee you, he won't get loose again. He's gonna be tied—"

"Clay!" shouted Bucky Wiseman. "It's Black Hawk!"

Every eye flashed to the little man whose bony finger was pointing due south between two wagons.

Huddling together, their eyes beheld three riders approaching. They were some two hundred yards off, coming at a casual walk. In the center was the Cheyenne chief, sitting erectly astride the albino stallion. His full headdress moved with the wind. Flanking the albino were two pinto ponies, spotted brown and white. Half-naked Cheyenne bucks rode them with dignity.

One of the bucks held a rifle above his head. A large white cloth clung to the barrel and danced in the wind.

To the rear of the trio, on the same ridge where Bostin had seen them the day before, sat three score painted braves on pinto ponies.

"Looks like I get my powwow," observed Clay Bostin, taking a deep breath.

A set of fingernails pinched his arm. "Clay, you can't go out there!" said Rachel, her voice shaking. "Those beasts are savages. They have no conscience. Don't you remember how we found you? Think of those poor people you were traveling with. Think of the wagon train we found. Remember Beth Ann Kiser!"

"I am remembering, Rachel," he said, squeezing both her shoulders hard. "This is our only chance. They have us outnumbered. We're almost out of ammunition. I don't want anything like that to happen to you."

Rachel's blue eyes misted over. In the emotion of the moment, Clay Bostin's tortured heart overtook him. It came out like water from a broken dam. "I love you, Rachel. I love you like I've never loved anyone in this world."

His throat sprang tight. Releasing the grip on her shoulders, Bostin turned and stepped between the wagons. As he walked toward the buckskin, his last words echoed in his brain. He had done the thing he had promised himself would never happen. Visualizing the look on her face when the words came out, he was not sorry that he had told her. There was something in her eyes...

Swinging into the saddle, he reined the big horse circular-fashion and, skirting the wagons, rode toward the approaching Cheyennes at the same casual walk.

Knuckling tears from her eyes, Rachel fixed her gaze on Clay Bostin's broad back. *And I love you, too, my darling*, she said within herself.

Bucky edged himself next to Rachel. His rough hand squeezed her trembling fingers. "I told you so," he whispered, with a glint in his eye.

Clay Bostin did not have far to ride. He met up with Black Hawk a mere forty yards from the wagons. Bostin raised his right hand in a sign of peace.

The albino halted, tossing his magnificent head, pink nostrils flared. The pintos followed suit, rear legs moving slightly back and forth. The buckskin nickered nervously, animal instinct sensing the strain of the moment.

Black Hawk sat rigidly, headdress bowing to the breeze. Silently, he welded his jet-black eyes on Bostin's face. They were cold and mysterious. Hard as polished marble.

The other two stared impassively at him.

An icy hand clutched at the white man's spine. He silently agreed that the savage was well named. He had the look of a hawk about him, the stern manner of the predator. His Indian nose was thin and humped, giving it a hawk-like appearance. There was an air about him. The air of the relentless bird of prey...the heartless killer, black-winged and menacing.

The stone-faced Cheyenne chief sat his horse, jaw squared, with white streaks of clay beneath his hardset eyes. Red clay was criss-crossed on his chest in heavy stripes. A yellow streak encircled his naked belly. Solid muscles were evident in his arms and shoulders.

Black Hawk broke the silence with his deep, resonant voice. "We meet again, White Eyes," he said in English. "I see you survived the stakeout. White man's God look on you with favor."

"Yes," said Bostin, pulling tight on the reins. The buckskin was unhappy with the situation.

"Lone Elk say White Eyes merciful. Doctor wound. Fill belly."

"That's right."

"Good. Lone Elk say White Eyes want powwow."

"Yes, Black Hawk. You wouldn't tell me the day you staked me out, so I don't know what caused the Cheyennes to put on warpaint."

For a moment, all three Indians stared at him, suspicion and distrust evident in their dark eyes.

Black Hawk spoke again. "Long time ago, when my father, Running Horse, was boy, this land belong to Cheyenne. When he young man, fifty grasses ago, White Eyes come. Kill our buffalo for sport. Steal from Cheyenne. We fight. White Eyes soldiers come like flakes of falling snow. Cover ground. Too many for Indian to fight. Make war on us. Take our land. Put us on reservation. Promise hunting ground where plenty buffalo, deer, elk. White man lie. Break promise."

Clay's line of sight shifted slightly, focusing on the mounted warriors who waited on the distant ridge. They sat waiting like the ageless hills they inhabited, motionless, expectant.

Black Hawk continued. "At season of new grass, year ago, white chief in east sign treaty. Cheyenne free to hunt this land. Two moons ago, send soldiers. Say we must move north to Sioux land. White Eyes chief big liar! Spirit of Cheyenne almost broken. We camp by river. Prepare to move north. Two white men, buffalo killers, come to camp. Rape Cheyenne girl."

Anger welled up into Black Hawk's eyes. "You have buffalo killers in wagon train." As he spoke, the Cheyenne chief looked past Clay Bostin.

"You mean, you put on warpaint because of what the two white men did?" asked Bostin.

"How is it white man say? Straw break horse's back."

"I understand, Black Hawk," Clay said in a friendly tone. "All of my life I have lived among Cheyenne and other tribes. Your father and my father were friends."

Again, Clay noticed that Black Hawk was studying the wagons behind him.

"I don't blame you for feeling as you do. There is no question you have been mistreated and lied to. If I were in your place, I would be angry also."

"That's right," the Cheyenne chief agreed.

"But you have been killing innocent people," pleaded Bostin. "The people in that wagon train you killed back there on the trail, they had nothing to do with your being mistreated. You staked me to the ground and left me to die. You shot and burned the family I traveled with." Gesturing behind him, Clay said, "You attack this wagon train. None of us ever did anything to your people."

Black Hawk's brow furrowed. "All white men bad. All white men speak with forked tongue. All white men who cross Cheyenne land *die!*"

Shaking his head vigorously, the man on the buckskin said,

"These people mean you no harm, chief."

"You lie!" Black Hawk's eyes bulged. "Men who shame Cheyenne maiden travel with wagons."

Clay was pretty sure no one saw the rapists except the girl. He was reasonably certain that Smith and Fielder were the culprits, but he dared not let Black Hawk know it. He would wipe out the whole wagon train to get to them.

"Why would you say that, chief? Lone Elk said no one saw them except the girl."

"They here. No doubt," said Black Hawk, reaching into a leather pouch on his waist. From the pouch, he produced the worn right heel of a riding boot. Bostin's face blanched and the Indian read it.

"You let Black Hawk walk into camp," said the Cheyenne chief. "See if man in camp walk strange, need this." He turned the heel circular fashion on the tips of his fingers, eyes fixed on Clay Bostin's face.

With a sigh, Bostin nodded. "He's there, chief. Both of them found us on the trail. They had no horses. We took them on the train to ride as far as North Platte."

"They must die," said Black Hawk huskily. His mouth drew into a thin, hard line. Again, he looked past Bostin, toward the wagons.

"I can't let you kill them" said Clay.

The Indian glared hard at the lantern-jawed man. "You find them worth dying for?"

"What do you mean?" queried Bostin.

"Your father friend to my father. I let you live if you give us buffalo killers. You say no, we kill all in train."

Clay thought of Rachel. His blood ran cold. He could not let her die. Pondering his next move, he studied the Hawk's stern face. The red man fixed his gaze, once again, toward the train.

Twisting in the saddle, Bostin saw two groups of people watching from between the wagons. Standing in the front of one group was Rachel Flanagan. Next to her was Sherry Manor. Clay was sure Black Hawk was eyeing one or both of them. His blood chilled again.

Chapter Fourteen

Black Hawk's expression was cold and inflexible. "We take buffalo hunters. You live. Refuse, you die." Waving his hand in the direction of the wagons, he roared, *"All die!"*

"Black Hawk, let me ask you...is murder worse than rape?" Clay Bostin had one ray of hope left. The Cheyenne chief was intelligent. Maybe he would listen to reason.

"Suppose," answered the stone-faced chief.

"You know it is."

Black Hawk closed his eyes and nodded.

"The man with the broken boot murdered a young man in this wagon train. He will be turned over to the authorities at North Platte. He will be punished by white man's law. He will hang."

Black Hawk shook his head. "Broke Cheyenne law. Must pay Cheyenne way."

The moment was critical. Life and death hung in the balance.

"I cannot turn them over to you," Clay said in a heavy tone. "I *will* not."

Black Hawk's face, stolid until now, twisted hideously with anger. He would not waver in his savage determination. The hiss of death was in his voice. "You die! *All* die!" Wheeling the albino furiously, he rode at a gallop toward his band of warriors, followed by the two bucks.

The angry words of Black Hawk carried to the wagons. Fear claimed the faces of the crowd as Bostin rode to them and dismounted. His heart throbbed savagely in his breast. He dared not lie to them. Once they knew Black Hawk's demand, they would rise up against him. Ill feelings were already running high toward the buffalo hunters, especially Dub Smith.

Immediately, they crowded around him.

"What made him so mad?" asked Cliff Adams.

"What does he want?" asked Jack Sutherlin.

"What was that in his hand?" came another voice.

Bostin's face was colorless. "He wants Smith and Fielder."

The two men just named were tied to wheels of separate wagons. Both looked at Bostin, eyes wide. Everyone heard the audible intake of Smith's breath. Lambert Fielder's mouth flew open. Cold sweat was immediately visible on the faces of both men.

"Are they the ones that molested the Cheyenne girl?" asked Cliff Adams.

"No!" shouted Dub Smith, straining against the rope which held him to the wagon wheel.

"He's got the heel to your boot, Smith," Bostin said, looking at the man with a cold stare. "He found it where the girl was attacked."

Smith's face blanched. He and Fielder eyed each other.

"Do I understand, Bostin, that if the Cheyennes get these two pigs, Black Hawk will let us go?" It was the deep voice of big Jack Sutherlin.

Clay Bostin nodded.

"You must have refused, the way he was acting," said Horace Nething.

"Had to," replied Clay.

Jack Sutherlin's face turned red with rage. Clenching his huge fists, he roared like a mad bull, "What do you mean, you *had* to? What's the matter with you, man? Those heartless animals are gonna smear our blood all over this country! Let 'em have 'em!"

Rachel and Bucky edged near Clay Bostin as the crowd voiced agreement in a clamorous outcry.

Suddenly, Martin Manor, who had been silent and sullen since the river incident, stepped in with the crowd and yelled, "We're gonna take 'em, Bostin! What you're doin' is crazy. Now, you just back off and stay out of it. We're not gonna get slaughtered just for some high and mighty principle you got in your head! We're taking them to Black Hawk!"

"No, you're not!" shouted Cliff Adams, stepping beside Bostin. All eyes were pinned on Adams. "That murderous Smith killed my son in cold blood and I'm not lettin' them Cheyennes have him until he stretches a rope! Let's hang him, then let the Cheyennes have his rotten corpse!"

Several voices spoke agreement.

"You're all giving in to panic!" shouted Bostin. "You take the law into your own hands...you're guilty of murder yourselves!"

Abruptly, Jack Sutherlin stepped up to face the tall wagonmaster, eye-to-eye. He was purple in the face and scowling murderously. "I've taken all the nonsense I'm takin' offa you!"

Sutherlin swung his big right fist and caught Bostin flat on the left jaw. Rachel leaped back and Bucky sidestepped as Clay went down. He rolled like an athlete and was immediately back on his feet. The crowd moved back to give them room. Bostin's hat lay on the ground. Bucky picked it up.

Sutherlin rushed him, fists flailing. Bostin stepped aside and struck him a crushing blow. Jack's head was hard. Pain shot into Bostin's hand, but the blow staggered the big man. Jack's hat rolled on the grass. Clay was aware that he was giving Sutherlin at least fifty pounds, but he knew he had to whip him. Sutherlin would take over if Clay lost.

Jack staggered momentarily, shook his massive head, and charged again. He caught Bostin in the ribs with a hard blow. Air whooshed from his lungs. The lean man countered with a left hook, tagging Sutherlin under the eye. It popped like an ax hitting frozen bark on a tree.

As the big man circled for a fresh assault, Clay eyed him cautiously. He caught a glimpse of Rachel's deep red hair glistening in the sun. Her face was white.

Sutherlin lunged in, aiming a punch at Clay's face. The agile man of the plains ducked the punch and drove a hissing right into his stomach. Jack's eyes bulged as he doubled over. Clay chopped him hard, square on the nose, and danced away. The big man's eyes watered. Jack rushed in again, bent low. He wanted to avoid another stomach punch. The first one had visibly hurt him.

Twice Jack pumped blows to the rawboned face of Clay Bostin. The tall man rolled with them and countered with three to the nose.

Sutherlin got in another good one to Bostin's ribs, but took two stiff ones to the jaw in exchange. His nose was spurting blood. He was sucking hard for air.

As the fighters circled, Bucky Wiseman glanced between the wagons southward. The Cheyennes had disappeared.

Big Jack lunged again, hoping to catch the younger man with a haymaker and finish it quick. Clay pulled his head out of the way, and sent a vicious, smashing blow to the mouth. Sutherlin staggered. Bostin set himself, put his shoulder behind it, and hit the man with all his strength. The blow sounded like a flat rock dropping into mud.

The big man flopped to the ground with a thud, rolled over...and lay still. Mrs. Sutherlin was immediately kneeling beside him.

Clay Bostin hitched up his sagging pants, ran a sleeve across his mouth, and eyed the crowd. "If any of you others have the same idea, let's get on with it now, while I'm warmed up," he said, with a raw edge to his voice.

Nobody moved.

Bostin swept the crowd with his eyes and waited.

"All right, then," he said. "Let's roll out of here. If we drive the rest of the day and keep moving all night, we can reach North Platte by ten or eleven in the morning. Black Hawk may yet attack before sundown. Be on the alert!"

Soberly, the travelers prepared to move out. Two of the men helped Jack Sutherlin wobble to his feet while two others secured Smith and Fielder.

As Bostin wheeled to head for his horse, he nearly collided with Rachel. The early afternoon sun reflected on her face. There was an unmistakable look of admiration in her eyes. Halting abruptly, he said, "Whoops! I almost stepped on you."

"You *did* walk a little on big Jack," she observed.

"Had to handle it," Clay replied, flexing his right hand. "You did a pretty good job on Smith, yourself."

"I had to handle it," came a quick response. A subtle smile was on Rachel's lips.

Clay said no more. He studied her deep blue eyes. It took Rachel a long moment to break the gaze. "Guess I better get to the wagon," she said, turning away quickly. She felt Clay's eyes on her as she walked briskly to the wagon. This was not the time to reveal her heart to the tall, handsome object of her affection.

Wagon wheels rolled once again. A large herd of buffalo ambled across the path of the seven wagons. Bison swished their tails and eyed the strange vehicles warily as the wagons threaded through the herd. Melanie and Suzanne Adams laughed and giggled at the awkward animals.

To the west spread the vast prairieland in seemingly endless fields of waving grass. Trees were becoming more plentiful and were visible all the way to the horizon in variously shaped patches. Sometimes they appeared in long, slender lines.

The graceful beauty of the rolling prairie could scarcely be enjoyed for the heavy dread that hung like a dark cloud over the slow-moving procession. Eyes grew red-rimmed from the strain of vigilantly scanning the land, watching for the first frightful sign of blood-hungry Cheyennes.

Clay Bostin darted back and forth under the watchful eye of Rachel Flanagan. The big buckskin, holding its head majestically, seemed aware of the noble rider in the saddle.

Bostin knew that the failure of Black Hawk to attack as yet was only part of a vicious plan to put a raw edge on their nerves. He would come sooner or later.

As the sun slanted westward, Bucky Wiseman tipped his dirty old hat low on his brow, providing shade for his eyes. Biting off a fresh chaw from the soggy tobacco plug, he stuck it in front of Rachel's nose. "Here, honey," he said with a wicked cackle, "this stuff'll cure what ails yuh."

Rachel wrinkled her nose, turning her head. "The only thing that ails me, you old buzzard, is the smell of that stuff!"

Slipping the plug in his shirt pocked, he said, "*Old buzzard?* I recollect thet there's the kind o' label you put on thet there Smith feller."

Turning slowly toward the old gent, Rachel said, "So?"

"Wal, I sorta thought you'n'me wuz frien's," Bucky retorted, rolling the tobacco from one side of his mouth to the other.

"Why, Bucky, we *are*!" snickered the auburn-haired lady. "*You* are a sweet old buzzard...and *Smith* is a dirty old buzzard!"

Bucky chuckled and let things go quiet. After a few minutes he said, "When you gonna tell 'im, honey?"

Planting an innocent look on her face, Rachel said, "Tell who what?"

"Don't play cat-and-mouse with me, kid. Thet young feller

needs to know that you love him, too."

"I'll find the right moment, Bucky," she answered. "I want it to be just right."

"He's eatin' his heart out, honey. With things as they are—I mean Black Hawk and all—don't wait too long."

"We're going to make it, Bucky. I just know it." Rachel wiped her hand over her face. "I worry about Alvin. I don't know how he will take it."

"There's lotsa wimmin in Frisco, honey. When he finds the right one, he'll realize that all these years it's been a brother-sister type thing, too."

"Oh, Bucky, you really think so?" Her eyes were pleading.

"Shore, honey. You jist take it from old Bucky."

Clay Bostin pulled the big buckskin alongside the wagon. "We'll stop long enough to have supper at sundown, Buck," Bostin said, looking at the old man. "As soon as it gets dark, we'll move on."

"Okay, pard," said Bucky. Turning his head, he spat a brown stream.

Looking at the girl, Clay asked, "You all right?"

Rachel nodded, dropping her eyes.

"I'll pass the word," said Bostin, pulling on the reins and dropping back.

When Bostin reached the Peabody wagon, Martin Manor looked at him soberly and said, "Mrs. Peabody says he's worse. She thinks he's gonna die."

"Only thing we can do is keep movin'," replied Bostin. "His only chance is the doctor in North Platte."

The lean-bodied wagonmaster studied the four horizons. Not a sign of Black Hawk. The sun was low in the western sky. It would set in another two hours. Certainly the attack would come before then.

Another hour passed. The orange ball was only half visible on the western horizon. Clay was riding about thirty yards in front of Bucky's wagon. Reining the buckskin around, he started toward the wagons, when his eye caught the outline of Black Hawks warriors on a ridge about half a mile south. Waving his arm, he cried, "Circle 'em! Circle 'em! Black Hawk!"

Instantly, Bucky Wiseman jerked his wagon into a sharp right turn. Suddenly, Bostin shouted, "Hold it!" as he saw the dark-skinned Cheyenne chief and the same two warriors separate themselves from the band. They were galloping toward the wagon train, white flag flapping.

"Go ahead and straighten out the line, Buck!" Clay commanded.

Soon the wagons were in a straight line again, with necks craning and eyes fixed on the approaching trio. Bostin waited until they were near, then rode slowly to meet them. Again he lifted his right hand in a sign of peace.

The anger was gone from Black Hawk's countenance. Clay had no idea what to expect. The savage chief spoke first.

"You son of Derek Bostin. Maybe tell truth."

"Truth about what?" asked Bostin, holding his face rigid.

"You swear by mother's grave buffalo hunters will hang?"

Clay knew Black Hawk was leading up to something. What it could be remained to be seen. "I can guarantee you the one with the broken boot will hang, Black Haw. The other one is not guilty of murder, but he will be severely punished for his crime against the Cheyenne."

Black Hawk's dark eyes studied Bostin solemnly. The albino stallion bobbed his head and blew.

"If you swear this is so, then I give you chance to live," the chief spoke with a deep voice.

"Chance?" queried Bostin.

Black Hawk extended his arm in the direction of the wagon train. Pointing a stiff finger toward Sherry Manor, who sat on the seat next to her mother, he said, "Give me woman with sunshine hair."

Clay was already shaking his head when Black Hawk swung his arm and pointed at Rachel. "And give me woman with sunset hair."

Bostin felt his blood run cold. He stared at the Indian in stunned silence. Slowly, a flame of indignation began to spread through Clay Bostin's system. When he opened his mouth to speak, his breath was hot. "We do not give our women away," he said heatedly.

Fury leaped into Black Hawk's eyes. Baring his teeth, he said, "Then we kill you and *take* them. Next time we come, we kill all...all 'cept two woman." Wheeling the albino, he rode away, trailed closely by his two warriors.

White-hot rage bolted through Clay Bostin as he rode back to the train. His eyes were like fiery bits of stone. People were piling out of the wagons, assembling at the lead vehicle. Everyone was there except the Peabodys.

Bostin slid off the horse.

"What is it, Bostin?" asked Jack Sutherlin. His swollen upper lip gave him a slight speech impediment.

The tall plainsman lifted his hat, sleeved beads of sweat from his forehead, and placed the hat to the back of his head.

"Well, come on, man," said Cliff Adams, "what is it?"

Bostin threw a glance at Sherry Manor, held it there for a few seconds, then set his gaze on Rachel Flanagan. Breathing heavily, he spoke through his teeth, "He wants Sherry and Rachel."

Bucky cursed.

"It wouldn't have come this far, Mister Bostin," shouted Mrs. Manor, slipping her arm around Sherry, "if you had given them Smith and Fielder!"

"That's right!" boomed Jack Sutherlin.

Cliff Adams voiced his agreement, upon which an uproar broke out.

"Wait a minute! Hold it!" yelled Bostin. "Listen to me!"

Slowly the crowd quieted, and excited voices trailed off.

"I've lived with these Cheyennes all my life," said Bostin with a suppressed calmness. "If we had turned the hide-hunters over to them, they would've come back and bargained our lives for Sherry and Rachel anyway. Black Hawk was eyeing them this morning."

"That's just your way of throwin' off the blame, Bostin," hissed Jack Sutherlin.

"You're not thinking, Jack," retorted Bostin. "The Hawk was willing just now to leave Smith and Fielder to white man's justice if we gave him Sherry and Rachel. His vengeance is not as strong as his lust. I tell you, he would have been back for these two women."

"So he's going to kill us all to get them," said Cliff Adams.

"That's his plan," replied Bostin.

"You saw what they did to those two girls in that wagon train back there," said Horace Nething to Bostin. "We can't let that happen!"

"We're not going to let it happen," responded the tall man with feeling. "We're going to make it to North Platte." Looking southward over his shoulder, he said, "They'll hit us at sunrise. It's too close to dark now."

Swinging his gaze back to the crowd, Bostin spoke again. "Let's eat supper now. We'll drive all night and set up the circle at dawn. We'll have to make every shot count. If we can withstand one more attack and kill enough Cheyennes to make Black Hawk retreat to lick his wounds, we can be in North Platte by late morning."

"We can do it, Clay!" exclaimed Bucky.

Jack Sutherlin looked at the old man with cold eyes. "You're kiddin' yourself, Wiseman," he said curtly.

"Yeah," put in Martin Manor, fixing his hard gaze on Sherry. "We haven't got a chance."

Sherry blinked with wide eyes and bit her lip. Mrs. Manor burst into tears.

"We'll all be dead an hour after sunrise tomorrow!" sobbed Esther Owen, embracing her baby.

"I know it looks bleak, folks, but let's don't give up," said Bostin. "As long as we stick together, there's still a chance." Scanning the crowd, he said, "We have some extra rifles since...since some of the others are no longer with us. Any of you ladies know how to shoot?"

"I can," said Maude Healy. "It's been a while, but I used to shoot magpies off the henhouse as a girl. I think I could knock a few savages off their horses."

Eyes darted back and forth. None of the other women spoke. Abruptly, Rachel Flanagan said, "I've never fired one, Clay, but I'm willing to try, if you want."

"I will, too," said Mary Lou Adams.

Clay looked at Rachel, then at Mrs. Adams. Finally, he swung his gaze to Cliff Adams. "Ammunition is mighty low, Cliff. What do you think?"

"We could let 'em shoot if the Indians come in on foot. Couldn't hardly miss. Mary Lou can use...Billy's...Billy's rifle." Adams said slowly.

"You show her how to work it, okay?" asked Bostin.

Adams nodded and ushered his wife toward their wagon. The group scattered to make hasty preparations for supper.

Procuring Jeremy Sutherlin's Winchester, Clay stood Rachel beside Bucky's wagon and showed her how to load the chamber and work the lever. When she had convinced him that she could do that, he said, "The rest is simple. You just press the butt of the rifle firmly against your shoulder, aim, and fire."

Placing his hands on her shoulders, he turned Rachel toward the sunset. Standing directly behind her, he said, "Now, put it up to your shoulder."

"Like this?"

"Yep. Now press your cheek against it and close your left eye. See the little bump out on the tip of the barrel?"

"Mm-hmm."

"Put that right smack in the crotch of the little V-shaped piece close to you. Aim that straight at your target and squeeze the trigger."

"Just squeeze?"

"Right. You don't *pull* it. That will throw your aim off." Lowering his face down next to hers, he placed his right hand over Rachel's. Pressing slowly on her finger, he said, "Just squeeze."

A lock of her hair brushed his cheek. His head leaped. Straightening up, he said, "Of course, you'll be firing from a prone position under the wagon. It'll be a little different."

Rachel nodded.

"I'll be right next to you," he said warmly. "If you have any trouble, I can help you. You'll have to fire between two wooden boxes. I'm going to protect you as much as possible."

She nodded again, smiling. Her eyes looked deep into his. Clay Bostin wanted to take her into his arms. He felt like his chest would burst.

Bucky Wiseman's words echoed in Rachel's mind. "He's eatin' his heart out, honey. With things as they are—I mean Black Hawk and all—don't wait too long."

Rachel's heart throbbed. "Clay...I—"

"Yes?"

"I—"

"What is it Rachel?"

"I...better go help fix supper." Handing Clay the Winchester, she hurried toward the center of activity.

Talk was minimal around the fire as the harried travelers ate morosely. Mrs. Sutherlin carried food to Mrs. Peabody, who refused to leave her husband's side.

Mary Lou Adams eyed Mrs. Manor sitting alone and scanned the faces within the firelight. Looking back at the ashen-faced woman, she said, "Vida, is Sherry not eating?"

Mrs. Manor set her weary eyes on Mary Lou. "She's not hungry, she says. Just wants to stay in your wagon."

"Poor dear ought to eat," said Mary Lou.

"Maybe she will when we're safe in North Platte," put in Esther Owen.

"I don't think so," said Sherry's mother sadly. "I don't think she will, until her father—" Standing up, Vida Manor dropped her plate and broke into sobs. Hastening toward the wagon, she disappeared into the darkness.

Moments passed. The quiet group was finishing the meal when a bloodcurdling scream came from the Adams wagon, followed by a heavy moan. Clay Bostin was the first to reach the rear of the vehicle. Mrs. Manor was holding a slip of paper in her trembling hand. By the light of the lantern, Bostin could see her pallid face.

"She's gone!" shrieked Vida Manor. "Sherry's gone!"

Chapter Fifteen

Snatching the paper from the hand of the terrified mother, Clay Bostin tilted it toward the lantern. His voice shook as he read it aloud to the gathering crowd.

> Mother—
>   *Even your love cannot shelter me from the shame and hatred Daddy has for me. I can't stand it any longer.*
>   *Maybe Black Hawk will be satisfied with just me. It's worth a chance. If I offer him myself, maybe he will let the rest of you live.*
>   *I'm sorry this has to hurt you. But it's better this way.*
>   *You're loving daughter,*
>   *Sherry*

Martin Manor's face appeared in the crowd. Elbowing his way to the wagon, he said, "What is it?"

Clay Bostin had never seen such hatred on a human face as that which twisted the visage of Vida Manor. Curling her lip over her teeth, she swore vehemently at her husband. *"I hope you're satisfied now, Martin!"* she hissed savagely.

Clay jammed the note into Manor's hand. As he read it, his face blanched, jaw slack.

Ignoring the burning eyes of his wife, Martin Manor said to Clay Bostin, "I've got to go after her!"

Wiping a hand over his mouth, Clay said gravely, "No, I'll go. I know the Cheyenne."

"Let me go with you," pleaded Manor, his eyes wild.

"I'll have a lot better chance alone," said Bostin calmly. "Besides, we've only got one horse."

"I'll unhitch one from one of the wagons," Manor replied.

"Too slow, Martin. I'll have a better chance alone." Turning to the mother, Clay said, "How long has she been gone?"

"I don't know," answered Mrs. Manor tearfully. "It couldn't be much more than an hour."

"Maybe I can catch her before she finds the camp," said Bostin with a note of optimism. "Just depends on how close they are." Turning to Mary Lou Adams, he said, "Will you stay with Mrs. Manor, ma'am? She's gonna need a mother's understanding."

"Yes," replied Mrs. Adams, nodding.

Bostin's eyes roved the crowd in the dim light. "I'll be back as soon as I can. You all better pray." Wheeling, he hurried to the buckskin. Checking the cinch, he spoke from the side of his mouth, "Bucky! Can I borrow your hunting knife again?"

"Shore, Clay," replied the old man. "I'll get it."

As Bostin dropped the stirrup into place, Rachel stepped close to him. "I know you must go, Clay. But, please. Please be careful."

From the corner of his eye, Clay saw Bucky coming back. Looking at the shadowed face of the Irish beauty, he said, "If it wasn't for a certain banker in California, I would have a better reason for being careful."

"There's no time now," breathed Rachel, "except for me to say *you have the best reason.*" Suddenly, she reached up, pulled his head down, and planted a warm kiss on his lips.

Bucky halted abruptly, eyes wide, mouth open. If the moment were not so serious, he would have shouted.

Clay Bostin's arms enfolded the girl briefly. Fire surged through his veins, bursting from his flaming heart. His head was spinning as he released her.

Bucky slapped the sheathed knife into Clay's hand, his eyes sparkling.

Feeding the sheath onto his pants belt, Clay snapped the buckle, adjusted his gunbelt, and said, "Bucky...take care of her. Get the wagons moving as soon as things are cleaned up. I'll catch up."

The old man nodded.

Clay set his gaze on Rachel. "I'll be back," he said. Instantly, he was in the saddle. To the sound of diminishing hoofbeats, he disappeared into the night.

The scene had not gone unnoticed by the camp. As Rachel and

Bucky walked back toward the group huddled by the fire, they passed Dub Smith. He was tied to a wagon wheel, seated on the ground.

"So the tall man is your lover boy, eh, baby?" sneered Smith.

Without warning, Bucky spit a brown stream, hitting Smith in the eyes. The buffalo hunter cursed violently, attempting to wipe the burning fluid out of his eyes with his upper arms.

Smith was still spewing violent oaths when Rachel and Bucky joined the circle. Maude Healy placed a stout arm around the shoulders of the Irish lass and said, "He's a mighty fine man, honey."

Rachel tried to smile.

Vida Manor stepped away from the Adams wagon and approached her husband, who stood slightly aloof from the group. Her face was a vitriolic mask of loathing. With ice in her voice and teeth bared, she said, "If Sherry dies, I'll kill you." Leaving Manor dumbfounded, she returned to the wagon and Mary Lou Adams.

Cliff Adams was pacing back and forth on the fringe of the crowd. Periodically, he stopped and looked at Dub Smith, whose eyes were still smarting. Smith tried to ignore Adam's hard stares but each time found it difficult.

The murderer of Billy Adams felt a rising fear growing inside him. Clay Bostin was gone. The raw-boned wagonmaster was not there to protect him. The look in Cliff Adam's eyes sent a chill down Smith's spine.

Casually, Adams moved next to Jack Sutherlin. Leaning close, he said, "Billy's killer is still alive, Jack. Justice will never be done if we don't handle it ourselves."

Sutherlin raised his eyebrows. Cliff's eyes were wicked by the light of the fire.

"We need to get it done while Bostin's gone," Cliff said with a tone of urgency.

Jack Sutherlin nodded. "You're right."

The two men entered the center of the circle, and Sutherlin's big voice boomed, "Billy Adams's cold blooded murderer will get off scott-free, folks, if we take him to North Platte. Too much fancy stuff goes on in these modern-day courtrooms. I say let's hang 'im while we can!"

Dub Smith's head snapped around.

Martin Manor seemed to come to life. Nodding vigorously, he moved near the fire. "Yeah! If it wasn't for him, Sherry would still be here!"

Vida Manor's face took on a sick look.

Horace Nething spoke up, "If it wasn't for them two hunters, the Cheyennes wouldn't have bothered us at all!"

"Let's hang both of 'em!" shouted Harry Owen. "Bostin won't be able to do anything about it once they're swingin'!"

Dub Smith was in a cold sweat. Fearfully, he pulled at the rope which held him to the wagon wheel. Three wagons further back, Lambert Fielder began to whimper.

"Wait jist a dadburned minnit!" shouted Bucky. "You all heard what Clay said. If you hang those fellers, *you'll* be murderers!"

"Is a lawman a murderer when he shoots down an outlaw?" rasped Harry Owen. "No! He's just ridding society of infectious scum!"

"That's right," agreed Jack Sutherlin. "None of us in this camp are safe with them two alive! They'd molest our women and murder us all if they ever got loose!"

"But you ain't the law!" screeched Bucky. "You ain't got no right to hang 'em!"

Cliff Adams cursed violently. "We got as much right to kill them as Smith had to kill my son!"

"A fine bunch you are!" interjected Rachel Flanagan. "Clay Bostin is risking his life for one of your own right now, and while he does, you disobey his orders! You'll be sorry!"

"Rachel's right," agreed Maude Healy. "You're wrong in this. Every one of you! It'll be murder!"

Jack Sutherlin's swollen face was red by the firelight. "Do you call judges murderers when they condemn killers to die? Is a hangman guilty of murder when he carries out the sentence? No!" Shaking his fist, he said, "Let's get on with it! There's a stand of cottonwood trees about three hundred yards to the north."

As Smith and Fielder were being untied, Bucky ran to his wagon, pulled out his buffalo gun, and trained it on the frenzied men. "Stop it, right now!" bellowed Bucky. "Stop it!"

Horace Nething gave the old man a blank stare. "What are you going to do, Bucky? Shoot us? Then what will *you* be guilty of?"

With that, Nething turned back to the task at hand.

"You can't stop them, Bucky," came Rachel's voice. "There isn't anything we can do."

The wives of the five men sat numbly, staring into the fire as if nothing were happening.

Carrying two ropes and three lanterns, Manor, Sutherlin, Adams, Nething, and Owen led the frightened buffalo hunters away. Rachel, Maude, and Bucky watched the three lights fade into the distance.

Lambert Fielder sobbed and begged for his life. "Please! Don't kill me! I didn't murder nobody!"

"You raped that Indian girl," sliced Jack Sutherlin. "A lot of innocent people have died because of that!"

"Yeah," added Harry Owen, "you're a murderer!"

Their feet made a swishing sound in the knee-high grass as the tall cottonwoods loomed ahead, silhouetted like hideous specters against the moonless sky.

Reaching the tall trees, the men carrying the lanterns set them on the ground. The shadows of the hanging party were cast upward against the giant cottonwoods.

"Let's put 'em both on the same limb, boys," said Cliff Adams. "Then they won't be lonely."

Dub Smith broke down and began to cry. "I'm sorry, Mister Adams," he said between sobs, "I'm sorry I killed your son. Really I am. Please don't hang me!"

"Here's a husky limb," said Jack Sutherlin, pointing upward. "It'll hold both of 'em."

Both ropes were slung over the limb. One end of each rope was left lying loose on the ground while crude nooses were fashioned on the other.

Smith still pleaded with Cliff Adams. "Please, Mister Adams. Don't do it! I'm sorry I shot Billy!"

"All the sorry in the world won't bring my boy back, Smith!" yelled Adams.

"Killin' me won't either!" reasoned Smith.

"But justice will be done!" snapped Adams.

Lambert Fielder stood trembling like a leaf in the autumn wind. He was weeping and mumbling incoherently.

Both men were pushed to where the nooses now swayed in the night wind, casting moving shadows on the underside of the great branches.

Cliff Adams, his eyes wild with excitement, forced a noose over Smith's head. Both men's hands were tied behind their backs.

Horace Nething looped the other noose over Fielder's head and cinched it tight. Fielder choked and coughed. Grasping Smith's rope, Adams said, "Jack, you get on this one with me. You boys help Horace."

As each of the men filled their hands with rope, Adams said, "When I count three, yank hard and hoist 'em high. We'll wrap the ropes around the trunk and tie 'em."

Dub Smith sobbed unashamedly. Fielder still wept and mumbled.

"One. Two. *Three!*" shouted Adams.

Smith and Fielder sprang skyward, kicking, choking, gasping, writhing furiously. The ropes were quickly secured to the trunk.

As the five hangmen walked in the direction of the wagons by lantern light, they could still hear the rattle of death escaping from the throats of the dying men. Harry Owen sensed the need of a drink. Horace Nething felt a wave of nausea. Martin Manor plugged his ears. Jack Sutherlin wished they had used horses, so their necks would have been broken. The sound of them choking was sickening. Cliff Adams was already finding that revenge was not as sweet as he had anticipated.

Clay Bostin strained his eyes against the night as he spurred the big buckskin southward. As the wind whistled in his ears, he watched for Sherry in the vague light of the stars. The blond hair would make her easier to spot.

He had ridden a couple of miles when the yellow lights of several campfires came into view. Fear struck Clay's heart. He had hoped the Cheyennes were camped father away. It would be more than three miles from the wagons. Sherry could be in the Indian camp by now.

Clay held the gelding to a hard gallop until he was within five hundred yards of the camp. The grass was thick, which helped to muffle the sounds of the hoofbeats, so he trotted another three hundred yards. Dismounting, he tied the big buckskin in a thicket of trees and, rifle in hand, continued on foot.

As he moved swiftly through the grass, the entire camp came into view. Tepees were scattered in no particular order. Several young bucks milled about the fires.

Suddenly Bostin's heart leaped in his breast. His eyes focused on the slender figure of Sherry Manor outlined against the firelight. She had not yet reached the edge of the camp. The Cheyennes were unaware of her presence. He judged she had about fifty yards to walk before she stepped into the light. She was at least seventy yards ahead of Bostin.

Clay sprang into a dead-heat run. He must stop Sherry before she reached the edge of the darkness. Calling to her would alert the camp. Forcing every ounce of strength into his legs, he darted across the uneven sod. Sherry was within ten yards of stepping into the camp when she heard Bostin's footsteps. Stopping in her tracks, she turned and peered into the darkness.

As Clay reached her, panting for breath, he whispered, "Come on, Sherry. I'll take you back."

Giving him a look of vexation, she said audibly, "No, I'm not going back."

"Shhh!" Bostin whispered. "They'll hear you!"

One of the Cheyennes raised his head and looked in the direction of the man and girl. A gust of wind swept through the camp, disturbing the fires. The Indian returned to whatever he was doing.

"Sherry," said Clay in a hoarse whisper, "they'll torture you!"

"I don't care."

Clay shot a glance at the camp. The same Indian was looking this way again. Another was asking him something.

Bostin took hold of the girl's hand gently. "Come on," he whispered.

Sherry jerked her hand free and cried out, "No! This is the only chance the wagon train has!"

A dozen or more braves jumped to their feet from around the fires. Suddenly, the camp was alive with activity. Bronze-skinned men were reaching for rifles, while others picked up bows.

Bostin seized Sherry forcibly. She screamed, struggling against him. Swiftly, he aimed a stiff punch at her jaw. Stunned, the girl collapsed.

A Cheyenne was running toward them, rifle in hand. Others were on his heels. Bostin drew a bead with the Winchester and fired. Working the lever, he fired at the second Indian as the first fell in a lifeless heap. When number two went down, the rest of them scattered, dropping earthward. Rifles began to bark.

Quickly, Bostin hoisted the dazed girl to his shoulder and plunged northward. He felt reasonably sure the Cheyennes would not leave the perimeter of light to follow him. Two of them were already dead. They had no idea who or how many were out there in the darkness. His main task now was to get out of firing range.

Bullets kicked up dirt all around them. Arrows hissed and thudded into the sod.

Sherry groaned and grunted as she hung belly-down over Clay Bostin's shoulder. Her head was to the rear, feet forward. The rugged man of the plains ran for all he was worth. A bullet struck a nearby rock and whined away angrily.

Soon he caught sight of the thicket of trees etched against a star-lit sky. A little further and they would be out of range. His legs were beginning to ache. His lungs felt raw.

The firing had stopped by the time Bostin reached the trees. He had not noticed that Sherry was no longer making any sounds. The gelding nickered as Clay drew near.

"Now, little lady," said Clay, dropping the rifle, "we'll get you back to—" Easing Sherry from his shoulder, his hand struck the arrow that was buried in her back.

"Sherry," he gasped. "Oh, no." The girl was dead.

Lowering her gently to the ground, Bostin pulled the arrow from her back. It had imbedded itself a depth of three, maybe four inches. Dolefully, he draped the lifeless form over the saddle and clucked to the horse.

Looking over his shoulder as he cleared the trees, Clay could see the Cheyennes running to and fro, like ants after someone had disturbed their hill.

Black Hawk would assume someone had attempted a sneak attack on his camp. Clay Bostin and his adopted wagon train would be prime suspects.

The long, lean man of the plains kept the gelding at a steady trot. The wagons, no doubt, were on the move. Though he dreaded the initial moment with Vida Manor, he wanted to overtake the train reasonably soon. Rachel was there.

For a little while the ecstatic memory of Rachel's warm and tender kiss made him forget the dismal gloom of the moment. *Strange,* he thought, *falling in love at such a violent and hopeless time.* Clay told himself that against all odds he and Rachel must make it through this nightmare. If she meant what he read in that kiss, the Irish lass was in love with him, too. They would have to talk about Alvin what's-his-name...but come blood, fire, or smoke, Clay Bostin would never give her up now.

The occupation of his thoughts dulled the passing of time. Suddenly, he recognized the spot where he had left the wagons. He was glad to know they were on the move. North Platte was no more than fifteen or sixteen miles away. If they could just withstand one more attack...

Bostin's attention was drawn to a strange sound coming from the dark cluster of cottonwood trees just to the right of the trail. *Sounds like hemp rope grating on a tree limb,* he thought.

Swinging the buckskin toward the trees, he could hear the wind rustling the branches. All of a sudden his eyes caught the two dark forms swaying listlessly in the wind.

Chapter Sixteen

The cool wind ruffled Rachel Flanagan's hair as she sat in the seat beside Bucky Wiseman. Pulling the blanket up around her ears, she said, "How will he do it, Bucky?"

"Get Sherry away from the Cheyennes?"

"Yes."

"I don't know, sweetie. It ain't gonna be easy."

"Oh, Bucky," said Rachel worriedly, "I'm scared."

"He'll make it," said the wiry old gent. "Clay Bostin is the kind."

"But—"

"Try not to think about it, honey. Jist look up there," he said pointing skyward, "and count the stars."

"I'm glad of one thing," said Rachel softly.

"Whut's thet?"

"I'm glad I did what I did."

"Reckon Clay was glad, too," said Bucky, a lilt in his voice. "Any man thet wouldn't like thet is either crazy or daid!"

"Oh, Bucky..." Rachel said, shaking her head. "I mean if...if he didn't make it...at least he would die knowing—" Rachel's words cut short. "No. I can't even think that way. He *will* make it."

"Thet's the spirit, little lady. You betcha he'll make it. An' a couple or three years from now, you an' thet chunk o' he-man will be settled down around Fort Laramie raisin' a whole litter o' younguns!"

Rachel tried to laugh, but it would not come. She was quiet for a few minutes. One of the horses blew. The wheels maintained their steady hum. The rattling of the traces filled the night air.

"Must be a wonderful thing to be a mother," Rachel mused aloud.

"Guess I'll never know," said the old man.

"Are you ever serious?" Rachel asked in a friendly tone.

"Not too often," he answered.

"Must be an awful thing, what Mrs. Manor is going through right now," said Rachel. "How terrible to bring a child into the world and then—" Rachel put her hand to her mouth and bit down on the index finger. "And that poor girl—" She bit down again.

More time passed. It seemed to Rachel Flanagan that the night would never end. Then she wished it wouldn't. Sunrise would bring Black Hawk, whether Clay was alive or not.

"What do you think Clay will do about the hangings, Bucky?"

"I don't rightly know, honey. He—"

Bucky's statement was cut short as he spotted the outline of horse and rider against the western sky. Clay had circled ahead, so as to approach the lead wagon first. As the old man pulled back on the reins, Rachel focused on the dark form.

"Clay!" erupted Rachel with a combination of joy and relief.

The other wagons ground to a halt. The pair in the lead vehicle quickly made out the limp form hanging loosely over the saddle. Sherry's long blond hair swayed in the breeze.

Rachel gasped.

"It's Bostin!" came a male voice from the rear.

Scrambling feet emitted a hollow sound into the night air as people scurried from the wagons, carrying lanterns. A hush came over them as their eyes fell on the inert shape draped over the saddle.

Vida Manor pushed her way forward, sided by Mary Lou Adams.

Clay Bostin slid slowly off the horse's rump, bracing himself for the inevitable. The lanterns clearly revealed Sherry's body. A terrible, hysterical cry came from Vida Manor's lips, a cry that seemed to emanate from the depths of a tortured soul. Clenching her fists, she threw her head back and howled like a wild beast.

Martin Manor stood frozen on the outer circle, the yellow light from the lanterns matching his face.

Vida howled again. Bostin stepped to her. "Ma'am, the Indians didn't—" Howling insanely the third time, Vida moved with the swiftness of a cat. Snatching the hunting knife from Bostin's waist, she charged Manor full speed and drove the blade savagely into his chest.

Bostin seized Vida from behind, pinning her arms. But it was too late. Martin Manor's face tightened, then sagged. His eyes bulged as he grasped the handle of the knife protruding from his chest. Blood flowed freely as he staggered momentarily, then fell dead. His eyes still bulged.

"Take her to the wagon," Bostin said quickly to Mrs. Adams.

"I'll help," said Rachel.

As the two women guided Vida Manor to the Adams wagon, Clay bent over, closed the dead man's eyes, and jerked the knife from his chest. Wiping the blade on the grass, he sheathed the knife.

Esther Owen ran behind a wagon, gagging. The other women walked slowly away. All five men remained.

"What happened, Clay?" asked Bucky, examining the hole in Sherry's back.

Jack Sutherlin lifted his lantern and studied it closely.

"I caught her just before she walked into the camp," said Clay dejectedly. "She refused to let me take her. Insisted it was the only hope for the train."

Cliff Adams shook his head. Horace Nething made a clucking sound. Harry Owen looked over Jack Sutherlin's shoulder.

"When I took hold of her," continued Bostin, "she yelled. The Cheyennes were stirring. I clipped her one. Shot a couple bucks, put Sherry on my shoulder, and ran for it. They started shooting. I didn't know she was hit till I got to my horse."

"Poor kid," said Cliff Adams. "What an awful way to die."

A scowl leaped to Bostin's face. Bolting Adams with a hard look, he said, "Not as bad as the way Smith and Fielder died."

Cliff's face blanched.

Bostin eyed the others in the same manner, then looked softly at Bucky. "Tell me about it, Buck."

"No, look here, Bostin," cut in Adams. "Them two had it comin' and you know it. We—"

"Shut up!" growled the tall man. "Bucky."

"Me an' Rachel tried to stop 'em, Clay. Maude, too. I even threw my gun on 'em. They went ahead anyhow." Dipping his chin, he said, "I couldn't shoot 'em, Clay."

"Course not, Buck," said Bostin.

"Wasn't *your* son Smith killed," said Adams.

"Fielder didn't kill Billy," retorted Bostin.

"If he'd a got loose, he'd a ravaged every woman in this train," said Sutherlin. "What would you have done if he'd put his slimy hands on Rachel?"

"You can't hang a man for what he might do, Jack," argued Bostin.

"He raped that Indian girl," parried Sutherlin.

"I'm not condoning his crime, Jack," responded Clay, his voice hard. "Nor Smith's. But in a civilized society, men are given a trial. The law handles it."

"Well, they're dead," interjected Cliff Adams. "You can't change that."

"No, and neither can you," said Bostin. "They day may come when you'll wish you could.

"What'll we do about their bodies, Clay?" asked Bucky.

"Leave them there," replied the wagonmaster. "Maybe Black Hawk will find them in the morning and have a change of heart."

"See there," said Adams, "we did this whole wagon train a favor."

"I said *maybe*, Cliff. Don't count too strong on it." Turning to the others, Clay said, "Let's put these bodies in the back of Bucky's wagon. We'll bury them at the cemetery in North Platte."

"What you gonna do about the hangin's, Bostin?" asked Horace Nething.

"I don't know," said Clay morosely. "Right now, my objective is to get this train to safety. Be ready to circle at dawn."

Mrs. Sutherlin drove her own wagon, while her husband took the reins of the Peabody wagon. Martin Manor and his daughter rode lifelessly in the back of Bucky's wagon...closer than they had been in years.

Dawn came, with its dread of Cheyenne attack. Bucky led the seven wagons into a close-knit circle. They were stationed on a rounded rise, where they could see for miles in every direction. One fire was lit, a hasty breakfast prepared. As the sky lightened, Clay went to the Adams wagon to check on Vida Manor. She sat on the floor of the bed, eyes wide open, staring but not seeing. She seemed totally withdrawn. There was no response.

As the sun lifted its rim over the edge of the earth, one person was stationed beneath each wagon. Extra guns and the meager supply of ammunition were dispersed evenly.

Walking to the circle, Clay admonished those in the wagon beds to lie flat when the shooting started. Vida Manor still sat erectly in the Adams wagon.

He eyed Rachel, who peered across the plains between two heavy boxes, fingering the rifle nervously.

All was quiet, except for the birds singing in the fields. Slowly, the sun floated upward, detaching itself from the earth. Nerves were stretched tight. The dew began to disappear from the grass. Clay Bostin paced the ring of wagons like a caged beast.

Silence.

The tall wagonmaster waited another quarter hour. Still nothing.

"You don't suppose they found Smith and Fielder?" came Bucky's raspy voice.

"I really don't think that'll satisfy 'em," replied Bostin. Scanning the horizon one more time, he said, "Let's move out!"

The miles seemed to drag slower than ever. Clay darted back and forth on the buckskin, eyes peeled. *Why don't they come?* He asked himself. *They know we'll have refuge and maybe cavalry at North Platte.*

Hardly had the thought settled in his mind when his eye caught a trace of black smoke straight ahead. North Platte. *On fire!* His heart sank. Twisting in the saddle, he pointed at the smoke, catching Bucky's attention.

"So that's it," said Bucky to Rachel. "Black Hawk went ahead of us."

"Oh, no," breathed Rachel unbelievingly. Standing up and bracing herself, she studied the scene. Billows of black smoke slowly eased skyward, being carried south by the north wind. "Clay, what are we going to do?" she asked, as the man on the buckskin drew near.

"We'll have to go on in, take a look," said Clay hollowly.

Word spread through the train. All eyes strained to see. That is, all except those of Vida Manor, who was not aware of anything...and Elmer Peabody, who hovered near death. Mrs. Peabody began to weep.

"Don't give up yet, ma'am," said Clay from the gelding's back. "It may not be as bad as it looks."

Most of the smoke had disappeared into the sky as Clay Bostin's ill-fated wagon train approached North Platte. About half the buildings had been burned. Some of those which remained were scorched badly. Heaps of ashes lay smoldering where three hours earlier buildings had stood.

Bodies were immediately visible, scattered in the street and draped over various objects. The pall of death hung heavily in the air. Riding slowly, ahead of the wagons, Clay bit his lip when his eyes suddenly fell on the muddled, loosely strewn bodies of a dozen troopers. Their blue uniforms were soaked with blood. Clay thought it strange that not one body he had seen yet had been scalped.

Women in the wagon train were weeping uncontrollably. Their hopes of safety and an escort to Fort Laramie had been dashed.

A quizzical look rode Bostin's face. "Hold 'em up here, Bucky," he said. "I'll be back in a minute." Spurring the horse, he rode between two smoldering ash heaps to the next street. Trotting up one street and down another, he returned after about five minutes.

"Strange," Clay said to Bucky, "some of the people must have known the Indians were coming. Near as I can tell, there's about forty, forty-five bodies."

Suddenly, Jack Sutherlin spoke up and said, "Bostin! There's a trooper over here, still alive!"

Bounding from the saddle, Clay rushed to the side of the fallen trooper. Corporal stripes adorned his blood-soaked sleeve. Kneeling down, Clay saw the rise and fall of the man's chest. "Get some water, Jack," Bostin said.

The young man's body was riddled with bullets. Leaning close, Clay said, "Corporal. Corporal."

With a moan, the dying trooper moved his head and fluttered his eyes. They were glassy. He could not focus them on Clay's face. He ran his dry tongue over his equally dry lips. Jack Sutherlin returned, followed by the other men. On their heels was Rachel Flanagan.

Bostin took the canteen from Sutherlin, twisted off the cap, and carefully cupped one hand at the back of the corporal's neck.

"Let me help," said Rachel, kneeling, supporting the dying man's head.

"Here's water, Corporal," said Bostin, touching the canteen to the dry lips. The trooper took some, coughed, then took some more.

Looking up at the group, Bostin said, "Check the others, fellas. Everybody. Make sure there isn't someone else alive. Don't rely on sight. Feel their pulse."

Instantly, the group went into action.

"Soldier, can you hear me?" said Clay, turning back to the mortally wounded man.

Taking another sip, the corporal nodded weakly. His lower lip quivered. "Y-yes."

"Black Hawk?"

"Yes."

"What about the people?"

The trooper tried to open his eyes.

"The people, Corporal. Did some get away?"

The soldier nodded. "We...we held...held them off. Most...most...got away. Horses. Wagons."

"Any more cavalry near?"

The trooper licked his lips and slowly shook his head. "'Bout a...hundred camped half...halfway b-between here...and the fort."

Bostin's eyes met Rachel's. He read the fear that lingered there. Looking at the corporal again, Clay said, "They take all your guns and ammunition?"

The soldier nodded. "Cleaned out...gun shop, too...bef...before they b-burned...it."

"They'll be well armed now," Clay said to Rachel.

Overhead, a giant cloud slid in front of the sun and cast a heavy shadow over the battered town. Along with it came another shadow...a dark cloud of despair.

"Clay, what are we going to do?" asked Rachel, a quiver riding her voice.

Bostin opened his mouth to speak when the young corporal jerked, coughed, and cried weakly, "Mother! Please, Moth—" His body slacked. Rachel felt his head become weighty in her hands.

"Oh, Clay," she blurted, "He's gone."

Bostin nodded, capped the canteen and stood up. Easing the

dead trooper's head to the earth, Rachel reached toward the tower-ing man. Gently, Clay lifted her upward. "Oh, Clay," she said, breaking into tears, "what are we going to do?"

Clay folded her into his arms and held her tight. Burying her face in his chest, she cried for several minutes.

The five men walked slowly toward Bostin. "No one else alive, Bostin," said Sutherlin. "What we gonna do?"

"We can't stay here," Clay answered flatly.

"But at least there are buildings," put in Horace Nething. "It would be easier to fight off them brutes from them than from the wagons."

"You see how well the buildings protected those folks and these troopers," retorted Bostin with a sweep of his hand. "No, we've got to head toward Cheyenne. This boy told us before he died that there's a division of troopers west of here."

"Won't they come lookin' for these?" asked Cliff Adams, nod-ding his head at the scattered troopers.

"Possibly," said Bostin.

"Then I say we wait here."

"Better to be movin' toward them," said Clay. "We'll have pro-tection that much faster."

"Makes sense, fellers," put in Bucky. "We ain't got much ammu-nition. The cavalry's got lots of it."

"The Hawk's got more now, too," said Clay. "They cleaned out the gun shop here in town before they burned it."

"S'pose it'd be all right to lift a little food from these houses, Bostin?" asked Cliff Adams. "We were gonna stock up here. General store is an ash heap."

"Leave a little money," replied Bostin, nodding. "Folks'll be comin' back."

"Wish we could have found the doctor for Elmer," sighed Harry Owen.

"His house is the third ash heap from the stone chimney," said Clay, pointing across the street. "Even if he got away with the people, he's out of medicine."

"Mister Bostin!" It was Maude Healy. She was standing next to the Peabody wagon. *"Mister Peabody just died."*

Chapter Seventeen

Elmer Peabody was buried in North Platte's tiny cemetery, alongside Martin Manor and his daughter. Maude Healy stood beside the new widow as Clay Bostin read Scripture. Rachel Flanagan, hair shining golden red in the sun, stood with Vida Manor. Vida showed no recognition of what was taking place. Her tearless eyes stared vacantly into space.

When Bostin had finished, Rachel led the unresponsive woman back to the wagons.

Cliff Adams approached Bostin. "What about all these other bodies, Clay?"

"We'll put them in that barn over there," Bostin said, pointing. "We don't have time to dig that many graves. We'll tell the army about them. That's the best we can do."

An hour later, stocked with food, the wagons moved westward out of North Platte. The horses' hooves sounded hollowly on the wooden bridge as the somber train crossed the Platte River.

Mrs. Peabody sat between Bucky Wiseman and Rachel Flanagan. Jack Sutherlin drove the Peabody wagon.

Clay Bostin found it necessary to be straightforward with the exhausted, frightened travelers. Black Hawk was playing cat and mouse. He was torturing this wagon train for giving aid to Smith and Fielder. But there was more. He had bargained for the hide-hunters and lost. When he had countered with the demand for Sherry and Rachel, he had lost again. There would be more harassment.

If Black Hawk had wiped out a dozen troopers, he could converge on this train and do the same. Before he did it, he would probably terrorize them some more. Bostin's only hope was to cross paths with the cavalry division while the vengeful chief played his irksome game.

Bostin had one other faint ray of hope. Before pulling out of North Platte, he pointed out to the people that there were many patches of blood on the ground, scattered about the battle area of the town. Evidently the troopers had scored high before they were finally overcome. This explained why none of the bodies were scalped. Black Hawk's warriors were wounded severely and his losses were heavy. When the last trooper was cut down, the Cheyennes had gathered their dead, picked up their wounded, and hightailed it for camp. Maybe they were hurt badly enough to slow them down.

Bostin was optimistic. Every moment without an attack brought them that much closer to the cavalry. The wagon train was headed in a straight line for Cheyenne. There would be no way to miss a division with that many troopers.

The sun eased across the southern sky. The tall wagonmaster would push the prairie schooners till sundown, then they must rest. The horses were tired. The people were weary.

As the afternoon wore on, Clay wondered what he would do about the hanging of Smith and Fielder. Certainly he could not ignore it. Those men deliberately took advantage of his absence and snatched the law into their own hands. Shaking his head as if to remove the troublesome thoughts, he turned to a much more pleasant subject. Rachel Flanagan.

Swinging the big buckskin so he could set his eyes upon her, he did just that. When her eyes met his, they lighted up, in spite of her evident weariness. She flashed him a warm smile...and his arms ached to hold her. Again, Clay Bostin resolved that this train was going to make it to Fort Laramie and safety. It *had* to. The Irish lady with the auburn hair was part of it.

The seven wagons groaned to a halt in a tight circle at sundown. Laboriously, the women cooked supper. They attempted to make conversation, but little progress was made.

Sullen and exhausted, the travelers ate their meal. Cliff Adams assigned the order for the night watches, informed Clay of the order, and retired to his wagon as the others were doing.

About eight o'clock a giant yellow moon pushed its rim over the eastern horizon. A soft breeze toyed with the canvas cover on the wagons. One of the horses blew. Another nickered. Bucky Wiseman ran out of things to say to Clay Bostin and bade him good night. The tall man sat alone by the dying fire, admiring the moon. Rachel was spending the night with Mrs. Peabody.

A million crickets played their familiar symphony while a lone coyote sang a solo somewhere in the distance.

Bostin was entertaining the notion of bedding down until his time for watch when soft footsteps rustled the grass. He rose to his feet, his gaze falling on Rachel's face in the light of the moon. Stepping close to him, she turned and looked at the big yellow disk in the sky.

"Breathtaking, isn't it?" she said softly.

"Sure is," replied Clay.

"It will be silver pretty soon."

"Oh, not for a long, long time."

Turning toward him, she said, "The moon?"

Clay Bostin's heart was in his mouth. "No. Your hair."

"Clay, I was talking about the moon."

"And I was thinking about your hair."

Neither of them planned it, but suddenly her hands were in his. He pulled her close. Moonlight danced in his eyes. She tilted her face toward his and their hearts blended simultaneously with their lips.

Clay folded her in his arms and held her close. She felt warm, delicate, small, with her head on his chest. Rachel could feel the throb of his heart.

"Strange, isn't it?" said Rachel

"Mmm?"

"That in the midst of violence, bloodshed, death, and human anguish...two people could find each other and fall in love?"

Clay placed a finger under her chin, tilting her face upward. "Do you really mean that?"

"What?"

"You love me?"

"Yes, my darling. I love you."

"I hate to bring this up, but what about Alvin Pinwheel?"

Rachel smiled. *"Penell,* Clay. *Penell."*

"Okay, but what about him?"

"I have never been in love before, Clay. Not until I met you. I had nothing with which to compare my feelings for Alvin."

"But now you're sure?"

"I'm sure, Clay. My only affection for Alvin is a sisterly one."

"But what about his for you?"

"Bucky says there are plenty of women in San Francisco...and Alvin has probably figured out our socially designed relationship for what it is, too."

"Bucky?"

"Mm-hmm."

"He talk to you about me?"

"Mm-hmm. Incessantly."

"That tobacco-chewin' old cuss!" Clay was shaking his head. "He did the same thing to me!"

"I guess we'll call him *Cupid*," said Rachel, smiling. They laughed together.

Holding her tight again, Clay said, "Rachel, we're going to get through this wild nightmare."

"Oh, Clay, we *must*."

"And when we do..."

"Yes, Clay?"

"I—I'd just as well get all my cards on the table..."

"Yes, Clay?"

"When we get to Fort Laramie..."

"Yes, Clay?"

"Will you...marry me?"

"Yes, Clay."

Morning came with a gray dawn that evolved into a rosy-red sunrise, turning the dew on the grass the same color and making the leaves on the trees look like shimmering diamonds. The morning breeze added a touch of splendor.

An hour after sunrise the horses leaned into their harnesses and the wagon train was once again on the move. Clay Bostin was riding point, about five hundred yards ahead of the wagons, scouring the rolling plains with his careful gaze. The sweetness of Rachel Flanagan during those moments in the moonlight still lingered with him.

Looking straight ahead, Bostin noticed a large cluster of trees. There was nothing unusual in this country about a stand of willows, oaks, and cottonwoods growing together in amiable community, but there *was* something unusual...

It took another minute to focus on them. Sure enough, there were two bodies swinging in the morning breeze. They were hanging upside down, ropes lashed to their ankles. Spurring the gelding to a gallop, Bostin closed in. His stomach did a turn as he drew the buckskin to a halt.

It was Smith and Fielder.

Their eyes had been gouged out and small rocks jammed into the sockets. Their ears had been cut off and stuffed into their mouths. Black Hawk was making his message clear. This wagon train was doomed. Every person in it would die violent and terrible deaths.

Quickly, the lean-bodied wagonmaster dismounted, looked back at the approaching wagons, and climbed the tree. Edging out on the limb that supported the swaying corpses, he cut the ropes. Hastening to the ground, he dragged the bodies into the deep shade of the small forest, depositing them behind a thick-trunked oak. He sauntered back into the sunlight and waited for the wagons to arrive.

"Whut was thet yuh drug into the woods, Clay?" asked Bucky, pulling on the reins. "Looked like a coupla corpses to me."

Clay nodded as others were leaving their wagons. "Smith and Fielder," he said flatly.

Bucky's eyes widened. Mrs. Peabody looked at Rachel, whose eyes were glued on Bostin.

"Smith and Fielder?" said Bucky. "Whut—?"

Cliff Adams sided Wiseman's wagon just as Bucky echoed the two names. "Smith and Fielder?" he said, casting a glance toward the trees, then fixing his gaze on Bostin.

"Smith and Fielder?" reechoed Horace Nething, as he came on Adams's heels.

"Let's wait till everybody assembles and I'll only have to tell it once," replied Clay.

Bostin waited until all were present except Vida Manor, quizzical looks on their faces. Lifting his hat, he ran his fingers through his thick, dark hair. Dropping the hat back in place, he said, "Black Hawk is getting nastier in his little game. He took the trouble to mutilate the bodies of the hide-hunters and hang them here where we would find them."

"Where'd you put 'em?" asked Jack Sutherlin.

"Back there," replied Bostin, pointing toward the shadow.

Sutherlin immediately wheeled and stomped in that direction, followed by Nething and Adams.

"You'll wish you hadn't!" Bostin warned.

Momentarily, Nething and Adams appeared, faces blanched. Sutherlin could be heard gagging and vomiting.

"What does this mean, Clay?" asked Bucky, still seated in the wagon.

"It's Black Hawk's little game to wear us down. Let's hope he keeps playing until we find the troopers." Doing a quick panorama, Clay said, "No sign of 'em yet. Let's keep moving."

As the terrified travelers removed to their wagons, Clay set his gaze on Rachel and approached the wagon. There was a haunted look in her blue eyes.

"Clay, I'm scared," said Rachel, her face pinched.

"We'll make it, darlin'," he said, reaching up and squeezing her hand. "By the way, did you tell Cupid over there about our engagement?"

"Not yet," said Rachel, looking past Mrs. Peabody at Bucky.

The old man's head jerked, eyes wide, "Naw! Yer kiddin'!"

"Nope," said Bostin. "I popped the question and she has agreed to become Mrs. Clay Bostin when we get to Fort Laramie."

Bucky took off is hat, waved it wildly, and let out a war whoop. Mrs. Peabody embraced Rachel.

"That's dadburned good news!" said Bucky, flashing his toothless smile. "You can name your first boy after me!"

Bostin laughed. "What *is* your name, Buck?"

The old man cleared his throat and with an air of dignity said, "Adrian Oswald."

Clay laughed again. "Guess we'll just call him *Bucky*," he said to Rachel. Setting his gaze on the scraggly-bearded old man, he wagged his head. "No wonder they call you *Bucky!*"

Wiseman turned his head, spat a brown stream, and said in a hurt tone, "You shore do know how to hurt a feller!"

The day dragged slowly and ended without further incident. Night blanketed the plain. The full moon turned the world silver as the wagon train bedded down.

Harry Owen took the first watch, walking around the outside

perimeter of the wagons. Rachel, Clay and Bucky sat alone by the fading fire. They discussed the imminent danger, the impending rendezvous with the cavalry, and the savagery of the Cheyennes.

Finally, Bucky stood up and stretched. "Wal, I guess ole Buck'll hit the hay," he said, scratching his ribs. "I s'pose this here ingagemint ends it all, huh, Rachel?"

As Clay assisted the Irish beauty to her feet, she gave the old man a puzzled look and said, "All?"

"Yeah, all them good mornin' and good night kisses we been injoyin'," he said with a sly look. Cackling, he turned toward his wagon.

"Bucky," called Rachel.

Wiseman turned around. "Yep?"

Rachel walked to him, pulled his head down, and held his wrinkled face between her hands. Puckering her lips, she dropped her eyes. Bucky's mouth dropped open, eyes bulging. The moonlight divulged a beet-red face. He shot a glance at Bostin and gulped, "M-Miss Rachel, I—"

Smoothly, Rachel planted a kiss on the end of his nose.

"Aw, shucks," he repeated and moved toward the wagon, embarrassed.

As Rachel returned to the towering man of the plains, she looked up at him and said dreamily, "I love you, Clay."

Taking her graceful form into his arms, he said, "I love *you*, little lady."

They stood together for a long moment. "How can it be, Clay?" said Rachel.

"What?"

"We've only known each other a few days...and yet it seems I've known you all of my life."

"Same here."

"I always thought you couldn't love someone until you've known them a long time."

"Love has no boundaries," Bostin said, looking into her eyes, "Even time."

"Know when I fell in love with you?" she asked, running the tip of her finger over his lips.

"Huh-uh."

"The night we picked you up and I held your head in my lap in the back of Bucky's wagon."

Clay smiled. "Even with this scar staring you in the face?"

Moving the finger to the jagged white line on his left cheekbone, she said, "I don't see it as a scar. It's part of you...a part that shows you are a very strong and brave man."

The tall man ejected an embarrassed chuckle. "Don't have to be brave to fight an Indian. Just desperate."

Sliding deeper into his arms, Rachel said, "I'm not a bit afraid when you hold me."

Nothing was said for several minutes. Then Rachel broke the silence. "Clay?"

"Mm-hmm."

"When did you fall in love with me?"

"The day I was born."

"Clay, I'm serious."

"So am I. All my life I've stored up a pile of love for that certain girl who would one day walk into my life. She was there in my mind...a vague image, but *there*. I didn't know what she looked like. I didn't know her name. But of one thing I was certain. I knew I would know her the minute I laid eyes on her."

"And?"

"There was the girl I had loved all my life."

"No room for doubt?"

"Not an inch."

The moon looked down on beams of silver light and acknowledged its approval of the tender, lingering kiss.

Chapter Eighteen

Clay Bostin had taken the second watch. Jack Sutherlin relieved him at two o'clock. Bostin had been asleep about three hours when suddenly he found himself wide awake. There was an uncomfortable sensation stirring deep within him.

It was unmistakable. The Cheyennes were coming. Rising to his feet, he looked eastward. A vague light fringed the horizon. The sun would be up in an hour. Hastily, he found Cliff Adams, who was now on watch.

"We better get ready, Cliff," Clay said in a serious tone. "They're coming at us at sunup."

Cocking his head sideways, Adams said, "You sound mighty sure."

"I am." Wheeling, the wagon master strode to where the big buckskin was picketed and let it inside the circle. Saddling the horse, Bostin checked his rifle and sidearm.

By the time the top rim of the sun appeared, the sleepy-eyed people were at their posts under wagons, guns in hand. Clay Bostin paced the circle nervously, studying the misty plains. Just as the prairie came alive with orange light, a wild, whopping wave of painted savages galloped full-speed from a shallow draw a thousand yards to the south.

"Try to hit Black Hawk!" shouted Bostin. Instantly, he dived under the Peabody wagon beside Rachel. Her face was white, lips blue. Sweat beaded her forehead. "You'll do all right, darlin'. Just aim careful and squeeze gently."

Clay levered a cartridge into the chamber of the .44 Winchester. As the Cheyennes drew nearer, Bostin counted a few more than twenty. Either Black Hawk figured this to be a cinch, or the toll was heavier back in North Platte than he had guessed.

"Hold your fire till you get a positive shot!" Clay shouted.

Black Hawk was in the lead, and then as the pintos parted to form a circle, he drew rein. Suddenly, a sheet of fire vaulted at the galloping riders. Bostin drew a bead and squeezed the trigger. A Cheyenne warrior peeled off his horse. Two more dropped in the first volley.

Clay was taking aim at a yelping buck when Rachel squeezed the trigger of her rifle. A chunk of flesh split off the Indian's shoulder. He screamed and fell from his mount. Rolling, he tried to gain his feet. Blood was spurting from the wound. He ran toward them like a wild beast. Clay's rifle bucked in his hands and the Indian dropped flat.

"Lower the muzzle just a little next time!" Bostin shouted to the girl, above the roar.

Her chance came immediately. An arrow twanged into one of the boxes in front of her just as a bronze-skinned Cheyenne rode into her sights and stopped. He was aiming his rifle. Rachel shot him dead center in the chest and the pinto no longer had a rider.

Abruptly, the Cheyennes galloped away and gathered outside of rifle range. Clay spoke to Rachel. "Good shootin', honey. They'll be backing a min—" Bostin's attention was drawn inside the circle to a pair of braves who had entered on foot. One of when drew a bead on Harry Owen while the other one went after Bucky Wiseman with a knife.

Bostin rolled and fired at the one about to pull the trigger on Owen. The Indian jerked at the impact of the slug, but his rifle discharged and Owen, who was still under his wagon, slumped to the grass.

Bucky and the young warrior were on their feet, squared off hand-and-wrist. The Cheyenne was trying to drive the knife into the old man's chest. Clay Bostin leaped to his feet, running across the circle to Bucky's aid, when Bucky suddenly spewed a brown stream into the Indian's eyes. The savage shook his head, blinking against the smarting fluid. Momentarily he lost his balance and the leathered old man turned the knife on the blinded Indian, shoving it into his belly all the way to the hilt. The savage screamed, staggered, and fell down on the knife.

Clay shouted a congratulatory word to Bucky and wheeled to check on Harry Owen. Esther was kneeling beside him. Before

Bostin could reach Owen, Jack Sutherlin hollered, "Here they come!"

Thundering hooves filled the air with a roar as guns spat fire again. As Clay dived under the wagon, he saw Mrs. Owen shoulder her husband's rifle and pull the trigger. Bucky's big buffalo gun boomed.

The screeching cries of the Cheyennes increased in volume as they came in close. Gunfire banged until it seemed it would shatter eardrums. Rachel dropped two more Cheyennes, all the while gaining confidence in her use of the weapon.

Blue smoke hung in the air. The bitter smell of gunsmoke stung nostrils and watered eyes.

A bullet struck dirt in front of Clay Bostin. Particles splattered his face. As he thumbed away debris, his vision cleared and he caught a glimpse of a rider coming head-on toward the circle. The Indian was going to try to jump the horse between two wagons.

Raising the muzzle, Clay fired just as Rachel's gun roared. The Cheyenne peeled over backward from the impact of the two bullets, but the momentum of the charging horse carried the animal into the wagon with a thundering crash. Rachel threw up her arms, instinctively trying to protect herself. Clay ducked his head. The wagon splintered, rocked, and settled as the frightened animal gained its balance and limped away.

"You all right?" Clay shouted.

"I think so!" came the answer. Rachel's hair was speckled with dirt and bits of wood.

Suddenly, Bostin heard a scream, followed by a rapid exchange of gunfire. There was no time to turn and look. Two more warriors, bodies striped with paint, had dismounted. They were coming at a full run, guns blazing. Bucky's big Sharps boomed just to Bostin's right. One of the charging Cheyennes went down. The force of the fifty caliber slug drove him into the other one, causing him to stumble. As the stumbling savage rolled over, Bostin put a bullet in his head.

Abruptly, the whooping band of savages turned tail and galloped away. As the firing stopped and the smoke cleared, Rachel screamed, "Clay!" She was pointing out on the prairie. There was Vida Manor walking stiff-legged, eyes blank, toward the retreating Cheyennes. The Indians had pulled up just out of rifle range. Clay saw Black Hawk gesture toward the woman. One of the bucks kicked his horse's sides. As he galloped toward Vida, Clay Bostin scrambled from under the wagon. He screamed, "Vida! Get down! Vida! Fall to the ground!"

Vida Manor kept walking. The Cheyenne rammed her head-on with his horse, spun the animal around, and taking aim, shot her through the head. The vicious savage was still sixty yards from Bostin. The lanky plainsman stopped, drew a bead on the Indian's bronze back, and fired. With a wild cry the Cheyenne toppled off the horse and lay motionless in the grass.

Suddenly, the Indians left Black Hawk and charged. Bostin was now at least fifty yards from the wagons.

"Clay!" screeched Rachel from the circle. "Get back! Hurry!"

Bostin moved backward, keeping his eyes on the ten charging bucks. They suddenly drew up where Vida's body lay in a crumpled heap. One of them dismounted and lifted Vida's limp form to his horse. Clay dropped to one knee. Steadying the rifle, he squeezed the trigger. The rifle bucked in his hand. Before the Cheyenne could remount his horse, he went down.

The others lifted their guns and began firing at Bostin, who went flat to the ground. Bullets kicked up dirt all around him as Rachel screamed.

Suddenly, Bostin heard the crack of a rifle just behind him. Then it came to him. Rachel's scream was too close. Twisting his head around, he saw her coming toward him on the run. Blue smoke was sifting from her muzzle. She swung the lever, aimed at the Cheyennes, and fired again.

"Get down!" yelled Bostin. But the Indians had stopped shooting and were galloping away. Vida's body slipped off the bare back of the pinto. The Cheyennes kept on riding and were soon out of sight.

Bostin stood up and took Rachel into his arms. She was trembling all over. "You little fool," he said tenderly. "They could have killed you!"

"That's what they were trying to do to you!" she panted.

"But, honey, you took an awful chance."

"They got my Irish up," said Rachel, blue eyes flashing. "You get an Irishman mad, you got something to contend with!"

"I think they found that out," said Bostin, looking in the direction where the Indians had disappeared.

Bucky Wiseman was coming toward them. "You kids okay?"

Clay nodded. "You walk Rachel back to the wagons, Buck. I'll go get Vida."

As Clay entered the circle a few moments later, carrying Vida Manor's limp form, his eyes fell on the six bodies which had been laid on the ground in a straight line. Swallowing hard, he placed Vida's body in the line.

Cliff Adams stood over the lifeless forms of his wife and two daughters. His left arm hung limply at his side, covered with blood. Tears washed his cheeks. Both girls had been stabbed to death. Mary Lou had been shot in the chest at point-blank range. Black powder burns mingled with blood on her dress.

Esther lay dead, next to the bloody body of her husband. Both had been shot.

Cliff looked at Clay Bostin. "Three of them came in on foot. Shot me first. I heard Mary Lou scream, but I was stunned and couldn't function for a moment."

"Me and Nething opened up on 'em, but one of 'em shot Mary Lou," said Jack Sutherlin soberly. "They must have got to the girls first." Tears were visible in the big man's eyes. His whole frame shook. Sutherlin was standing next to the body of his wife. Looking down at her, he said, "She picked up Esther's gun. Tried to fight 'em off. They shot her in the back."

"What abut the Owens' baby?" asked Maude Healy, heading for the Owens' wagon.

Rachel walked to Cliff Adams. "Come over here and sit down," she said, motioning to a wood box. "Let me look at your arm."

Maude Healy spoke from the Owens' wagon. "Baby's gone!"

"Gone?" echoed Bostin.

"Cradle's empty," said Maude. "Only one thing it could be. Them filthy Cheyennes took her."

Bucky Wiseman cursed. Turning to Bostin, he said, "What'll we do, Clay?"

"It's too late to do anything, Buck. They've killed her by now. I know how Cheyennes think. We'll find her little body somewhere on the trail ahead of us."

Cora Nething began to sob. Her husband put his arm around

her shoulder.

"Clay," said Rachel, approaching the tall man, "Cliff has a bad gash in his left shoulder. The bullet went clear through. He's bleeding bad. You want to take a look at it?"

Bostin nodded. As the two turned toward Adams, they saw him roll off the box to the ground. Kneeling beside the unconscious man, Clay examined the wound. "Main artery to his arm has been severed," he told Rachel. "If we don't get it stopped, he'll bleed to death. May already be too late."

Together, Clay Bostin and Rachel Flanagan wrapped Adams's shoulder, strapping it tight with cold, wet compresses. The blood soaked through. Clay shook his head. "We haven't stopped it, honey," he said. "He needs a doctor."

Rachel bit her lip, fighting tears. "Oh, Clay, *why?* Why do they have to be so brutal and heartless? They're nothing but inhuman brute beasts."

"They're savages," said Clay in an even tone. "It's the only way they know."

"I realize they've been mistreated," said Rachel, "but it's hard to understand how human beings can be so cruel."

Bucky Wiseman approached. "We killed eleven of 'em, Clay. Five had bows. Others had .44 Winchesters. Army stuff. We found thirty-one cartridges among 'em."

"Good," replied Bostin. "Would you count all the ammunition? I'd like to know exactly what we have."

Nodding, the old man walked away.

Blood was dripping now from the bandages on Cliff Adams's shoulder. Clay looked at Rachel and shook his head.

Adams stirred as Bostin poured water into his mouth. His eyes fluttered. Looking into Bostin's angular face, he said, "I—" He clenched his teeth against the pain. "I want you...to...know. I'm...sorry...sorry about the l-lynching. I was...wrong. I was j-just so...upset over...over Billy. I—"

Adams's eyes rolled back. His mouth sagged, his body went limp.

As Clay Bostin laid Cliff's inert form next to Mary Lou's body, Bucky approached. "Horace 'n' me counted ten Winchesters, three navy Colt .44s, and yore Colt .45. We have three buffalo guns. Mine, plus Smith's and Fielder's. An' then there's thet Spencer single-shot Black Hawk had pointed at you. But we ain't got no forty-four-seventy bullets. We have ninety-three cartridges left for the Winchesters or the Colts. I only have thirteen left for my Sharps. How many you got fer yore forty-five?"

Clay tapped his finger around the gunbelt on his slender waist. "Got fifteen, including six in the gun."

Bucky looked-skyward, tapping his fingertips on his palms, moving his lips silently. "Thet's a hunnerd 'n' eleven bullets left," he said morosely.

The leathered old gent went through his silent calculations again. "Oh, yeah," he said, twisting his nose, "I forgot to carry the one."

"A hundred and twenty-one," said Bostin, "and somewhere out there are a couple thousand Cheyenne warriors."

"Let's jist hope the bulk of 'em is a long way from here," said Bucky.

"A hundred and twenty-one bullets," repeated Bostin, "and eight people to fire 'em if everybody handles a gun."

"Looks like Mrs. Peabody and Mrs. Nething will have to get with the crowd," observed Wiseman. "How did Rachel do?"

"Not bad at all, Buck," replied Bostin. "I was too busy to keep count, but she got two...three...maybe four."

The old man smiled, exposing the gap between his teeth.

"You did all right, yourself, old boy," added Clay. "Spittin' in that Indian's eyes was fast thinkin'."

"Aw, shucks," said Bucky, waggling his head. "That's nuthin' fer a old Injun fighter like me."

Horace Nething's arm was still useless from the first attack. He kept watch while the three men and four women dug a single trench, which would be a common grave for their dead. The women wore gloves to prevent blisters. The midmorning sun added to their labor by slamming hot rays against their bodies.

By noon the trench was finished and the eight corpses were tenderly laid to rest. Jack Sutherlin wept like a little boy as Clay Bostin read from the old Bible.

The solemn group returned to the wagons. Clay examined the Peabody vehicle, under which he and Rachel had fought Indians.

The side was battered where the pinto had crashed into it. He decided it could still function properly. They needed all seven wagons for protection when the next attack came.

This put every member of the group on a wagon to drive. Bostin rode the buckskin. As the wagons began to move, the tall man of the plains eyed Rachel. She sat straight-backed, wearing a pair of Bucky's gloves, holding the reins as if the horses were dead-set on jerking them from her hands.

Pulling alongside, he said, "Just relax, darlin'. Let the animals do the work."

First in line was Bucky. Then came Rachel, followed by Maude Healy. Behind her came Mrs. Peabody, Mrs. Nething, and Horace Nething. Jack Sutherlin, still weeping, brought up the rear.

The afternoon grew hotter under the late spring sun. Clay Bostin rode point. From time to time he circled the train, keeping a sharp eye on the rolling hills. At one instant, as the sun was lowering, he thought he saw movement about two miles ahead. Squinting against the bright sun, he focused on the spot where the moving objects had appeared. Nothing.

As Bostin approached the place a half hour later, he saw a pile of head-sized rocks in the middle of the trail. Drawing nearer, he could see something dark lying on top of the pile. He was right. He had seen movement. Cheyennes.

A piteous groan escaped his lips. The small dark object was the charred body of the Owen baby. Swimming from the saddle, Bostin looked on in horror. The Cheyennes had wrapped the infant with thick layers of burlap, evidently while still alive, soaked her in oil, and set fire to the burlap. The helpless baby had been cooked alive.

Clay Bostin's rawboned frame shook violently. His face turned crimson with fury. His lips went white. He had known the Cheyennes would kill the baby, but to do it like this...

The wagons pulled to a halt. Rachel Flanagan was the first person at Bostin's side. The towering, muscular man was weeping, his frame still shaking. Rachel fixed her eyes on the burnt remains. Her knees turned watery. Squeezing Bostin's arm, she gasped, "Oh, no!"

The others were gathering, eyes glued on the dead infant.

"I'm glad Harry and Esther didn't have to see this," said Cora Nething.

Clay Bostin breathed vehemently through his teeth, "Dirty...filthy...devils."

Bucky pulled a shovel from the back of his wagon. Moving north of the trail about ten paces, he dug a tiny grave. The infant's charred little frame was wrapped carefully in a blanket and buried in the sod. Every eye was moist as the travelers turned back to the wagons.

Clay Bostin seemed frozen to the spot. He stood staring down at the small mound. Rachel tugged at his arm. His frame was rigid. "Just an innocent, helpless baby," he said in a heavy monotone.

"Come on, Clay. We must keep going," said Rachel softly.

Abruptly, he became aware of Rachel's presence. She took his hand and squeezed it.

"If I had that devil alone for five minutes, I'd make him curse the day he was born," hissed Bostin. "When I get you safely to the fort, I'm going after him."

"We'll talk about it later," said Rachel, pulling him away from the tiny grave.

Clay shook his head. "Now they've got *my* Irish up."

Chapter Nineteen

The haggard travelers ate their evening meal in silence. No one had anything to say.

Clay Bostin sat next to Rachel, alone with his thoughts. Where were the troopers? How much longer would this horrid nightmare go on? Was he to find the love of his life...and then lose her, all in a matter of days?

Suddenly, he pictured Black Hawk taking Rachel in his fiendish hands. Beads of sweat gathered on Bostin's brow. The awful fact leaped into his mind. If it came down to it, he would have to end Rachel's life, quickly, with a bullet. The repugnant thought hung in his mind, like a chunk of rotten meat. Horrible as it would be, Clay knew he would do it before he would let those savages use her, abuse her, and then torture her to death.

"...the matter?" Rachel's words filtered into this thoughts.

Looking into her face, he said, "What?"

"What's the matter?" she asked again.

"Oh, nothing," he answered, removing his hat and mopping his wet forehead. "I was just thinking about the Hawk."

The evening passed. Clay kissed Rachel good night and took the first watch. He was strung too tight to sleep. He thought of how beautiful this Miss Flanagan was, even with fear and fatigue on her face. She had made a point of keeping herself clean and presentable throughout the wearisome journey. Her dresses were showing the abuse they were experiencing, but she made them look good. He tried to imagine how she would look all spiffed up, waiting for him in the doorway of a log cabin in the foothills of the Wyoming Rockies.

One thing I'll tell you, Clay Bostin, he said to himself, if it all ends here on the plains, you were a mighty lucky man to have her love for a few days.

Morning came casually, with the sun chasing away the gray of dawn.

Everyone ate a light breakfast. Before pulling out, Clay took a few moments to school Mrs. Peabody and Mrs. Nething on the use of a Winchester .44. He encouraged them by using Rachel as an example of "getting the hang of it" fast.

They had been moving for nearly three hours when Bostin, astride the buckskin, spied Black Hawk's full headdress waving in the breeze. As usual, he approached from the south.

Clay drew rein and waved to Bucky. The wagons came to a halt, all eyes fixed on the three riders trotting toward them. One of the redskins held a white-flagged rifle over his head.

Riding slowly toward them, Bostin eyed twenty-five or thirty mounted Cheyennes about half a mile to the rear. His blood ran hot as he drew abreast of the three savages. If Black Hawk's face was stolid, Bostin's was pure granite. His eyes were riveted to the jet-black pools in the wicked face of the Cheyenne chief.

The Indian spoke in a heavy, deep tone. "Black Hawk give White Eyes one more chance."

"You're losin' a lot of men in this scrap, Buster," snapped Bostin. His voice was cold, like a gust of wind off a frozen lake.

Ignoring the statement, Black Hawk said, "Give me woman with sunset hair, wagons go to Wyoming unmolested."

"What kind of a beast are you?" demanded Bostin, taking his own turn at ignoring statements. White-hot fury was surging through his veins. "Is the Hawk so weak he must fight babies?"

The Indian's face stiffened. Fire touched his eyes. Clay knew the bucks who flanked the chief would not violate the white flag that flapped in the breeze. To do so would lower them to the level of double-tongued white men.

"Did you ever fight a real man?" Bostin growled.

Anger was now evident on Black Hawk's dark visage.

"A man who tortures and kills helpless babies is a low-down, snake-in-the-grass, yellowbellied, milk-faced coward!" Clay Bostin's words lashed the Cheyenne chief with the burning sting of a bull-whip.

Black Hawk fought to hold his composure.

"You fight me right now," challenged Bostin heatedly. "Bare

hands. To the death."

The albino bobbed his head and blew.

Fear brushed Black Hawk's stolid face. He was strong, muscular. He had proven himself in many a knife fight. But *bare hands*... There was clearly murder in the dark, flashing eyes of this rawboned man of the plains.

The two bucks looked at their leader. One of them spoke in Cheyenne, "You no let White Eyes provoke you into fight. No use. We attack again. Put bullet in head." The other buck spoke in agreement.

Black Hawk felt a wave of relief. Deep inside, he knew it was cowardice, but he would cover it with a façade of "good sense."

"Black Hawk not waste strength on White Eyes. Kill you in gun battle."

"Another thing I've noticed, Buster," lashed Bostin angrily. "You always stay in the background. You afraid of bullets?"

Ignoring Bostin's words again, the chief said, "Make offer one more time. Give me woman with sunset hair. You...others, live."

Clay Bostin spat with contempt. "Not in a million moons, Buster." Wheeling the big buckskin, he rudely rode away, leaving the trio to their thoughts.

The frightened people awaited Clay's words as he drew close to the wagons.

"What is it this time, Clay?" asked Bucky.

"He's giving us our last chance," answered Bostin dryly. "He still wants Rachel."

The rest of the day was without incident. The wagons creaked to the rattle of traces as they continued westward. Dark clouds moved in from the north, casting a gray pall over the sunset. The wind picked up as darkness blanketed the land.

The dwindling group of travelers sat around the fire, trying to cheer each other up. The wind gusted periodically, scattering ashes and blowing smoke in people's eyes.

The fire was almost out as the languid emigrants arose to prepare for bed. Suddenly, from the darkness out on the prairie, came a bloodcurdling howl, accompanied by the approaching hoofbeats of a single horse.

A soft *whump* was heard in the center of the circle. The hoof-beats faded away.

It was too dark to see the object. Clay struck a match. It was immediately snuffed by the wind.

"I'll climb in the wagon and light a lantern," offered Bucky.

Patiently, the huddled group waited until the old man climbed out of the wagon in a ring of yellow light. Quickly, he ran to the spot. Every eye followed the glow of the lantern.

Clay Bostin breathed something no one could distinguish. Women gasped. Men groaned. Bucky swore.

It was the exhumed body of the Owen baby. Three arrows were stuck in it, each one piercing clear through.

The little body was buried again, by lantern light. The depraved, virulent malignancy of Black Hawk's savage mind was evident to his intended victims. They were dealing with not only a barbaric fiend but a madman.

Black Hawk's tactics were working. No one in the wagon train slept that night.

Hoping for sight of the cavalry division, Clay Bostin led his train westward the next morning. The day passed with no attack from the Cheyennes. Two more days passed. Still no attack.

Midafternoon on the next day, Clay was riding point. The land was beginning to show them a rougher terrain. They were moving closer to Wyoming Territory.

Where are those troopers? Clay asked within himself.

Suddenly, movement caught his eye off to the left. There, on a southern ridge, about half a mile away, were five mounted warriors. They were riding in plain sight, parallel with the wagons, at the same pace.

When Bucky saw them, he drew rein. Clay trotted the gelding to Bucky's wagon and said, "Keep going. They're not ready to jump us. This is more of the Hawk's game to rattle our nerves."

Explaining the same thing to each driver, Bostin had them rolling again. The brazen quintet stayed with them until sundown. On this night the fatigue overwhelmed their fear and everyone slept except the man on watch.

For six days the five Cheyennes kept the same distance and the same pace. Beside the fire that night Clay Bostin said, "We're only four days out of Cheyenne. Somehow we've missed that cavalry division. We need to stay alert. Black Hawk will come at us any time now. There is no doubt he intends to wipe us out before we reach Cheyenne."

"You suppose he's gatherin' reinforcements along the way, Bostin?" asked Jack Sutherlin.

"Possible."

"What chance have we got?" asked Cora Nething.

"We're still alive, Cora," said Rachel. "As long as there's life, there's hope."

Cora tried to smile.

The heavy clouds hid the moon. The night was dark. Clay and Rachel sat next to Bucky's wagon and huddled together against the wind. Bucky was on watch.

"Tell me about our home, your parents," said Clay to the girl.

"Not much to tell," replied Rachel. "I was born and raised in Chicago. My parents came to this country from Ireland. My father's name is Walter. My mother's name is Elsie. Her maiden name was O'Toole."

"You're full-blooded, huh?"

"Aye," she answered with a giggle. "Sure, now, ye ought ta be a figgerin' that out, me boy," said Rachel, donning a heavy brogue.

Clay laughed and hugged her tight.

"You would love my parents, Clay," Rachel said warmly, "but you would probably find them a bit stuffy. Father made it big in real estate. We live in a snooty neighborhood, only mingle with the upper class. That's why they arranged for me to marry Alvin."

"Arranged?"

"That is the word," Rachel said with a sigh. "It was just a social arrangement. I thought it was fine, though. I would be the wife of a big-time banker. Alvin would provide the social standing and level of living to which I was accustomed. As far as I knew I was in love with him. Everything was cut, hung up, and dried."

Squeezing Clay's strong, rough hand, she said, "And then..."

"And then?" Clay echoed.

"And then I came from quiet, sedate, respectable Chicago...to find my true love in a wild, raw, bloody, windswept land."

Clay was silent for a long moment. "Except for the Cheyennes, how do you like it?" he asked.

"I love it, Clay. The wide open spaces speak to me."

"Wait'll you see Wyoming," he said quickly. "Fort Laramie is just a little ways east of the Rockies. If Nebraska speaks to you, Wyoming will *shout*."

Rachel clung hard to the rawboned man. "Oh, Clay, we've *got* to make it. I know I will love Wyoming. If for no other reason, I will love it because it is your home, too!"

"You don't think you'll miss the big-city life and all the refinement?"

"Not if I can be Mrs. Clay Bostin and spend my life loving you!"

Clay folded her in his arms and kissed her.

"Tell me about *your* home, *your* parents," said Rachel.

"Well, Mom died when she was twenty-four," began Clay.

"That's my age," said Rachel.

"I was three at the time," added Clay. "She was giving birth to my sister. Complications set in. Both of them died. I only have vague recollections of Mom."

"There are no other brothers...sisters?"

"Nope. Just me. Come to think of it, how about you?"

"I have an older sister. Katie."

"Oh?"

"She's twenty-six."

"Is she as beautiful as you?"

"She has it all over me in looks."

"Impossible."

"She married a wealthy businessman. Lives in Boston. Has two children. Tell me about your father."

"Dad is sixty-one. He's still Indian agent in Wyoming Territory. Tall. Rugged. Handsome."

"Sounds like somebody else I know," said Rachel, squeezing his hand again. "I am anxious to meet him."

"You'll love him," responded Clay. "He'll love you, too."

The wind popped the canvas on the wagon, reminding them of the present situation.

"Oh, Clay," she said, "hold me!"

Clay Bostin wrapped his arms around Rachel's delicate form.

He could feel her warm breath in his ear. Several minutes passed. Rachel spoke in a half whisper. "Clay, if somehow...somehow we don't...make it, I want you to know that I would change nothing. Knowing you...loving you these few days is worth more than a lifetime with someone else."

"Me, too," said Clay. When he kissed her, he felt the warm moisture of her tears on his face.

Swirling masses of clouds filled the sky as a new day was born. Each person in the wagon train had private thoughts about this being their last day on earth.

Light rain was falling as the wagons went into motion. Clay noticed that the five riders were nowhere in sight. This was a bad sign. Black Hawk might be crouching for the kill.

Bostin felt they were safe as long as it was raining. He had seldom known Indians to engage in battle in bad weather. The rain lasted till just past noon. The sky began to clear. By two o'clock the sun was shining. The tall man of the prairie studied the surrounding hills and fields. The kill-hungry Cheyennes were somewhere near. No doubt they were watching every move.

The sun grew hot. A slight breeze eased the discomfort somewhat. Clay halted the train at a bubbling stream. The water was a bit muddy from the rain, but the horses did not seem to mind. After a brief respite, the wagons rolled westward again.

About an hour later, the man on the big buckskin was sighting along a low plateau off to the left when suddenly a long row of mounted Cheyennes rode over the top. They were only about five hundred yards away. Instantly they kicked their horses to a gallop and started yelping.

Bostin spun the gelding and raced toward the wagons. Bucky had already seen the Indians and was leading the train into a tight circle. The old man allowed Clay to ride inside before he closed it off. Drivers were peeling off their seats, guns and ammunition in hand. Bostin took the time to yank the battered wooden boxes out of Bucky's wagon and toss them under Rachel's wagon. He could hear Jack Sutherlin giving last-minute instructions to Cora Nething and Mrs. Peabody.

Black Hawk was coming for the kill. The barking braves opened fire while still galloping. Their shots were going wild. As they drew well within range, Clay hollered, "Let 'em get a little closer!" He waited ten seconds. "Now! *Fire!*"

Pinto ponies skidded on the wet grass as guns roared and bullets whined. Clay Bostin's diminishing forces fought like seasoned soldiers. Half-naked savages began bouncing on the ground. Gunsmoke was everywhere.

Jack Sutherlin saw Cora Nething take a bullet between the eyes. He quickly spotted the Indian that shot her. The savage was working the lever of his rifle. Taking aim, he shot the man in the stomach.

Clay Bostin, making his shots count, could hear Bucky's big gun boom, again and again.

Suddenly, out of the smoke, a screeching warrior was on foot, running straight into Bostin's sights. The Winchester belched fire. The warrior let out a mortal yell, stumbled, and fell, his face popping the ground.

Rachel saw a brave who was having trouble with his horse. The frightened animal was spinning in a circle. Just as the rider came face forward, the Irish lass squeezed off a shot. The Indian's face contorted in a ghastly mask of death, just before he fell head first off the horse.

From the other side of the circle, Horace Nething let out a yell as three bucks came crawling under the Peabody wagon. Mrs. Peabody lay dead, an arrow through her neck.

Bucky's gun boomed as Bostin twisted around, bringing his gun to bear. Nething's Colt roared at the same time Bostin's rifle fired. All three Cheyennes went down. One of them rolled over, lifted his gun, and fired at Horace. The bullet whizzed past Nething's head, splintering wood. Bucky's buffalo gun thundered. This time the warrior went down for good.

Bostin was still twisted around when he heard Rachel scream. Jerking back, he saw two bucks who had appeared out of the smoke, grasping at the girl. They were trying to pull her out from under the wagon. Her rifle lay in the grass as she struggled against them. Realizing he would be slow swinging his rifle around, Clay released it and whipped out the Colt .45. The gun roared, and one of the Indians released his grip on Rachel's arm, screaming in pain. He staggered, then kicked the gun from Bostin's hand.

The other savage dragged Rachel away from the wagon. She struggled and screamed. Instantly, Bostin bounded to his feet and swung a haymaker, connecting solidly. The wounded brave flopped to his back. Like a panther, Bostin lunged for the Cheyenne who had Rachel. Just before Clay reached him, the Irish lass raked the Indian across the eyes with her fingernails.

The muscled man of the plains twisted the savage's hands off the girl, setting her free. Rachel ran and dived under the wagon, picking up her rifle. As Clay wrestled with the young buck, another left his horse to aid his fellow warrior. Rachel drew a bead on his back and fired. The Indian stiffened, bowed his back, raised up on his toes, and fell like chopped timber.

Guns roared. Arrows hissed. Smoke billowed. Clay Bostin flipped the Indian to the ground. The red man rolled, struggling to get free, but Clay wrapped his legs around his middle and sunk his fingers into the savage's long, black hair.

Bostin was like a maddened beast. This wild barbarian had dared put his hands on Rachel Flanagan. Locking the man's body tight with his legs, Clay left one hand in the thick hair and grasped the chin with the other. With one violent jerk, he twisted the Cheyenne's head, snapping the neck with a loud crack.

Dropping the lifeless form, Clay bounded back for the wagon. The wounded buck was stirring, coming back to consciousness. Clay hear Rachel's rifle roar at another charging Indian as he drew the hunting knife and plunged it into the wounded buck's heart.

The screeching Cheyennes pulled away as suddenly as they had come.

Rachel leaped into Bostin's arms. He held her tight as he watched the half-naked Cheyennes gallop away. Black Hawk was waiting for them at a safe distance. In a moment they were gone. There would be no second wave today.

The eagle eye of Clay Bostin caught movement among the dead Indians. One brave was wounded but crawling toward a rifle. Quickly, Clay released the girl, ran to the Cheyenne, and killed him with the knife. He wiped the blade on the Indian's breechcloth and returned to Rachel.

"No sense wastin' a bullet," he said evenly.

Horace Nething sobbed and shook violently as Bostin and Sutherlin lowered his wife's body into the grave, alongside Mrs. Peabody. Maude Healy had suffered a surface wound in her right arm. A bullet had seared through the flesh, missing the bone. Rachel had bandaged it. The stocky woman stood beside the graves, holding the wounded arm.

Thirty minutes later, five wagons moved out, leaving behind the two mounds, nine dead Indians, two discarded wagons, and four horses. The horses were set free to roam the prairie.

A quick count revealed that they now had thirty-seven .44 cartridges, which included a few picked off the dead Cheyennes. Clay had fourteen bullets left for his Colt .45. All of Bucky's .50 caliber bullets were gone. Clay Bostin knew they could not withstand another such attack. It was imperative that they meet up with the cavalry division by nightfall.

Chapter Twenty

Darkness descended upon the prairie, with no sign of the army troopers. Rachel Flanagan cooked supper over a crackling fire. A light wind was blowing. Maude Healy barely touched her food. The pain in her arm was extreme and demanded her attention. Rachel explained ruefully that there was nothing in the wagons to relieve the older woman's pain.

After the meal, Clay Bostin discussed their plight as the six survivors sat around the fire.

"They will probably hit us at dawn," said Clay somberly. "They know how many of us are left. Their losses have been heavy and they respect us."

"Does that mean they'll come with a big number?" asked Jack Sutherlin, his big shoulders dropping.

"Possibly."

"I woulda thought they'd come at us with a cupple hunnerd an' done the job all at once," said Bucky.

"They would have, if they had that many, Buck," replied Bostin. "Apparently the bulk of the tribe is away off somewhere. They've been pickin' up a few braves along the way. Our only hope is that we've cut 'em down enough that they won't have a large number to throw at us."

Bostin paused for a moment, then said, "I'll take that back. That isn't our only hope."

Eyes widened.

"If we could kill Black Hawk, they would run like scared coyotes. We'd be in Cheyenne before they could elect a new chief and come after us."

"But he won't come within range," said Sutherlin.

"Maybe there's a way to *draw* him in," said Rachel.

Clay eyed her cautiously. "I don't like the tone of your voice, little lady."

"It's *me* he wants, isn't it?"

"Yes." Clay's face reddened.

"He must have sent those two who grabbed me, right?"

Bostin nodded.

"So he wants me alive, right?"

"I don't like what this is leading up to," said Clay warily.

"Now, just listen a minute." Rachel patted his arm. "If I would start walking toward him when they attack, then fall, he might just ride toward me."

Clay Bostin's face pinched. "Rachel, I won't let you—"

"They won't shoot me, Clay. He wants me alive."

"Yeah, till he's through with you."

"If I can lure him close enough for you to get a shot at him—"

"No!" cut in Clay. "Even if I was crazy enough to let you go out there, a stray bullet could hit you!"

"None of us want you to take a chance like that, honey," said Maude Healy.

"But it may be our *only* chance," retorted the Irish lass.

"No!" said Clay.

There was absolute agreement in the tiny group that they would all die before they would allow the girl to take the chance.

Clay turned to Bucky. "Bucky, is it all right if I give Rachel your hunting knife?"

"Shore," said the old man.

Clay stood up, released his buckle, and slipped the scabbard off his belt. Extending it to Rachel, he said, "Find something to wrap around your waist and put this on it."

"I got a belt in my wagon, Clay," spoke up Bucky. "I'm a leetle bigger around than she is, but I can poke a hole in the belt an' make it fit."

"Thanks, Buck," said Bostin. "The rest of us need to stick butcher knives under our belts. The ammunition is mighty low. It'll be hand-to-hand in the next one."

"Now I know how they felt at the Alamo," said Horace Nething.

"There's one big difference here," said Bucky. "We're gonna come through it!"

"You just stick to that, Bucky," said Clay. Turning to Rachel, he asked, "Honey, why don't you take Mrs. Healy and bed her down? Make her as comfortable as possible."

Bostin waited till the two women were out of earshot. Speaking in a low tone, he said, "I want you fellas to promise me something."

Each man nodded.

"If I go down and Rachel is still alive..." Clay swallowed hard. "Will you see to it the Cheyennes don't get her?"

Clay Bostin's meaning was understood. Each man agreed that he would end Rachel's life before they would allow her to fall into the hands of the brutal savages.

Horace Nething took the first watch while the others bedded down. Clay Bostin took Rachel into his arms before they parted for the night. He kissed her tenderly and said, "I love you for what you offered to do."

"Clay, I just—"

Pressing the tips of his fingers to her lips, he said, "No more about it, darlin'."

They talked for a few more moments, kissed again, and Rachel made her way in the darkness to Maude Healy's wagon. She would spend the night near the wounded woman.

Clay Bostin was on watch when dawn came, lining the eastern horizon with a dull gray. Hearing movement inside the circle, he stepped between the wagons and made out the form of Rachel Flanagan.

"It's Mrs. Healy, Clay," she whispered. "I think her arm is infected. I've heard that coal oil sometimes helps. I thought I would try it."

"There's a full can of it in that box over there on the ground," advised Clay.

Skirt swishing in the still air, Rachel walked to the box and, after fumbling for a moment, pulled out the can of coal oil. Finding a small pan, she poured it half full of the oil. Clay could hear the gurgling outside the circle.

As Rachel set the can down, her eyes fell on the small collection of .44 revolvers which lay near the box which held the coal oil. Fingering for the handle of the gun on top, she grasped the cool grip and stuck the barrel under the knife belt on her waist.

The sky was rosy pink when the four men stood outside the circle and scanned the horizon.

Rachel checked the loads in the pistol. Slipping it under the belt at her left side, she borrowed a large shawl from Mrs. Healy's wagon and threw it over her shoulders. The morning was cool and no one would question her wearing the wrap. It would serve to conceal the gun.

Rachel carried the can of coal oil from the Healy wagon and set it on top of the wooden box. She eyed the cluster of pistols. Would someone notice one was missing?

Suddenly, the four men dashed between the wagons. "Here they come!" exclaimed Clay. Turning to Rachel, he said, "How's Mrs. Healy? Can she use a gun?"

"I'm not sure," said Rachel, "I—"

"I can use a handgun!" shouted Maude, climbing from the wagon.

"They're over by the box," said Clay, pointing.

"I'll get her one," offered Rachel, moving toward the pile of guns.

Clay Bostin counted only sixteen warriors, including Black Hawk, who reined up at his usual distance.

One thing was different. Billows of black smoke trailed behind the galloping bucks. *Five arrows!* Clay had expected them before this. Five of them held burning arrows, while the others shouldered rifles.

The warriors bearing the smoking arrows would make a pass just ahead of the others. As the arrows ripped into the canvas covers, the bucks with rifles would open fire.

Hooves thundered. Arrows hissed. Guns barked. Cheyennes screamed.

Bellied down beside Rachel, Clay found himself trying to count the shots being fired from beneath the wagons. A blazing arrow had found its mark in the canvas cover over their heads. Three wagons were on fire.

Clay saw a buck flip off his horse, blood spewing from his side. He lined the sights on another, squeezed the trigger, and watched him die before his body hit the ground.

Smoke from the burning wagons swirled around them. Tossing a glance to his rear, Bostin saw a bronzed body running on the inside of the circle, heading for Maude Healy. Dropping the Winchester, he whipped out the Colt and fired. The Indian staggered, shot Maude, and turned toward Bostin. Clay fired again. The man dropped to his knees, raised the rifle, and Bostin's gun belched fire again.

Bucky hollered from the next wagon, "Clay, I'm outta bullets!"

Leaning over and picking up his rifle, the lean-bodied man tossed it to him. "Use mine!"

Another Cheyenne broke through. Clay shot him before he could lift his gun.

Jack Sutherlin charged across the circle, grabbed two of the dead Indians' rifles, and plunged back under his burning wagon. Clay flattened down next to Rachel again. "How's your ammunition?" he bellowed, lifting his voice above the booming guns and the roaring fires.

"Getting low!" shouted Rachel.

Clay fired twice more, not being sure of his accuracy because of the smoke. Looking back again, he saw a buck running across the circle. Swinging the pistol around, he heard the helpless, hollow sound of a hammer striking an empty chamber. Dropping the pistol, he sprang to his feet. The Indian fired and missed, hitting the wagon at Clay's back. The single-shot Spencer was still useful as a club. The Indian swung it at Bostin. The agile plainsman ducked and planted a hissing right fist in the red man's midsection.

The Indian staggered, a sick look on his face. Clay snatched the rifle from his grasp, got a firm grip on the barrel and, swinging it savagely in a wide arc, crushed the Cheyenne's skull. The rifle stock shattered, breaking off the hammer, trigger guard, and trigger.

Just as Bostin let the broken gun slip from his fingers, another brave came at him with a knife. Twice he dodged the swishing blade, looking for a chance to get the redskin off balance. The knife flashed again. Bostin eyed a burning blanket, half hanging from a blazing wagon. The bottom part of the dangling blanket was not yet on fire.

As the lithe Bostin sidestepped the deathly blade, his eyes fell on the pan of coal oil left on the box by Rachel. The savage backed up and came again. Swiftly, Clay grasped the pan and flung the oil in the Indian's face. While he shook his head and thumbed at his smarting eyes, Bostin sunk his fingers into the dangling portion of the blanket and snapped it full force into his face.

The Indian ejected a bloodcurdling scream as he became a human torch. While the man writhed and screamed, Clay lunged for his Colt, broke it open, punched out the empty shells and thumbed in fresh ones from his belt.

All the wagons except Bucky's were blazing beyond control. The horses were whinnying, ears erect, eyes wide.

As the screaming Cheyenne collapsed to the ground, smoke pouring from his peeling skin, Bostin stood in the middle of the circle. He was turning every which way, shooting between the wagons at the wild savages. He knew that within a few more minutes those firing from under the wagons would be forced to move. The heat would drive them out when the fire reached the wagon floors.

Clay broke the Colt to reload. There were only two bullets left in his belt. As he thumbed them in the cylinder, he tossed a glance toward Rachel's firing position.

She was gone.

A cold chill shinnied up his spine. Blinking against the smoke, he swung his gaze in a complete circle. Panic ripped through his system. He screamed her name. Abruptly, the wind changed directions, altering the course of the smoke.

Clay Bostin's mouth flew open when he saw her. She was walking through the broken circle of trotting painted ponies, heading straight for Black Hawk.

Gunfire continued to pierce the air. Rachel Flanagan, shoulders draped with a heavy shawl, moved toward the Cheyenne chief, who was perched astride the albino stallion. The expression on his face suddenly changed. Slowly, he let the stallion move toward her. Rachel appeared to stumble. Black Hawk struck the horse with his heels, galloping toward her. As he pulled the albino to a stop directly over her, Rachel swung the Colt .44 from under the shawl, hammer back.

Before the Cheyenne leader could react, she squeezed the trigger. The gun bucked in her hand and Black Hawk fell from his horse. The frightened stallion reared, pawed the air, pranced frantically on his hind legs, then hammered the earth with his forelegs. Rachel tried to dodge the hooves, but one struck her foot.

Clay Bostin was already bounding toward Rachel when one of

the Cheyennes screamed something in his own language. Quickly, several bucks rode to their fallen leader, hoisted him upward, and placed him on the albino. Another buck jumped aboard. Supporting the bleeding chief, he thumped the stallion's sides. The suddenly silent Cheyennes galloped away. Bostin could have shot one or two, but his attention was on Rachel.

Kneeling beside her, he said, "You little fool! You precious little fool!"

Gritting her teeth in pain, she said, "I got him, Clay. I got him! See! They left. I got him!"

Bostin gathered her in his arms, cradle-style, and carried her toward the wagons. Bucky was pulling his wagon away from the others to keep it from catching on fire. Jack Sutherlin was unhitching the frantic horses, turning them loose from the blazing wagons.

Sutherlin had not yet reached the wagon just behind Bucky's. When the old man pulled away, the frightened team in the next wagon bolted. Across the prairie they sped at full speed. After about two hundred yards, the wagon broke loose and became a tumbling ball of fire. The horses kept on going.

Bucky leaped from his wagon and ran toward Bostin. "Is she okay, Clay?" he shouted.

Bostin eased the auburn-haired lady to the soft, plush grass. "It's her foot, Buck," he said nervously. "The albino stepped on it."

Rachel winced as Clay commenced to remove the shoe from her right foot.

"You oughtta be whopped for pullin' a fool stunt like thet, leetle lady!" said Bucky. "But I shore am proud of yuh! Is thet dadburned Injun daid?"

Rachel sucked air through her teeth as the shoe came off. Face twisted, she said, "He was still alive when they picked him up. I've never fired a revolver before. My aim was a little wild."

"You hit him, sweetheart," said Bostin emphatically. "That's all it took." Tenderly, Clay palmed the swelling foot, examining it closely. "I think it's broken," he said, shaking his head.

"Maude's dead, Bostin," said Jack Sutherlin, approaching. "They shot her four times."

Rachel's eyes moistened. "Oh, no."

"Horace got it in the same arm again," said Jack advisedly. "He's stretched out over here on the grass."

"I'll be right back, darlin'," Clay said to Rachel. Briskly, he strode to the prostrate Nething. Kneeling down, he looked into the man's dull eyes. The wounded arm was bleeding heavily.

"Lotta pain, Horace?" asked Bostin.

Nodding with effort, Horace said, "Yeah."

"We'll get that arm wrapped right away," said Clay.

"Wait..." Nething's tongue was thick. "Jack doesn't...know about the one in...my back."

Bostin's eyes widened. Nething coughed. Blood appeared at the corners of his mouth.

Slowly, Clay turned him on his side and eyed his back. There was a large stain of blood on the grass. The hole was almost dead center in the man's back. There was no question a lung had been punctured.

"Clay—" Nething coughed again and swallowed blood— "just leave me and get...out of here."

"Nobody's leavin' nobody," announced Bostin. "We still have Bucky's wagon. We'll pull over here and load you inside."

"I'm done for Clay. Just go."

"Nope," said the lean man. Bostin stood up and walked back to the others. "He's got a slug in his back, too." Looking down at the girl, he said, "Rachel, I'll wrap your foot up tight. Then, would you sit by Horace while Jack, Bucky, and I bury Mrs. Healy?"

Rachel nodded.

Using strips from an old pillowcase from Bucky's wagon, Bostin carefully wrapped Rachel's foot, which was speedily turning a blackish-blue color.

The three men alternated with Bucky's two shovels and soon dug the grave to a sufficient depth. There was no blanket in which to wrap the woman's body. Rachel offered her shawl, but Clay felt she would need it. They wrapped Maude's face in one of Bucky's old shirts. Bostin carried Rachel from Nething's side long enough to conduct a brief service for Maude Healy.

The service ended, Clay lifted the Irish lass and carried her back to the bloody spot where Nething lay. The man was no longer breathing.

Turning toward Jack and Bucky, Clay said, "He's dead, fellas.

We'll need to dig another grave."

While Bostin and Sutherlin dug the grave, Bucky moved among the dead Indians, gathering what ammunition he could. After the words were spoken over Horace Nething's grave, Bucky said, "Clay, them Injuns was low on bullets. We've got thirteen forty-fours, all total. Jack has two in his rifle. I was down to one. I got ten offen them dead Injuns. How many you got?"

"Two," answered Bostin, tapping the .45 in his holster.

"My rifle was empty, Clay," spoke up Rachel, "But the revolver I shot Black Hawk with still has five left."

"Where is it, hon?" asked Bucky.

"Out there where I shot him," answered Rachel, pointing.

"I'll get it," said Bucky, shuffling across the grass.

The two wagons were now reduced to smoldering heaps. Clay was thankful the Cheyennes somehow missed Bucky's wagon. Rachel insisted on riding in the seat with Bucky and Jack. Clay hoisted her upward. The other two men climbed up beside her. Bostin walked toward his horse, when suddenly he stopped, snapped his fingers, and said, "Wait a minute." He had just remembered the Indian he had killed, crushing his skull with the man's own rifle. It was a Spencer .44-70.

Looking toward the wagon, he said, "Bucky, did you search the Indian over here with the busted head?"

Scratching his beard, the leather-faced old man said, "Come to think of it, I guess I overlooked thet one, son."

On the dead warrior's waist, Clay Bostin found a leather pouch containing five .44-70 cartridges. Pocketing the bullets, the tall man raised his voice, "Got five for the Spencer in your wagon, Buck!"

Chapter Twenty-One

Three days passed. Dawn broke warm and clear on the fourth day. Rachel prepared breakfast from a sitting position. The swelling had subsided some in her foot, but she still could not put her weight on it.

"You reckon we'll make Cheyenne today?" Bucky asked Clay around a mouthful of food.

"We will if the Cheyennes leave us alone," replied Bostin.

"You think there's still a chance they'll dog us?" asked Jack Sutherlin.

"Depends," replied Bostin. "If the Hawk recovers enough to where he can ride, they'll come. You can bet they're moving the camp right along with us." Pointing his fork due south, Clay continued, "I'll wager those redskins aren't more than a mile from that ridge over there."

When they finished eating, Clay knelt at Rachel's feet. "Let me look at the foot, darlin'," he said, unraveling the makeshift bandage. "Mmm," he hummed, "swelling's down a little more. Sure is purple. Must've broken every vein. I'll sure feel better when we get the doctor in Cheyenne to look at it."

Bucky stood up. Fishing in his tattered shirt pocket, he produced a chunk of soot-colored tobacco and bit off a sizable piece. Rolling the acid bite from one side of his mouth to the other, he said, "This is my las' chunk o' this stuff. Dug it outta the wagon this mornin'. Shore woulda been a shame if'n them dadburned savages had torched *my* wagon."

"A terrible shame," said Rachel caustically, wrinkling her nose.

Once again, the wagon wheels made tracks in the rich grass. As the axles squealed and the traces rattled, Clay Bostin made a wide circle on the buckskin, eyes roving the land. The terrain was becoming more rugged. Small rock formations appeared, jutting abruptly from the earth, standing eight to ten feet high. The first ones appeared a light sand color. Rachel noticed that as the wagon moved farther west the rocks took on a more reddish tint.

The sun passed its zenith. Clay trotted the gelding alongside the wagon. "You'll be able to see Cheyenne when we top that next rise," he announced.

Bucky flashed a toothless grin. "Well, Rachel, we'll have you in thet there doctor's office in two shakes of a lamb's tail."

The lady with the auburn-hair felt a wave of relief wash over her. Could it really be? Was the Lord in heaven going to let her become the wife of Clay Bostin? Was this fiendish nightmare really over? Would there be no more— The black dot racing over the distant rise interrupted her thoughts. Someone was driving a buckboard, lashing the horses violently.

Clay Bostin spurred the gelding straight ahead, hastening to intercept the speeding vehicle. As Clay drew near, he could see a man and a woman in the seat. In the back were two children, both girls. The tall man raised his hand, palm forward.

The buckboard slowed down, then came to a stop as Clay approached. The horses were lathered and breathing hard.

"Don't go into Cheyenne, mister," said the man, eyes wild.

"What's the matter?" queried Bostin.

"Cheyennes on the warpath," said the man excitedly.

"Black Hawk?"

"Yessir."

"You see him?"

"Nope, but others did. We don't live in town. Got a place about four miles this side. Friend slipped past 'em, came runnin' to tell me. Said Black Hawk is sittin' on his ghost horse about a half mile south of town, sendin' his warriors in, makin' a pass two or three times a day, shootin' and killin'."

"No cavalry?" asked Clay.

"S'posed to be out this way patrollin'," said the harried man. "Only other is in Fort Laramie. I'm hopin' to find 'em out here. The fort is fifty miles the other side of Cheyenne. You ain't seen nothin' of 'em?"

"Nope," said Bostin. Jerking his head over his shoulder, he said, "Wagon behind me is all that's left of a wagon train. The Hawk has dogged our tracks more than halfway across Nebraska. Burned out North Platte.

The man swore.

"We're gonna swing north, mister, head for the fort," advised Clay. "You want to tag along?"

"Too far," the man answered, shaking his head.

"John," the woman spoke up, "Maybe we ought to go with them. At least—"

"We'll find the troopers, dear," cut in the man. Flashing Bostin a quick look, he said, "Luck mister." Snapping the reins, he put the team into a gallop.

Bucky, Rachel, and Jack eyed the buckboard as it met them and passed. Bostin sat his horse and waited for the wagon.

"What's burnin' his tail?" asked Bucky.

"Black Hawk is making attacks on Cheyenne," answered Bostin, a troubled look in his eyes.

Rachel's heart sank.

"We'd better head north, skirt the town, and beeline for the fort," said Bostin.

"Are they sure it's Black Hawk?" asked Rachel.

"This fella hadn't seen him," replied Clay, "But he said others had."

"Wish I had shot straighter," said Rachel, ice in her voice.

Within an hour they were passing just north of Cheyenne. Clay Bostin listened intently, expecting to hear the sound of gunfire coming from south of town. At the moment, all was quiet.

By sundown they found themselves surrounded with scattered formations of towering red rocks. The setting sun turned the western sky a blazing farrago of orange, red, pink, and purple. "Oh, Clay! Look at the sunset! I've never seen anything so gorgeous!"

"I have," he said flatly.

Rachel knew by the look in his eyes what he meant. Her arm was already around his neck. Pulling his face toward her own, she kissed him softly. "Thank you, my love."

"Hey, you two!" shouted Bucky. "Yore embarrassin' me!"

Ignoring him, Clay said, "Wait'll we get to the fort and you see the sun set over the Rockies. It'll pull your eyeballs loose!"

Supper was beans, weak coffee, and hardtack. The bulk of the food had burned in the other wagon.

"You think Black Hawk will come after us Bostin?" asked Jack Sutherlin.

"If thet was really him them town people saw," interjected Bucky. "May have been some other Injun a sittin' on his nag."

"Don't think so, Buck," said Bostin. "Must have been a flesh wound. It was him they saw, all right. Cheyennes have a custom. Nobody rides a chief's horse unless he is dead. Then, the only man can have the horse is the chief's son when *he* becomes chief. Black Hawk is too young. He couldn't have a son old enough to be chief."

"What happens if the chief dies and they elect a new one?" asked Rachel.

"Then, in honor of the chief, the horse is retired. No man ever sits on the horse's back again."

"Had to be Black Hawk, then," said Sutherlin.

Clay nodded silently.

Morning came, heralded by a stunning sunrise. Clay told Rachel he had ordered it special for the future Mrs. Bostin.

As the wagon began to roll, the rawboned man riding the buckskin warned Rachel and the two men that Black Hawk was certain to come. They were forty miles from the fort. The crafty Cheyenne chief would plan to attack them before they got much closer. The men were to protect Rachel at all costs. Black Hawk would be seething for revenge for the trick she pulled on him. The bullet wound he suffered would intensify his desire to torture her.

It was midafternoon when the attack came.

Clay was riding alongside the wagon. Suddenly, from a knoll about five hundred yards to the south, Black Hawk's screeching yell signaled the attack. A dozen wild-eyed warriors picked up the call. Goading their horses, they came at a full gallop.

"Hit it, Bucky!" shouted Bostin.

"Hyah!" bellowed the old man, popping the reins. The wagon lurched. The horses seemed to sense the danger. The vehicle swayed with the excessive speed.

Clay Bostin kept the buckskin adjacent to the wagon. As the whooping savages drew nearer, he turned in the saddle to look back.

Black Hawk's albino was staying just a few paces to the rear of the charging horde. Clay could make out a bandage around the chief's midsection.

White puffs of smoke were bursting from the muzzles of the Cheyenne rifles. Jack Sutherlin left the seat and crawled through the canvas opening, Winchester in hand. Within seconds he appeared at the rear, inside the wagon. Rachel leaned to the right side, holding another Winchester, waiting for the Indians to ride closer.

From the rear of the bouncing, swaying wagon, Sutherlin opened fire. The jostling of the wagon was spoiling his aim.

Clay shouted at the top of his lungs, "Wait till they pull alongside! Aim for the horses! Bigger targets!"

Sutherlin turned to acknowledge Bostin's command, when a black hole suddenly appeared in his forehead. The rifle was inside the wagon as it slipped through his fingers. As his body stiffened, he raised up on his knees, tilted over the tailgate, and peeled out of the wagon head first. His big frame hit the ground hard and bounced wildly, arms and legs flailing like a rag doll. The horse of the same Indian who shot him tried to dodge the flopping body. Its footing failed. Horse and rider went down in a bone-cracking crash.

Quickly, Clay Bostin reined the buckskin to the rear of the wagon. Leaning out of the saddle, he grasped the rear canopy rib, and while Rachel held her breath, he vaulted into the wagon.

The Cheyennes were gaining on them. As those in the lead drew abreast, Clay raised Jack Sutherlin's rifle and, steadying himself as much as possible, opened fire. The lead Indian's horse did a violent somersault, slamming its rider to the ground. A warrior on a fast horse was pulling in on the left side. Bucky palmed the Colt .44 with which Rachel had shot Black Hawk. The Indian fired and missed. Bucky fired twice and missed. The Indian worked the lever and shouldered the Winchester.

"Shoot the horse, Bucky!" yelled Clay.

The old man loved animals. Every fiber in his system rebelled against shooting the horse, but he knew Clay was right. The animal offered a larger target. This was life and death. Bracing the revolver on his left elbow, Bucky took aim and fired. The Indian's rifle fired first, sending a bullet right past Bucky's right ear. The Colt .44 found its mark and the pinto went down.

Rachel saw a redskinned rider pulling up on her side as Clay took out another one to the rear on the other side. The bounding, fishtailing wagon made accuracy difficult. The first four bullets missed the yelping savage's horse. The fifth one hit the horse in the breast. The Indian screamed as he plummeted earthward.

Bucky spent his last two shells and dropped the revolver to the floorboard.

The canvas covering was speckled with bullet holes. It ripped and tore with the wind flapping it fiercely.

Clay's rifle was now empty. Bullets were singing dangerously close. Crawling forward in the wagon, Clay yelled to Rachel, "Come back here and lie down flat! Hurry!"

As the girl complied, Clay took her rifle and said, "How many bullets left?"

"Three!" came the answer.

Shouldering the rifle he said, "Stay down!" With the third shot, another buck took a hard ride to earth. Dropping the Winchester, Clay picked up the Spencer .44-70 that had been left with him when Black Hawk had staked him out.

Reaching in his pants pocket, Clay felt the five cartridges. His blood ran cold. Five bullets left. Seven Cheyennes, including Black Hawk, who still rode to the rear of his galloping warriors. Purposely, Clay left one bullet in his pocket. He would fire the four in his hand, but the last bullet he would save for Rachel. Black Hawk would never put her through a vile orgy of torture.

The first three bullets whined harmlessly past the hard-riding savages. Clay thumbed the fourth in the chamber. Lying flat, he lifted his head barely over the tailgate. To his surprise, Black Hawk was goading the albino closer. They had one chance...

A bullet tore into one of the boxes as Bostin crawled around Rachel and stuck his head through the canvas opening. His eyes fell on the lathered team. "Bucky!" shouted Bostin. "Black Hawk is pulling closer! If you slow down real fast, he'll come within range. I've got one shot left. Gonna try to hit the albino! When I say 'Go,' count to five and slow 'er down. Don't jerk it, just ease it back. When you hear me shoot, take off as fast as those horses will go!"

"Gotcha!"

Turning around, Clay looked past the flapping canvas. Black

Hawk was even closer. The bucks had stopped shooting. Clay hoped they were out of ammunition.

Rachel looked up at him, fear in her eyes. Clay thought of the last bullet in his pocket. He patted her shoulder. Taking a deep breath, he hollered, "Go!" Springing to the back of the wagon, he braced himself raising the rifle. As Bucky drew back on the reins, the wagon slowed. The surprised Cheyenne chief yanked back his own reins, but it was too late. Bostin fired the Spencer and the albino pitched forward, spilling Black Hawk head-over-heels to the ground.

The remaining six riders pulled up sharply to attend their fallen leader.

The wagon picked up speed. Rachel sat up and eyed the scene. The young bucks were kneeling in a circle around Black Hawk.

Suddenly, something popped at the rear of the wagon. The speeding vehicle swayed heavily. The right rear corner dropped to the earth with a thud. Clay saw the wheel go reeling off to the side and shatter against a rock.

Bucky pulled the dragging vehicle to a halt. Jumping from the seat, he eyed the broken wheel to the rear and swore.

Clay was instantly out of the wagon. Both men threw their gaze toward the Cheyennes. The Indians were placing Black Hawk in a seated position on a pinto pony. Slowly, they mounted up, looked toward the crippled wagon, conversed for a few minutes, then rode south. They soon rode into a ravine and disappeared.

"They're out of ammunition, Buck," said Clay. "But they'll be back. They still had arrows, but they don't want to take on rifles with just arrows. If they only knew our ammunition was gone..."

Clay turned and lifted Rachel from the slanting wagon. "How far are we from Fort Laramie, Clay?" she asked.

Bostin eyed the landmarks for a moment. "About twenty-five miles," he said with a strained voice. "Do you think you can ride?"

"I think so," she replied.

"I'll cut the team loose from the wagon," offered Bucky. "I think they got enough left in 'em to carry us twenty-five miles."

Without warning, two bronzed riders on pinto ponies pulled out of the long ravine about fifty yards in front of the broken-down wagon. They were coming at a full gallop, arrows strung in bows.

"Get down, Bucky!" shouted Bostin, lowering Rachel carefully to the ground.

Bucky had stepped behind the horses to unhook the harness from the doubletree. Hearing Clay's warning, then hearing the rumbling hooves, he squatted where he stood.

As the charging Cheyennes drew near, they parted, one going on each side. Bowstrings hummed. Arrows hissed, striking horseflesh. The two savages kept on going as the horses screamed with pain. Both were mortally wounded. Within two minutes they were dead.

Wiseman stood over the dead horses and cursed the Cheyennes and their ancestors. "Whadda we do now, Clay?" he asked, face red with anger.

"We don't dare let them catch us out in the open," answered the tall man. Looking toward the lowering sun, he studied the situation. Rachel eyed him as a little girl would look at a strong, wise father.

A towering rock formation stood northwest about a half mile away. It sat in a mound of sod. The sod sloped upward to a point about twenty feet above ground level. From there it was solid red rock. The top was about fifty feet high.

"We need a safe place for you two to hide while I head for Laramie," said Bostin. "I think we can get up in that rock."

"Yuh think they'll come back before dark?" Bucky asked wearily.

"Depends on how far away they've camped. I don't think the Hawk was hurt too bad. It's at least two hours until the sun is totally gone. They won't attack after that." Clay hoisted Rachel cradle-style. "Can you carry the guns, Buck? I'll let Rachel hold the water."

"No sense takin' the guns, Clay," advised the old man. "They won't do us no good without bullets."

"If the Cheyennes find the guns here, they'll know we're out of ammunition," Clay said evenly.

"Oh. Yeah," said Bucky, wagging his head. "Ole Buck ain't thinkin' too good, is he, son?" Quickly, he began to gather the guns.

"Don't forget the Spencer," said Clay, placing a large canteen in Rachel's hand. Lifting a knapsack, he said, "There's a little jerky and some hardtack in here."

"It's a long way to that rock," said the Irish lass to the tall plainsman. "I'll get pretty heavy."

"You *are* a huge thing, aren't you?" chuckled Bostin. "I bet you weigh as much as a sack of potatoes."

The trio found that nature had provided a crude staircase up the east side of the towering rock. Near the top was a level area which was partially covered. It made a comfortable hiding place and offered a good view of the land to the south and east.

Rachel sat on a small ledge, while the men sat Indian-style on the rock floor. As they chewed jerky, Clay said, "As soon as it's totally dark, I'll head for the fort. I can have the army here before sunup. Cheyennes may have watched us climb up here. If they did, Black Hawk will lead them here at sunrise."

"I been thinkin'," said Bucky. "Why don't *I* go for the troopers an' you stay with Rachel?"

"No, Bucky," said Clay. "I'm the one—"

"Now, jist wait a minnit," cut in the old man. "If sump'n' should go haywire with our plans and them dadburned Injuns should git us, I think you two kids oughtta be together. Every minnit counts."

Clay looked longingly at the beautiful face of the girl in the fading light. To Bucky he said, "But I can travel faster than you, Buck."

"You jist think so, sonny," the old man snapped. "I kin make it as quick as you. Guarantee it."

Though the light was dim, Clay observed a spark in the flinty eyes.

"Okay," answered Bostin resignedly. "But you have to have the troopers here before sunup."

Bucky stood up and walked to the edge of the level area. Scanning the land in the last light of day, he said, "Feller kin see quite a stretch from up here. With a lotta ammunition, he could hold off the Cheyennes for a long time."

"I want to look at your foot before all the light is gone," Clay said to Rachel. As he unraveled the wrapping, he saw that it had swollen more. "All the bouncing' in that wagon sure didn't help it, darlin'," he said, wrapping the foot again.

A few stars appeared overhead.

"Well, I guess ole Bucky better hightail it outta here," said Bucky. "He's got twenty-five miles to hoof it."

"You sure you can make it, Buck?" asked Bostin.

"Only thing kin stop me is if I run into a pack o' purty girls. I kin fight off three or four, but sometimes they attack by the dozens. A feller jist can't help bein' irresistible!"

Rachel was still perched on the ledge. "Come here, *Mister Irresistible*," said Rachel, "I want to hug your neck."

As the pretty lady wrapped her arms around the old man's neck, she began to cry. "You be careful," she said, sniffing. "Those Cheyennes may be out there waiting for you."

Bucky swallowed a hot lump. Blinking against his own tears, he was glad it was now too dark for anyone to see them. "Now, don't you worry yore purty head over me. I'm gonna make it to the fort and bring back scads o' help, so's you 'n' this little short feller here kin git married 'n' have little Bucky."

As Rachel released him, he reached for Clay Bostin's hand in the dark. "Clay, take good care o' this Irish lassie, here. I'll see you with the sound of a bugle before sunup."

Bostin squeezed hard. "She's right, Buck. They could be waitin' out there. You be careful."

"I will, Clay. Adios." The old man faded into the night.

Clay held Rachel in his arms for a long time. Weariness finally overtook her and her breathing evened out and she slept. Sitting on the level rock floor with his back against the stone wall, he thought of the bullet in his pocket. If Bucky didn't make it... If the cavalry didn't come by sunrise...

Chapter Twenty-Two

Rachel Flanagan had been asleep in Clay Bostin's arms for nearly two hours when suddenly a long-forgotten but familiar sound met his ears. *Death drums.*

The Cheyennes were having a special ceremony. It was their heathen celebration of the proposed final victory over an archenemy. There was no question in Bostin's mind who the Indians had in mind. The savages had watched them climb the rock. They were trapped. The drums carried the solemn message. *Death would come to their enemies at sunrise.*

Easing the sleeping girl to the floor, Clay stepped to the edge and looked southward. The Cheyenne camp was just over the ridge south of the trail, less than a mile away. Several flickering fires lit up the camp. Clay knew the sound of the drums would go on all night. When they went quiet in the morning, the attack would come.

The rugged man of the plains had to face a cold, hard fact. If Bucky did not make it to Fort Laramie...even if he did not make it *in time*, Clay Bostin would have to end the life of the woman he loved. To save her from unthinkable torture, followed by a slow, agonizing death, he would have to put the last bullet in her head.

A wave of nausea washed over him. There had to be another— suddenly, Bostin's thoughts turned to what Bucky had said earlier, "Feller kin see quite a stretch from up here. With a lotta ammunition, he could hold off the Cheyennes for a long time."

Clay remembered the ammunition taken from the troopers and stolen from the gun shop in North Platte. Most of the Indians would be occupied with the ceremonies. If he could sneak into the camp, chances were good he could load up with ammunition and return to the rock before dawn.

After several minutes the plan was formed in his mind. He must go after the ammunition. It was their only hope of survival if Bucky didn't make it to Fort Laramie. They didn't have food or water to last long up on that rock, but ammunition would buy them time.

Returning to the enclosure, Bostin awakened Rachel. "Honey, I'm sorry to have to wake you," he said apologetically, "but we must talk."

"It's all right," said the girl groggily. "What is it, Clay?"

"Do you hear those drums?"

"Yes."

"The Cheyenne camp is straight south, about a mile."

"Mm-hmm."

"I'm going to sneak into the camp and get some ammunition. If something should happen to Bucky...or if he should even be late, we don't have a chance. But if I can get several hundred rounds of ammunition, we could hold 'em off for a long time."

"But how are you—?"

"They have a ceremony going. I've seen them before. It'll go on till sunrise. Everybody's involved. There probably won't be more than one or two guards."

"Whatever you say," agreed Rachel.

Clay swallowed hard. "Now, darlin', I want you to listen close."

"Yes, Clay."

"I have saved one bullet for the Spencer."

"Yes."

Clay was glad it was pitch black in the rock enclosure. He could feel the whiteness of his face. "If...if something should happen to me... I mean, if I didn't make it back...you will have to use the gun on yourself."

Rachel made no sound.

"Rachel..."

"Yes, Clay."

"Do you understand?"

"Oh, Clay, I *couldn't!*"

"Honey, listen. Do you remember Beth Ann Kiser?"

Rachel waited several seconds in the dark. "Yes."

"Black Hawk would treat you ten times as bad. Do you understand?"

"Yes." Rachel could hear Clay's boots scraping on the stone, then his hands searching for the Spencer.

Bostin found the gun, slipped the bullet into the chamber, and closed it with a loud click. "Rachel," he said softly, "remember when you pulled back this hammer to stop Dub Smith?"

"Uh-huh."

"If I don't return and the Cheyennes come up here, you cock the hammer, invert the gun and put—" Clay swallowed hard again— "put the muzzle in your mouth. Reach down with your toe and press the trigger."

Rachel could not speak. Folding her in his arms, Clay held her tight and said, "Honey, you have to promise me you'll do it."

Her body trembling violently, Rachel said, "I—I promise."

"I'll need the knife."

"Oh." Rachel's trembling fingers fumbled with the belt around her waist. Presently the buckle opened. "Here it is," she said, extending it toward him.

Clay slipped the scabbard onto his own belt.

Rachel wept softly as the strong man held her. Tears touched his face as he kissed her. "I love you," said Clay.

"And I love you, my darling."

He kissed her once more...and was gone.

The drums beat out their steady rhythm as Clay Bostin found his way across the rugged land to the edge of the camp. There were about a dozen fires scattered around the perimeter of the Cheyenne camp. A giant fire roared in the center of the area. Women, children, and old men sat on the ground in small groups. The younger men wore bright paint and feathered headdresses. To the beat of the drums, the painted savages chanted and danced wildly around the fire.

Black Hawk was visible sitting in the place of honor just outside the circle. The fluttering flames cast hideous, sinister shadows against the teepees.

It took Bostin considerable time to move soundlessly around the camp and locate the primitive wagon which contained their guns and ammunition. Three braves stood by as guards. Clay had also noted at least six who walked the perimeter of the camp as sentries. Each man patrolled a line covering about a hundred feet. Clay decided the two sentries who walked closest to the ammunition wagon must be disposed of first. The three guards at the wagon would be next.

Choosing the first victim, the sinewy-bodied Bostin moved toward him, bellied down. He would have one chance, and no more, to silence the sentry. One slip and it would be all over. Stealthily, he crept up behind the Indian. Like a cat Bostin sprang, cupping his left palm over the sentry's mouth. His right hand jammed the nine-inch blade into his chest. Jerking the blade out, he dragged the limp form and deposited it in the darkness.

The second sentry would not be as simple. He patrolled in a direct line of sight with a number of those who sat on the ground. Bostin's only chance to get him would be at the turning-around point where this sentry's territory met that of the dead one.

Three times in a row, as the sentry pivoted, at least one Cheyenne was looking in that direction. The sentry walked very slowly. Clay estimated that at least an hour had passed since he had killed the first one. He must get him the next time.

Bostin was poised for the kill as the painted savage came near for the fourth time. He was about to spring when a small boy came running, saying something to the Indian. Flattening to the ground, Clay sighed quietly.

The tall plainsman was foiled again on the fifth opportunity, but after the sixth the sentry lay dead in the shadows as Bostin crept toward the ammunition wagon. Clay's mind was spinning as he moved in the darkness. How was he going to take out three at one time?

The drums continued their monotonous beat as Bostin neared the wagon. He saw only two guards. Where was the third? Taking two would be much easier.

Abruptly, the third appeared, returning from the teepee area. He could hear them talking, but with the din at the big fire filling the air he could not make out what they were saying. A note of optimism touched him. Maybe one would leave temporarily as the other one had.

Time was getting by. All three guards remained at their post. Clay lay motionless on the ground. His thoughts turned to Rachel, alone on top of the rock. What must she be going through by now? He wanted to hurry the operation, but there was no way. One wrong move would finish everything. He must be patient. Wait for the proper moment.

The thundering drums seemed like hammers pounding in his head. Hours passed.

Clay's attention was drawn to a pair of bucks who were walking from the ceremony area toward the ammunition wagon. As he watched, it was apparent they were changing the guards. All at once a chill swept over him. *What if they change the sentries?* Whatever he was going to do, it had to be now.

Bostin felt a wave of relief as the original three walked away, leaving only two to guard the wagon. The two Indians were standing shoulder to shoulder with their backs toward him.

As soon as the three were safely out of sight, he lunged. The powerful left arm of Clay Bostin closed viselike around one Cheyenne's slender neck, cutting off his wind...while the razor sharp blade of the knife plunged full-length into the neck of the other.

The one in Bostin's arm reached for his own knife. In a flash, Bostin yanked the knife loose and sunk it into the second one's heart.

The pulse throbbed in Clay Bostin's temples. As he hurriedly pillaged the wagon, the eastern horizon caught his eye. A dull gray light was glaring at him. *Dawn!* Furiously, he grasped an army tote bag. It was too dark to read the caliber markings on the cartridge boxes. Chances were best that they were .44s. With panic biting at his spine, he jammed box after box between the stiff canvas sides. When it was full, he slung the shoulder strap over his head and picked a .44 Winchester. Tearing open a box, he quickly filled the magazine with seven cartridges, levered one into the chamber, and wheeled.

Bostin's heart leaped in his breast. A painted Cheyenne stood before him, pulling his knife. The tall, rugged man of the frontier had fought Indians most of his adult life. Hair-trigger instinct, born of many bloody battles, moved his lithe body a split second ahead of the hissing blade. Clay countered, swinging the butt of the rifle, catching the red man on the jaw. The Indian rolled his head enough to escape taking the full force of the blow. He staggered slightly and came with the knife again.

The weight of the tote bag hindered Clay Bostin's agility. He moved enough to evade the knife, but the momentum of the young buck knocked him down. Instantly, the savage sprang on top of him, knife raised.

Clay's left hand checked the swing of the Indian's knife hand. It was a contest of strength. The warrior's breath was hot and fetid in Bostin's face. Moments passed.

Summoning all of his strength, Clay unbalanced his opponent in one violent lunge. The two men rolled over, cartridge boxes spilling to the ground. In a lightning-quick move, the powerful plainsman had both hands on the wrist which held the knife. Clay Bostin's arms were like spring steel. The Indian's eyes bulged as his own knife shafted his midsection. His body jerked twice and went limp. Suddenly it struck Bostin. The drums had stopped!

Hurriedly, Bostin gathered the scattered boxes. It was light enough, now, to read them. All .44s. Picking up the rifle, he darted from the camp, glancing east as he ran north. The top rim of the sun was throwing orange shafts at the sky.

Straining every fiber of his body, he ran. Fear threw a cold sweat on his face. His heart pounded like a runaway trip-hammer. His lungs were on fire. His aching legs screamed for rest.

He ran. Throwing glances at the rising sun, he ran. For the love of Rachel Flanagan, he ran. For the *life* of Rachel Flanagan, he ran. Knowing the Cheyennes were already heading toward the towering rock, he ran.

Now he was in the bottom of the long ravine which paralleled the trail to Fort Laramie. A few more strides and he would top the ravine. His legs were weakening. *Can't stop!* he told himself. *Can't stop!* It would only be a hundred yards to the rock tower once he hit level ground.

Clay Bostin's mouth was as dry as desert sand when he crested the ravine. He could hear the pounding of his heart in his head. His attention was instantly drawn to the west. Less than a mile away brass buttons and cavalry gear glistened in the early morning sun. The long column was coming at full speed.

"He did it!" shouted Bostin. "Bucky! Bless him, he did it!"

Turning toward the rock, Clay's eyes focused on the tail end of a band of Cheyennes scrambling up the natural staircase. From where he stood, only the lower part of the rough-hewn steps was visible. He could not tell how many savages were climbing toward Rachel.

"No-o-o-o!" he screamed. His weary legs were carrying him at a full run toward the rock.

And then it came.

The loud roar of the Spencer cut the air, spelling death and echoing like thunder out of the rock enclosure. He stopped in his tracks.

Clay Bostin's heart froze. He went cold inside. Screaming the name of the woman he loved, the frenzied man charged toward the rock. Behind him, he could hear the bugle blaring.

By the time Bostin had cut the hundred yards in half, an alarmed handful of Cheyennes emerged like frightened rabbits from the rock. Eyeing the column of troopers two hundred strong, they scampered across the flat land, heading for the ravine.

Clay found himself bounding madly up the crude rock stairs, and icy hand of terror squeezing his heart. As he breathlessly reached the top, his gaze fell on the full headdress of Black Hawk. The feathers were twisted and crumpled under his lifeless form. A blue hole centered his chest.

Quickly, Clay Bostin's eyes lifted to the face of Rachel Flanagan. The beautiful young woman stood hip-shot, back braced against the rock wall, favoring her injured foot. Her cheeks were shining with tears. She held the empty Spencer loosely in one hand. At the sight of the tall figure outlined against the orange sky, she let it slip from her fingers. The rifle made a clattering sound as it stuck the hard surface.

Clay Bostin gathered the Irish lass in his arms, his own eyes swimming with tears. The subdued sound of pounding hooves was broken by the shrill blast of a bugle.

"It's all over, darlin'," he breathed. "It's all over."

Tilting her face upward, she said softly, "No, my darling Clay. *It's just beginning.*"

Other books by Morgan Hill:

Ghost of Sonora
Dead Man's Noose
Lost Patrol

A Man Who Laughs at Peril

Lieutenant Boyd Locklin's assignment to escort a wagon train through Apache territory ends in the massacre of those around him—but he emerges with a pretty young woman, the lone survivor. He goes on to acquire bitter enemies and face life-or-death duels—unharmed. But what will happen when he leaves his family for the unknown horizon of the Civil War? Will he emerge from prison camps and rattlesnake pits with the same carefree courage as before? Follow Locklin on an incredible itinerary of hair-raising battles with death!

Bandit or Freedom Fighter?

In the veiled and shadowed history of the West, there rides a mysterious horseman. His headless shoulders testify to his death at the hands of the law—in a state that forbade Mexicans like him to own property. A state that turned a deaf ear to the rape and murder of his beautiful young wife. This is the Ghost of Sonora. Was he man or myth? Was Joaquin Murieta the Napoleon of Banditry, as the California Rangers have charged, or *El Patrio*, the great liberator of the Mexicans of California? Here is his story. You make the decision.

Safely to the Gallows...

"You may put a rope on my wrists," the captured outlaw Duke McClain taunts Sheriff Matt Blake, "but you'll never put one on my neck." A death sentence awaits McClain in Tucson for his robberies, massacres, and senseless murders—but it lies across miles of unforgiving desert, full of cruel traps and bloodthirsty villains. Although Blake is determined to bring the outlaw to justice, a single thought echoes in his head with every thirsty step: A lot of things might happen before they reach Tucson...